SCALP DANCE

A SAM CHITTO MYSTERY

SCALP DANCE

LU CLIFTON

FIVE STAR
A part of Gale, Cengage Learning

 GALE
CENGAGE Learning®

Farmington Hills, Mich • San Francisco • New York • Waterville, Maine
Meriden, Conn • Mason, Ohio • Chicago

GALE
CENGAGE Learning·

Copyright © 2016 by Lutricia L. Clifton
Permission to reprint the map of "Tribal Jurisdictions of Oklahoma" was
granted courtesy of the Oklahoma Department of Transportation.
Five Star™ Publishing, a part of Cengage Learning, Inc.

LIBRARY OF CONGRESS CATALOGING-IN-PUBLICATION DATA

Clifton, Lu.
    Scalp dance : a Sam Chitto mystery / Lu Clifton.
    pages cm
    ISBN 978-1-4328-3129-5 (hardback) — ISBN 1-4328-3129-1
(hardcover) — ISBN 978-1-4328-3128-8 (ebook) — 1-4328-3128-3
(ebook)
    1. Indian reservation police—Fiction. 2. Murder—Investiga-
tion—Fiction. 3. Choctaw Indians—Fiction. 4. Oklahoma—Fiction. I. Title. II. Title: Sam Chitto mystery.
PS3603.L534S23 2015
813'.6—dc23   2015022037

First Edition. First Printing: March 2016
Find us on Facebook– https://www.facebook.com/FiveStarCengage
Visit our website– http://www.gale.cengage.com/fivestar/
Contact Five Star™ Publishing at FiveStar@cengage.com

Printed in the United States of America
1 2 3 4 5 6 7 20 19 18 17 16

For my sons, Christopher and Jeffrey

ACKNOWLEDGMENTS

In understanding the Choctaw Tribal Police organization, I am indebted to R. D. Hendrix, Director of Law Enforcement for the Choctaw Nation. Director Hendrix also demonstrated incredible patience as I endeavored to fathom the inner workings of the Checkerboard jurisdictional system. As fiction writers are prone to do, I exercised artistic license in developing characters and plot in *Scalp Dance;* if I have portrayed anything incorrectly in so doing, it is through no fault of Director Hendrix.

I am also indebted to the Choctaw School of Language for help with Choctaw phrases and terms.

In understanding basic police procedures, I thank Brian Thiem, a retired police officer with years of service working for many government agencies, including those on Indian reservations.

TO THE READER

In August 1994, the 103rd Congress signed into law the *Violence Against Women Act.* This law created new penalties for gender-related violence and new grant programs encouraging states and tribes to address violence against women. Congress reauthorized the act in 2000 and 2005, with President George W. Bush signing the latest act into law on January 5, 2006. Because of these acts, many tribes received grants to create programs to educate women and girls on how to avoid domestic violence and rape. As I write this book, violence against Native American women persists in significantly higher percentages than with their Caucasian, Hispanic and African American sisters.

The setting in this book is genuine; the towns and byways depicted are based on first-hand knowledge of southeastern Oklahoma, my birthplace. The characters and events are purely fictional. The view the reader receives of the old Choctaw religion is as someone with an interest in long-lost mythology and cultural beliefs. Regarding references to the geology of Oklahoma, the reader receives this author's interpretation of it after much reading and research.

PROLOGUE

The four men forming the circle shuffled uneasily, dark faces beaded with sweat, black eyes turned from the man on the ground. The hollow call of an owl caused an involuntary shiver. It was the darkest part of the day, a phenomenon involving radiational cooling of the atmosphere. The men in the circle knew nothing about the scientific reason for the phenomenon. Or cared. To them, it was that time when darkness and light exchanged roles. A time when even August heat could be chill.

Periodically, three of the men glanced toward the head man, who stared eastward. As the sky took on a scarlet hue, he cleared his throat and began reciting the words he had been given. Faltering at first, then resolute.

"The Master of Breath will judge you, determine your punishment and how long it will last. Your ghost will wander in this world for that time. Perhaps hundreds of years. Maybe less . . . maybe more. The Master of Breath will decide this, but it will be equal to the pain you have caused. This we do know. No one will mourn your passing, and when your time of punishment is over, you will *not* be reborn."

The man on the ground stared wide-eyed, his eyes darting around the group. He attempted to spit out the gag in his mouth, but it was useless. The men in the circle knew how to tie knots. His bound hands and feet were proof of that. He struggled to gain purchase on the hard ground beneath him, but he could not. His hands and feet were being held in place with more knots, tied to stakes. He could feel a hard object under his neck, which was elevated from his shoulders and head so that his throat stretched in an arc. Even if he were not gagged, he would have difficulty speaking, the pressure on his vocal cords was so great.

"It is time," the spokesman said, looking toward another in the circle.

Nodding, the man removed a knife from a sheath at his waist. Quickly he knelt and knotted a lock of hair between his fingers. With his other hand, he incised a square around the knot. Then he pulled, fast and hard. The knot of hair came free, and with it, a whimper.

As he completed his task, the man across from him removed a sword-like instrument from a leather case. Dropping the case to the ground, he swung the instrument overhead, putting muscled shoulders and back into the downward swing. The sound of splintering bone echoed through the stillness.

Their task done, the men broke the circle. Wasting no time, they took what they needed and left. The sound of their vehicle's motor was accompanied by early-morning birdcalls, the flutter of wings taking flight. Nothing more.

None in the vehicle spoke. Not because they felt remorse for their actions that day, but because a man's spirit had been dispersed, never to be born again. Though no sounds were made, their communal thoughts melded into a prayer that none there would ever know such punishment. There was no worse fate imaginable than for one's spirit to be destroyed . . . forever.

CHAPTER ONE

One, two, three . . . four.

Sam Chitto eyed the men standing in the trailer's shadow. The singlewide sat on U.S. 70, accounting for the state patrol officer's presence. A *Hugo, Oklahoma* city limit sign across the road explained why the town cop was there. The man in the tan uniform had a sheriff's department insignia on his sleeve, accounting for his interest. A fourth man, wearing the black-and-gray uniform of the Choctaw Nation Tribal Police, waved him into the driveway. Pulling his white Tahoe alongside another one just like it, he killed the engine and waited.

Tommy Rideout climbed into Chitto's SUV, fanning his face with a campaign hat. "What took you so long, Sam?"

Rideout was young, fresh out of training, and did his uniform proud. Biceps stretched sleeves taut, damp cloth outlined tight abs. Chitto wondered if he'd ever been as fit.

"Got here soon as I could, Eight."

Chitto had trouble with names. He had field responsibility for District 9 but handled multiple-district responsibilities when needed. Like today. While still a rookie, he had resorted to using associations as identifiers—a physical characteristic or a place; easier yet, a number—which led to using the district number to ID the respective field officer. The rationale made sense. People came and went. The Nation's districts remained the same.

"This what it looks like?" he asked, eyeing the three officers in the distance.

"Yep. Mexican standoff. Girl's been raped and it's not clear whose land this trailer's settin' on. You bring a checkerboard?"

"*Raped,*" Chitto hissed. "When you called, you said I needed to mediate an incident."

"Well, see . . ." Eight dipped his chin, staring at the floorboard. "The, uh, the girl was right next to me—listening—and, uh . . ."

Chitto listened to his words fade. Though new, the young officer had what it took to be a good, solid tribal officer. He believed in protecting the Choctaw and their land, and didn't go looking for trouble.

"Okay, then," Chitto sighed. "Let's see if it's in our jurisdiction, or out." He pulled a map from the glove compartment and unfolded it. The patchwork of colored blocks—the checkerboard—represented the homeland of the Choctaw since the Removal, the forced march of the Choctaws from Mississippi to Oklahoma in the 1830s. Subsequent chopping and changing of tribal boundaries by successive governments had created a nightmare of jurisdictional problems for modern peacemakers.

The problem drove Chitto and every other lawman to distraction, not least because of the amount of time wasting it caused. Here today were five officers—most of them standing around twiddling their thumbs—forced to wait for a consultation involving a map to determine whose jurisdiction this particular crime fit in.

But that wasn't the worst of it. Frustration among investigating officers occasionally escalated into arguments and disputes worse than the crimes being investigated. More than once, an officer's performance bordered on idiotic. More than once, the suspect slipped out the back way and was never brought to justice. Those with a perverse sense of humor found the situation laughable. But they weren't the ones dealing with the fallout.

To Chitto's thinking, the whole thing could be brought back to politics. And politicians. The good-old boys. Back slappers with hidden agendas. Chitto had little use for politicians. Truth be told, he hated them with a vengeance.

"It's in. Belongs to us," he said a minute later. Noticing Eight's hesitation, he waited for him to voice the cause.

"The guy's still inside. I'll send these other boys packing if you'll handle him. Call just came in on my cell 'bout a domestic dispute. I could follow up on it while you're finishing up here."

Chitto stared at him. "You telling me the perp's inside with the girl?"

"Yeah." Eight glanced toward the trailer. "But she's okay. She bashed him after . . . when he was done with her. Dragged him into a closet, wedged a chair under the doorknob, called us. She cold-cocked him a good one. Think he's sleeping one off, too. Smells like a bottle of Jack."

Chitto's chest felt like a hollowed-out gourd. The People called the tribal police ahead of other agencies—those that bothered anymore. Women rarely reported assaults. A few years before, the Nation had been granted government money to fund abuse-prevention programs. All ten and a half counties that fell within the Choctaw Nation boundaries had received train-the-trainer instruction with the money. How to teach young women and battered wives ways to avoid rape and domestic abuse. Still, the numbers were staggering, and most times, the assailant walked free.

"He, uh, he doesn't look Indian." Eight ran a hand over dark, burr-cut hair. "So you know what that means."

Chitto knew only too well. Making an arrest in the checkerboard was quite literally a game of checkers, the ability to make a move dependent on whether the victim and suspect were native or non-native, whether the incident occurred on native or non-native land, whether the Nation had a cross-deputization

15

agreement in place if on non-native land. A crime committed against a native by a native on Indian land was handled in the state court. A crime committed against an Indian by a non-native on Indian-held property was filed in federal court, and sometimes required the tribal police to contact the U.S. attorney's office to see whether an arrest should be made or paperwork filed for a later indictment. Because an arrest started the clock—putting the attorneys under the gun to build a solid case—tribal police typically filed paperwork in lieu of an arrest. Chitto didn't have to make a call today. He knew what the answer would be.

"Well, hell." Chitto sighed again. "Okay, take care of that other incident."

"Will do. Oh, I called for a victim's advocate from the county. Be here any minute."

"That's good, real good."

Eight paused as he opened the door, the hint of a grin showing. "It, uh, it smell like cigarettes in here to you?"

Shaking his head, Chitto laughed quietly. "That's just nostalgia you smell. Now get the hell out of my car."

Eight was still grinning as he made his way toward the three officers next to the trailer. It was common knowledge that Chitto kept a pack of Marlboro Reds in his glove compartment. No one knew the reason it was there or why it was replaced from time to time with a fresh pack. All they knew for certain was that he had given up smoking four years before—cold turkey. Trading chewing gum for smokes, he bought a pack of Doublemint weekly and stored it next to the Marlboros. His habits had made Chitto the butt end of jokes, not to mention earning him a reputation for being somewhat eccentric, all of which he sloughed away like water off a duck's back.

Chitto pulled out a stick and folded it into his mouth. Not a day went by when he didn't want to pull out a cigarette instead.

But he didn't. He kept the Marlboros there as a reminder of a promise he'd made and intended to keep. The aroma of tobacco served to remind him that, whatever else his shortcomings, he was a man of his word.

Opening the car door, he paused, easing scorched air into his lungs. The burnt-out yard provided no relief from record-breaking heat. Summer temperatures typically ran in the nineties, but this year, the norm had been a hundred or better and the skies had granted little rain. On the fifty-mile drive from his office in Durant, he'd noticed trees and bushes turning yellow, dropping leaves early. Still, animals in the field sought out their measly shade.

Retrieving his camera from the backseat, he heard tires crunch on the caliche driveway and watched Rona Guthrie pull up in a sedan with a Choctaw County insignia on the side panel. The victim's advocate. This dark-haired, dark-eyed woman was a crusader when it came to women's rights and outspoken about the need for more convictions. In spite of the oppressive heat, her white blouse and beige pantsuit were crisp.

"You boys finally sort out which square this checker's on?" Not waiting for a reply, she headed for the front steps, the wooden kind that spoke to the impermanence of a home on wheels.

Chitto hustled ahead of her, planning to brief her on the situation.

"Know the drill, Sam." She pushed past him. "How's she doing? Take her statement yet?"

"Just got here myself."

Following her inside, Chitto spotted a girl sitting on a worn sofa, a nervous-eyed dog at her feet. Australian shepherd, a herding dog with a protective nature. Bared teeth brought Rona to a quick stop. Chitto stepped in front of her, watching the girl calm the dog.

"Lieutenant Chitto," he said, pulling a business card from his shirt pocket. "This is Mrs. Guthrie from the county. We're here to help you."

"Name's Domino," the girl said, taking the card. "His chain's at the back door."

As Rona sat down next to the girl, Chitto hooked a finger in the dog's collar and led it to the back stoop. Pausing, he noted the lock on the door hadn't been jimmied. Beyond that, he saw a patch of yellow grass, no fence. A battered red Bronco was parked in the alley, front end jutting into the yard. Driver's door half open. Liquor bottle in the grass next to it.

Returning to the front room, he eyed the girl. Faded jeans, loose cotton shirt and tennis shoes did not detract from her natural beauty. What did was a split bottom lip and eyes all but swollen shut. A cast-iron skillet lay on the floor at her feet. In legal parlance, a weapon of opportunity.

A strong girl. Proud.

Noticing Chitto studying her, the girl turned her face to the floor.

Always the same . . .

Pulling a kitchen chair into the living room, Chitto laid aside his camera and ran the procedure. "Your name?"

"Teresa Walker with no H. I mean, Teresa, there's no H in it."

"Thanks, I'll remember that. Age?"

"Fifteen. Just turned fifteen last week . . ."

Chitto swallowed as the girl's words trailed off and jotted down the rest of her answers.

Place of incident: There at her aunt's trailer house on Highway 70, west of Hugo.

Aunt's Name: Betty Tomlinson.

Time of incident: Lunch hour, when she came home from school to eat a sandwich and let her dog out.

He glanced at his watch. "Did you say lunch hour?"

"Yeah. I got a free period before lunch, so I come home to let Domino out."

He glanced at the kitchen. A loaf of white bread and jars of peanut butter and jelly on the counter. Sandwich, uneaten.

He looked at her again. "You didn't lock the door after you let the dog out?"

She frowned. "He just needed to pee. I was gonna let him back in soon as I ate."

Just what anyone would've done.

"Okay, then what'd he . . ." He let the question hang, not wanting to verbalize what had been done to her.

She covered her face with her hands.

He reached for his camera. "Need to take a couple of pictures."

"That's enough," Rona said after he'd taken a few shots. "I'll take her to the clinic. You'll get a copy of the report."

"Not yet," Chitto said, looking at the girl. "How'd this guy know you were here alone, Teresa? Sounds like he might've known your routine."

The girl blinked slowly. "He's, uh, he's married to my aunt. But she's divorcing him 'cause he's a drunk. She works at the casino there near the airport, that's where she met him."

Which explained why the dog likely didn't bark or attempt to protect Teresa, he thought.

Another, more disturbing, thought pushed into his mind. The man was the girl's uncle, at least by marriage. Still, familial ties were as strong as blood ties.

Or should be, said a voice in his head.

"You know the assailant's name then?"

"Yes, sir. It's Buster, Buster Tomlinson. Think that's a nickname, but it's all I ever heard him called."

"Member of the Nation?"

She shook her head.

"That red SUV out back there belong to him?"

"Yes, sir."

"Okay." Chitto flexed tight shoulders. He'd come to the part he hated. "Look, here's the way it works." Briefly, he explained the steps he needed to go through to bring her attacker to trial. "So, you see, because the guy's not Indian, I write the incident up, turn it over to the U.S. attorney's office and they handle it. I'll file the paperwork today—soon as I get back to the office— but it could take a while. Sometimes the courts are pretty backed up."

The girl's face hardened. "Yeah, that's what I've heard." She turned, listening to a scratching sound at the back door.

"You go with Mrs. Guthrie," Chitto said, glancing at the door. "I'll let Domino back in, close up the house before I go."

"Thanks."

"No problem." Chitto did not feel worthy of the courtesy Teresa Walker paid him. He felt a need to apologize to her. "Anything else I can do?" Looking around the room, he saw a telephone on the floor. "Maybe call your aunt?"

She glanced at the phone, too. "Tried. Not at work yet, but she was goin' to the Walmart first. We're out of some things."

Chitto nodded, wondering if the rapist locked in the closet figured he'd find the aunt home and, when she wasn't, decided the girl would fill the bill.

"Mother, then?" At times like this, girls turned to their mothers, grandmothers and aunts. The comfort givers.

"Mother," she repeated. "Yeah . . . I don't know the number, but I'll learn it."

Rona gave Chitto a look that said, That's enough. He nodded and watched the two leave, his mind on the girl's parting words. Why wouldn't she know her mother's phone number? Why was she living with her aunt? Neither answer was necessary for his official report, but it was the kind of loose end that kept him awake nights.

A pounding in the adjacent room channeled Chitto's attention back onto the job. Walking to his car, he retrieved his nightstick, half hoping he got the opportunity to use it. But that rarely happened. When all was said and done, he'd file a report not deemed critical enough to warrant pursuing. Other things, like terrorism and drugs, had higher priority.

He blamed history for the situation, one event in particular. The Removal. The forced march of the Choctaws from Mississippi happened in the 1830s. Survivors of the march were given a part of Indian territory, a steaming basin wedged between the Canadian River on the north and the Red River on the south, the Ouachita Mountains on the east and grassland prairies to the west. Later, the federal government overhauled old treaties, restructuring ownership of the land—slicing and dicing the whole into smaller pieces—making allotment Indians of the Choctaw. Sometime after that, another government treaty replaced the previous one, opening up land not yet allotted to Choctaws to immigrant farmers and miners. The mix of tribal and non-tribal lands presented a checkerboard of problems for the law-enforcement community—federal, state, municipal and Indian—and created a land lawbreakers joked about.

Chitto returned to the trailer, ready to deal with the perp. As he pulled the chair away from the closet door, another question popped into his mind: Did Teresa-with-no-H take the rape-prevention training?

Of course she didn't. Why would she? A fifteen-year-old girl shouldn't have to take rape-prevention training to let her dog out to pee.

The drunk in the closet fell on his face when Chitto opened the door. Plaid shirt and khakis hanging open, belt unbuckled. Breath smelling like a whiskey keg.

21

"I'm bleedin'." A prominent Adam's apple jerked up and down when he talked. "Need a doctor." He fumbled with his zipper.

"Other things you need worse 'n that." Chitto jerked Buster Tomlinson's arms behind his back so he could cuff him. "Ever think about castration?"

"What the hell you doin'?" Tomlinson struggled free. He was a half head shorter than Chitto, twenty pounds heavier and sober enough to be aware of limitations brought on by insobriety.

"What's it look like I'm doing? I'm gonna have you hauled to lockup."

"For what?"

"Can't let you out on the roads in your condition. You're an endangerment to the public. You can sober up in the county jail. Night in the slammer will do you good."

And, Chitto thought, buy me time to get an indictment working.

"But my car's here. How the hell am I gonna get back to get it?"

"Won't have to. I'm having it towed to impound. It'll be there waitin' for you when you get out. As a matter of fact, be a good idea you *never* came back this way."

"That girl's the one needs arrestin'. What the hell she hit me with?" Tomlinson swiped blood from his head with a shirtsleeve.

"Looky here." Chitto held the nightstick in front of his face. "You think I'm not aching for a chance to use this? My opinion? Nothing's lower than a rapist, 'specially when the girl's his kin."

Tomlinson steadied himself as best he could. "That girl's no kin to me. And those squaws, they like it rough."

"What'd you say?" Chitto waited, watching Tomlinson swallow, then swallow again. The Adam's apple sliding up and down like it was on a pulley.

22

The nightstick in Chitto's hand seemed to put Tomlinson in a cooperative frame of mind. "Go ahead," he said, holding out both wrists. "Hell, I'll be out 'fore supper."

Chitto shoved hard, bouncing Tomlinson's head off the wall. "That very well may be," he said, "but I'm making you a promise. I aim to see you get your just due."

"Yeah, right." A snicker. "We both know how this is gonna turn out."

Reaction moving faster than reason, Chitto's nightstick connected with Tomlinson's right shinbone. The next thing he knew, he had the stick across the man's Adam's apple. Tomlinson had no choice but to look him in the eye.

"Listen good." Chitto spoke in a bare whisper. "I make a promise, I keep it."

Ignoring the man's howling, Chitto hauled him outside and locked him in the backseat of the Tahoe. Returning to the trailer to take care of Teresa Walker's dog, he saw Eight pulling into the driveway. The young officer hurried to catch up with him.

"Had another call but thought I might oughta check in with you first." He glanced over his shoulder. "What's with him? He's yelling something 'bout police brutality."

"Still too drunk to drive. We're cross deputized in this county, so I'm gonna call the sheriff and have him haul the guy in. Car, too. Wouldn't hurt my feelings, that guy disappeared off the face of the Earth."

Eight eyed the nightstick hanging at Chitto's belt. "You, uh, you think I should handle it? Maybe you could take this other call; it's here in Hugo."

"What kind of call?" Chitto freed Domino from his chain and let him into the kitchen. Turning the inside lock, he pulled the door tight.

"Old man got mugged at a local bar. He's Indian; that's why

they called us. Said he came in talking about some guys getting killed."

"At the bar?"

"Well, see, that's not clear. Now he's sober, he's clammed up."

Chitto walked with Eight toward his SUV, eyeing the man in the backseat. Anger surging again, his thoughts went to the first criminal in the universe. How could a deity of any breed see fit to allow Lucifer and his like to survive?

"Yeah. Call the sheriff's office, have a deputy come get him," he said. "I've had all of him I can stomach for one day."

Compassion was a questionable virtue.

CHAPTER TWO

Late summer haze lay across the land like a gauzy blanket. Nosing his Tahoe into a parking space at the Choctaw clinic in Hugo, Chitto slogged toward the front doors. He was there to check on an old drunk that had been mugged. A senseless crime. His morning had been like that, and most of the calls had dealt with drunks.

That was it, he reasoned, trying to understand his reaction with Buster Tomlinson. He'd let the drunk get under his skin, cause him to react with anger. No, he thought, thinking over the past year. He'd come close to losing it before he'd made Tomlinson's acquaintance. The signs were clear. He was as close to burnout as the ground he walked on.

He felt the heat of anger again, this time at himself. There wasn't room for that kind of reaction in law enforcement. At least, not his version of it, which read, *The tough go legal.* The law was the law and you upheld it, no matter how bad it stunk. But even now, he could see that Adam's apple sliding up and down.

Maybe I've reached the end of the track . . .

By the time he pushed through the front doors of the clinic, Chitto's knit shirt was plastered to his back, his dark slacks wrinkled. Field lieutenants were given the option to wear plain dress, which paid off in summer. Usually. Though coolers ran continually, the air inside was muggy, thick with antiseptic smells. The smell of sickness. Death. A smell he'd spent two years trying to forget.

"Sonny Boy Munro," he said to the round, gray-haired woman at the reception desk. He showed his ID. "Mugging victim."

She bobbed her head as she checked the computer screen, searching for the sweet spot on her trifocals. "Mister Munro's in Emergency. Go down that hallway right there, make a left at the dead end and . . ." She glanced up at him. "But I reckon you know the way."

" 'Fraid so, ma'am."

Pushing through doors at the end of the hall, Chitto flagged down a man wearing a white coat and stethoscope.

"Munro?" The doctor pointed him towards a bed in the corner where an elderly man sat. Legs spraddled. Cigarette hanging from his mouth, unlit.

As he approached, the old man pitched the cigarette in a wastebasket, pointing to a *No-Smoking* sign on the wall as explanation. Chitto nodded, figuring the cigarette had been sucked dry of nicotine. Addicts could be creative when it came to filling their needs.

Sinking into a chair next to a hospital bed cranked into a sitting position, he studied the bed's occupant. He had seen him recently, but didn't have time to inquire where. He pulled a pen from his pocket.

"Tell me what happened, what you remember."

"Nana kiyo." Nothing.

Shaking his head, Chitto went through the drill. Writing down what little information an eighty-year-old man smelling of liquor and urine could provide about his attack. He admitted being out on his feet at the Red River Tavern. Two men helping him outside. A *clunk* and the lights going out. As for other information, his mind was a blank. No description of his assailants. No memory of who else was in the bar.

Chitto eyed the report. "You said someone was killed."

"I didn't see no one killed."

Another look at the report. "Says here you mentioned more than one."

The old man shook his head.

Chitto pocketed his pen. "How'd you get to the bar, Sonny Boy?"

"Walked."

Glancing at the report sheet once more, Chitto frowned. "Says here you live outside Bokchito. That'd be a pretty good walk."

"Yeah, a pretty good walk."

"No car?"

"It don't run."

"So you walked . . . what? Ten, fifteen miles?"

"Got nothing better to do. Walk over to 70 sometimes, hitch a ride."

"And you planned on walking back in your condition." It was more a comment than a question.

The old man rubbed the back of his head. "They took my bottle away. Them doctors did."

"They give you something to eat?"

"Don't remember. You gonna make 'em give me back my bottle? I got to go home."

Chitto took in the stooped shoulders, creviced skin, hollowed chest. "Need to stay here a couple days 'til that knot on your head goes down. Get some decent food in your belly."

Sonny Boy swung his legs over the side of the bed. "No. I am going home."

"Whoa there, Grandfather." He laid a hand on the old man's shoulder. "That's not a good idea."

"Need to feed my sow." Though his drunk's eyes were blurred, Sonny Boy's look was steady. "I don't feed her, she'll

27

eat the little ones."

"Maybe you could call someone to check on them. You have family you can call?"

"Kids ain't worth a plugged nickel." Sonny Boy blinked slowly. "Got a granddaughter. She is a good girl."

Chitto pulled a cell phone from his pocket. "You know her number? I'll give her a call, you tell me her number."

"I don't know that." Sonny Boy rubbed the lump on his head again, wincing. "I got to go home. They's more dances coming up. I sell them pigs to make money."

Dances? Chitto's memory sharpened. Along with others in the department, he worked a ceremonial dance recently at Tuskahoma. They trailered horses up and rode herd on the crowd. Sonny Boy was one of the singers.

Chitto ran into his mother there, too. A tribal councilwoman, Mattie Chitto was one of the officials at the annual event. She took a break from her official duties that day to join him for dinner on the grounds. Corn-and-pork soup, made the old way.

"Had some *tafula* there at the old capitol a few days ago. That your doing?"

"Yeah. I sell two porkers to them people up there. Got six more sold."

Chitto mulled this over. The entire state of Oklahoma was one big celebration in the fall. The end of the old year, the beginning of the new—according to Indian time. The old man raised pigs to sell to the various nations for their harvest festivals.

Running a hand across his mouth, Chitto ordered his day. He needed to work up the Teresa Walker rape incident he'd covered earlier, finish a couple of other things before he called it a week. But Bokchito was on the way back to Durant.

"Tell you what. Let me check with the doctor, see what he says about your condition. He says it's okay, I'll take you home." He wagged a finger in front of the old man's nose. "You stay right here 'til I get back, Sonny Boy. You don't, I'm gonna be pissed. You hear me?"

"Nothing wrong with my ears."

The doctor felt Sonny Boy's injury looked worse than it was and he could go home if someone kept tabs on him. He wrote out instructions that dealt with icepacks to reduce swelling and handed Chitto a packet of low-dose painkillers.

"And no one else was reported as being injured or killed at the bar?" Chitto asked.

"No . . ." The doctor rubbed the back of his neck. "But the old man was sure convinced of it when he came in. Not just killed—scalped."

"Scalped." Chitto shook his head, feeling tired.

"And another strange thing." The doctor pulled a manila envelope out of a drawer. "Wallet hadn't been touched. Take a look; damn thing's stuffed full. Must've just cashed his dole check. That seem strange to you? That a couple of goons would haul an old man out of a bar, knock him out and not take that kind of money?"

Chitto flipped through the wallet. Several hundred in bigger bills, many smaller ones. He mouthed "Thanks" to the doctor as he walked away.

At the corner bed, Sonny Boy was slipping feet into rundown, canvas loafers.

"Check this out," Chitto said, handing over the wallet. "See if it's all there."

Sonny Boy fumbled with the money. "Yeah, most of it. Drunk up some."

"All right then, here's the deal. I'll take you home but someone's got to check on you. That granddaughter of yours live around here? She lives close, I'll give her a call, tell her to check on you."

29

"Got a number out to the house. She is a good girl. She learns of my hardship, she will come see me."

"Okay then. Meantime, I'll call some people I know, see if they can help you get back on the right path. Know who I mean?"

"Yeah. Been down that road before."

Chitto hesitated. "You've been in the program then?"

"Long time ago."

"What made you pick up the bottle again?"

Sonny Boy focused watery eyes on Chitto. "Because I am an honored man."

Nothing bothered Chitto more than incongruities. In Choctaw tradition, a man was honored for notable deeds, much as a woman was honored as caretaker of the children, the elders, the home. Being given such respect was strong reason to live an upright life, and nothing was more dishonorable to the People than to be known as a drunk.

"I'm not following you."

"The stones, they talk to me."

Anyone overhearing those words would have dismissed them as ramblings from an old man suffering dementia or DTs. But Chitto had trained to be a geologist and anything to do with stones drew him like a magnet. He still followed the field, subscribing to *Earth* magazine and the journal *Geology*. Unlike the more radical thinkers of the day, he didn't believe the Earth was sentient, but he did believe it was anything but static. He'd spent hundreds of hours examining rocks in an effort to understand how they came into being, how they had affected— and were affected by—their surroundings. The rock cycle. The carbon cycle. The water cycle. Mankind's cycle. The evolution of humanity was tied to the evolution of the Earth. Life was possible only because of the planet's unique conditions.

"What'd the stones say, Sonny Boy?"

"They are angry."

"Angry? Why would they be angry?"

"Because the daughters weep."

The lawman in Chitto took over. "If you've got daughters in trouble, Sonny Boy, I can help them."

The old man stared at him. "Got no girls. Only boys."

Chitto could think of nothing more to say. All he knew with certainty was this old man had a story and he wanted to know what it was.

"Think you lost your way, Grandfather. Those people that run the program will see you get back on the right road again. This time, you stay on it. Okay?"

"Sure thing."

CHAPTER THREE

Chitto rolled down the car window. Though hot enough to scald his nasal passages, natural air was better than what emanated from the old man.

"I think I wet myself," Sonny Boy said.

Chitto glanced his way. "Probably happened while you were unconscious. You know, when you were knocked out. We have no control over our bodies when we black out."

"Yeah. I don't do that. I keep myself clean, keep my things clean."

Sonny Boy was true to his word. Inside a weathered house with a pyramid roof, Chitto found sparse rooms orderly, the plank floor swept clean. The first thing the old man did was head for the shower. While he was bathing, Chitto did a quick walk through the house. He found no evidence that anyone else lived there, nothing to indicate women in distress.

Sonny Boy emerged from the bathroom wearing clean overalls and cotton shirt, thin hair plastered wet to his head. Chitto pursued him as he carried dirty clothes through a bare-bones kitchen, watched him drop them on top of a washing machine on a screened back porch. Before he could stop him, the old man pushed through the back door and made straight for a barnyard back of the house.

"How many you count?" Sonny Boy held tight to a stock fence surrounding a white sow and several piglets. Other pens held more pigs—some weaner sized, some larger—all of them squealing.

Manure stunk, no matter what animal produced it, but hog manure exists in a league of its own. Some town councils wouldn't permit pig farms within smelling distance of the city limits. Standing where he was, Chitto understood the rationale. The rotten-egg and ammonia smell sucked the breath out of him.

"Seven," he said, breathing shallow. "No, eight. I count eight in all."

"Good. That's how many they was when I left."

"Think we got here in the nick of time." Chitto crawled over the fence and righted a feed trough. As the four-hundred-pound sow began rooting in the trough, he left the pen on the fly.

Sonny Boy let out a hoot as Chitto cleared the top rail.

"That is one big pig." Chitto managed a grin, too. "What kind is she?"

"Yorkshire. Good bacon pig, not worth a plugged nickel for lard. Choctaw pig is a good lard pig. Not much call for lard no more. People buying corn oil."

Chitto nodded. Corn oil was all he saw when he picked up the few things he needed at the Safeway. That and olive oil. But he didn't know anything about olives, so he stuck with corn. Mary had taken care of those kinds of things. Being a schoolteacher, she got off work in plenty of time to shop. Not that it mattered. Now that she was gone, meals were simple. Fast food. Whatever he could fry in a skillet. Anything that hadn't gone moldy in the refrigerator.

"Keep their mash in this here barrel." Brushing away black flies, Sonny Boy pried the lid off a galvanized can next to the fence. "Tight lid keeps vermin out." He indicated a flat-back bucket hanging from a yard spigot. "You want, you can give them clean water while I stir up their mash."

Glancing at his watch, Chitto discovered he was on his lunch hour. "Guess I got time."

Freshening the pigs' water, he looking around the property, hunting for something to account for Sonny Boy's angry stones and hurt women. The yard was scraped down to bare dirt; a barbed-wire fence separated the house from an overgrazed pasture. No rocks of any size either place, nor anyone of the female persuasion. Other than one whopping big Yorkshire sow. Near the pigpens, a shed held various farm implements, weathered crossties supported a rusted-out Ford pickup, a chain and hoist draped a nearby tree. Sonny Boy not only sold pigs, he also did some butchering.

Shading his eyes, Chitto looked toward woods at the back of the property. Fifteen acres, maybe twenty. Once the woods probably extended for miles, but now, cornfields pushed up to it. A rough shelter sat in the midst of the woods, perhaps a quarter mile distant, a track leading to it looking like it had seen recent activity.

"Who lives back there?" Chitto pointed at the shelter.

Sonny Boy paused his mixing of pig mash to look. "Nobody. Leastways, not all the time."

Before Chitto could stop him, the old man picked up a pitchfork and tossed a heap of manure into a wheelbarrow. When he wobbled on his feet, Chitto knew he'd gone the distance.

Taking over, he wheeled the barrow to a pile of dung behind the barn, dumped it, wheeled it back. Holding Sonny Boy by the arm, he led him toward the house. Inside, he turned a box fan in the front room on high.

"Sow's okay, all the pigs are good now. You stay inside the rest of the day. While I'm here, call that granddaughter you mentioned, the one that'll come out to check on you."

"Yeah, I'll do that." Sonny Boy took a seat next to a table

with a telephone on it and pulled a handwritten list out of the drawer. "They's some pop in the kitchen, you want one." He took his wallet from his pocket. "I can pay you for your help."

"Not necessary." Chitto eyed the wallet, wondering again why the muggers hadn't taken the old man's money. "Pop's plenty good."

In the kitchen, Chitto helped himself to a Pepsi from the refrigerator, plus one for the old man. Pulling a tray of ice from the freezer, he dumped it into a plastic bag and listened to Sonny Boy talk on the phone. Finding white bread, peanut butter and grape jelly in a cupboard, he fixed a sandwich, shook potato chips onto a plate, and retraced his steps to the front room.

En route, a taste bitter as gall filled Chitto's mouth. Teresa Walker had fixed the same sandwich and never gotten to eat it. He'd forgotten about that sandwich, left it on the counter. Unwrapped. Ants would be having a picnic with it about now.

Hell of a homecoming for Teresa-with-no-H . . .

Chitto set the plate of food on the table next to Sonny Boy. "Granddaughter coming over?" He popped the top on the two soft drinks and handed one to the old man.

"Be over soon. Works at the Seven-Eleven there on 70. Runs the cash register, keeps the beer locker full of beer."

"You tell her not to bring any alcohol when she comes?"

"Not old enough to buy likker." The old man worked on his food, talking as he chewed. "She will do what she says. She is a good girl, real sorry to hear of my hardship."

"All right then. If you're in good shape, I'll get back to work. Your head starts to hurt, take one of those pills the doctor gave you. And keep that ice on that lump." He indicated the plastic bag he'd filled with ice cubes and the pill bottle on the table.

Sonny Boy picked up a remote control and waved it at the television set. "Yeah. I'm in good shape."

35

Chitto paused, rubbing a hand across his mouth. "Seems strange those guys knocked you out and didn't take your money, Sonny Boy. Why you suppose they did that?"

A shrug. "Maybe they didn't like what the stones were saying to me."

Chitto sighed. Weeping women. Talking stones. Dead men— *scalped* dead men. One for the books.

"Okay. You remember anything important, call me." He wrote his cell number on the back of a business card and laid it next to the phone. "I'd like it if that granddaughter gives me a call tomorrow or the next day, lets me know how you're doing." He tapped the card. "Night or day, doesn't matter."

"I'll tell her that, yeah."

Chitto couldn't resist a grin. Sonny Boy had forgotten about everything but the game show flickering on the television. Drunks were blessed in that way. In all likelihood, he wouldn't hear from the old man again. But maybe that was a good thing. Most of the time, his only contact with people was for bad reasons. He'd just as soon not see him again under those circumstances.

Resuming his journey to his office in Durant, Chitto made a mental note to contact the Choctaw AA so Sonny Boy could regain the honorable path. And as soon as he was done wrapping up other things, he'd pay a visit to the Red River Tavern. Too many things about this mugging didn't add up.

CHAPTER FOUR

"Anything urgent, Wanda?"

"Well now, lemme see . . ."

Wanda Gilly was a thin, gray-haired woman with a smoker's hack and voice that sounded like gravel washing through a culvert. Adjusting her bifocals, she picked up a stack of pink slips on the front of her desk. An old-timer, she relied on pile management rather than electronic devices to keep up with the various officers. She didn't take to change quickly, which is why she caused a stir the year before when she changed from wearing dresses to pantsuits. Pant legs creased like a knife. Shirt starched crisp as a new dollar bill.

Chitto watched her fumble pink slips, his impatience building. He needed to wrap up the Walker and Munro incidents and clear his desk. Working the celebration at Tuskahoma the previous weekend and filling in for other lieutenants in outlying districts added up to twelve straight days. Twelve straight *long* days. He was in bad need of a weekend off. Remembering Sonny Boy, he corrected his thinking. Even after he finished the reports, he had one more stop to make before he could think about downtime. A visit to the Red River Tavern.

"Field officer over in Talihini's working a robbery case," Wanda said, giving one slip a quick read. "Lieutenant's been out on sick leave, wants you to interrogate the suspects." She flipped to the next one. "Another officer's having a suspect take a polygraph, wondered if you could be there for the follow-up . . ."

Chitto shook his head. Lately, he spent more time in districts other than his own. The Choctaw Nation covered 11,000 square miles divided into twelve districts, much of it nothing but prairie tallgrass and blackjack. Four field lieutenants and twelve officers covered the area. Another lieutenant and five officers covered the hospital in Durant, working shifts 24/7. A DARE officer stationed in Wilburton handled education in the schools, trying to imprint the dangers of drug abuse before it became an addiction. Enough work for all of them—more than enough.

"Nothing needs handling today, but Dan wants you in a meeting in . . ." She eyed the clock on the wall. "Thirty minutes. Briefing with another agency. He's waitin' on someone to show up."

Chitto ran through reasons another agency might be called in on a Friday afternoon. He hoped he wasn't in for a bout with Ramon Rodriquez. FBI agents in general were pompous pricks, and Rodriquez was the pick of the litter.

Word on the street was, as a kid, Rodriquez belonged to the *Hermanos dos Rios* gang, loosely translated as Brothers of the River, and still carried a blade in his boot. Chitto doubted the rumor. For one, Rodriquez had no tattoos to denote his affiliation, at least not visible ones. For another, as a rule gang members didn't cross over to the side of the law if they valued their skin. To his thinking, Rodriquez started the rumor to make himself appear *macho*. To top it off, he dressed like a pimp. Most agents wore jackets over chinos, especially when they went to court. Rodriquez decked himself out in sport coat and tie every day. Chitto's opinion? The guy was cotton candy. Fluff that would disintegrate in heavy humidity. And hell, when wasn't it humid in southern Oklahoma?

"FBI following up on that drug cache we stumbled on last

month?" he asked.

"Don't know," she snapped. "Dan set up the meeting himself."

"What's goin' on?"

"How the hell would I know?" She raised an eyebrow. "I'm just the secretary."

He snuffed a laugh. The running joke was Wanda ran the department. A veteran of thirty-plus years, she had outlasted three directors and officers too numerous to count. Daniel Blackfox, the current director of law enforcement, and officers alike relied on her for everything from Alka-Seltzer to the most up-to-date information. She vacillated between mothering people to death and being a cranky bitch. In the best of times, being left out of any loop irritated her no end. Right then, she was pissed.

Taking the pink slips, Chitto made his way through the noisy office. Plans were in the works to move the department to the vacated day-care center behind the tribal complex. Currently being refurbished, the building was being divided into thirds, with law enforcement on one end, land management on the other and a cafeteria between. Construction sounds and dust filtered through the windows. Workers filed in and out like ants, checking in with Wanda, the self-appointed site supervisor.

Chitto put his mind on finishing reports, but his thoughts wandered to the pending meeting. Typically, a briefing involved multiple agencies. County, state, federal. More often than not, the FBI was there. Anything promising publicity attracted it. If not the FBI, maybe a county sheriff up for reelection that needed some front-page coverage. The BIA? He gave his head a shake. Bench jockeys, the Bureau of Indian Affairs tended to look on from the sidelines. And Dan was handling it personally. Why?

Doesn't matter. We'll be given a support role, unless . . .

He swiveled his chair, staring out the window. The view was uninspiring. Ranch-style homes dating to the 1980s. Construction vehicles strung along the curb like oversized Lego blocks. A grassy field across the road. Which left little to interfere with the thought that had popped into his head.

Along with some of his counterparts in other nations, Blackfox was demanding more involvement in crimes committed on Indian lands, especially from the FBI. Chitto knew this attitude was due to officer complaints. Hell, he'd been verbal enough—

"You eat?" Wanda appeared in front of his desk.

"What?" He looked up at her. "Oh, not yet."

The office was located on the second floor of the Choctaw Nation Tribal Complex. Originally a college, the tall, red-brick building was in a quieter part of Durant, more residential than business, but not far from fast-food places. McDonald's. Jack in the Box. Pizza Hut. Carl's Jr. But Southeastern University was back in session, adding four thousand students to the population of Durant, pushing it upwards to twenty thousand. Not wanting to battle a long line at a drive-through, Chitto had bypassed them all.

"That's what I figured." Wanda set a paper plate filled with meat and potato casserole on his desk. "Today was potluck, lots of leftovers. Thought you might help me out. Didn't want to stare at this the rest of the weekend."

Chitto grinned, wondering if Wanda thought an investigator couldn't see past an obvious lie. Nodding his thanks, he watched her leave.

He ate hungrily. Home cooking was not his usual fare. Alternating keying data into electronic report forms and forking the plate, he finished it and the Munro and Walker reports simultaneously. As he pitched the remnants of his lunch into the waste can, he became despondent and wondered why.

Was it guilt because he'd enjoyed another woman's cooking?

Or could Mary's outer shadow still be there?

He shrugged off the feeling. It wasn't Mary's nature to be jealous. It was this business with the fifteen-year-old girl. Teresa-with-no-H was in the hospital, getting who knew what kind of poking and prodding that added to her humiliation.

His anger boiled up again at Tomlinson standing there, cocky because he knew he was on tribal land. He ached for the chance to split the rapist's head wide open. Since he couldn't, he hoped Teresa's father and uncles would do it for him.

Sliding down in his chair, he frowned his frustration. Her family's hands were as tied as his. They would be collared for assault and battery because the tribal police could arrest Indians—and they knew it.

So much for justice.

Five minutes before the scheduled meeting, Chitto walked to Wanda's desk. "Get this to the U.S. attorney's office soon as you can." He set his digital camera next to the report. "Pictures on this memory card, too. Need the camera back before I leave."

Glancing at the report, Wanda's mouth went straight. "*Jeezuschrise*— not another one."

"Yeah, and put a rush on it. I'm keeping my finger on this one."

"Why? You never done that before."

Chitto walked away without giving her an answer because he didn't have one. All he knew was the girl called Teresa-with-no-H had gotten under his skin.

Pushing through a door marked *Director Daniel Blackfox*, Chitto saw two men present. Blackfox at his desk, not a gray hair showing though he was in his fifties, and across from him, a man Chitto did not know but who seemed familiar. Long-ago familiar. A few inches shorter than he was, maybe five ten. Late twenties. Slim built. Military-style haircut.

Rummaging through papers, Blackfox spoke without looking up. "Take a seat, Sam."

Facing the stranger, Chitto eased into a chair and sorted through his memory rolodex. A glimpse of the emblem on the man's duty notebook revealed he was *Chickasaw Lighthorse Police*. Still, nothing clicked.

He extended a hand. "Lieutenant Sam Chitto. Know you, but can't remember from where."

"Been a while." Producing a lopsided smile, the man gave Chitto a firm handshake. "Tubbe. Sergeant Frank Tubbe, Chickasaw Nation. We went through CLEET at the same time."

CLEET. The Council on Law Enforcement Education and Training Program required for employment. Eight, nine years before. Just after he finished a double major in geology and criminal justice at Norman. Tubbe was straight out of high school. A young rooster, ready to flex his spurs. A jagged scar on his head an indication he'd tested those spurs.

"Took a slight detour," Tubbe said, as if reading his mind. "Military duty for a while, then Gunnison County sheriff's department. Colorado."

Chitto knew Gunnison County. Remote country. Rough. Main attraction, hunting and fishing. Skiing. A good place to kick back. Or do some serious defusing.

"You still talk like a college professor?" Tubbe asked, grinning.

Chitto laughed softly. "Not so you'd notice. Colorado's pretty country. Why'd you come back?"

"Feet got cold."

"Enough reminiscing," Blackfox broke in. "Need to move fast on this one." He looked between Chitto and Tubbe. "Some jurisdictional issues but something smacks about this one, telling me we need a look-see. Murdered man just discovered on the Tuskahoma council house grounds. Feds will be notified quick enough, but I want the lowdown before they bury everything in some moldy cellar. ME's on the way. Choctaw land so we'll be running things from our end. Chitto's in charge. Any questions?"

Chitto stifled an urge to laugh. Hell, yes, he had questions. Especially as it would be his ass in the sling if the FBI found him running his own investigation.

"Fill us in, Dan."

"Victim decapitated, head found with the body. Wallet in his pocket identified him as Delbert Wilcox. Pontotoc County, over near Ada. From what I gather, married to a member of the Chickasaw Nation. I'm figuring he was a member, too. Talked it over with the Chickasaw people; they sent Tubbe over to work that side of it. Given the victim was Chickasaw."

Tubbe let out a grunt.

Blackfox looked at him. "Need to say something, Sergeant?"

"Ah . . . yes, sir. Did some checking after you called. Victim's not on the rolls. He's the husband of Emma Love Wilcox; she's the Chickasaw. Called the house before I left the office. Her daughter answered, said her mother was at work. Rest of the family appears to be unharmed. Plan to inform them of his death soon as I get back."

"Smart move," Blackfox said. "Making sure the husband was the only one involved." He looked at Chitto. "Sam, want you to concentrate on the location, try to determine how this Wilcox ended up on our land. A ceremonial held up there last week between the second and fifth of this month. Believe you worked it." He tapped the calendar on his desk. "That ended four days ago. If there's a connection, why'd he just show up today?"

Chitto looked at Tubbe. "Wife file a missing person's report?"

"Uh . . ." Tubbe's neck reddened. "Needs more investigation. Check on that soon as I get back."

A grin tugged at Chitto's mouth. The rooster didn't look so

cocky anymore.

"Good place to start," Blackfox said. "I'll contact state and county agencies on the QT, see if anyone's been picked up on the highways looking suspicious. Like maybe covered in a helluva lot of blood. Sounds like this Wilcox bled out there on the ceremony grounds. From what I was told, he was a big man, so he probably fought back."

That statement brought Chitto out of his chair. "Like to look at the scene right away."

Tubbe rose from his chair, too. "Wouldn't mind having a look-see myself." He looked at Blackfox. "If that works for you, sir."

"Work it out with Chitto. He's in charge."

Tubbe turned to Chitto but did not speak.

Chitto tried to read the response. Skepticism. Disapproval. No, Tubbe was still thinking like a military man. Preferred working with the head honcho, someone with lots of brass on his shoulder.

"Tag along if you want—got no problem with that. Wouldn't mind talking to that widow over in your territory."

Tubbe made another grunt.

Blackfox looked at him. "Anyone knows why Wilcox would be over here on Choctaw land, she would."

"Guess that makes sense." Tubbe looked at Chitto, the grin making another showing. "Lead off. I'll follow you."

"One more thing," Blackfox said, talking quietly. "Try not to roil the waters on this one. FBI will get their day; today just isn't it. So run hard and fast."

At the door, Blackfox laid a hand on Chitto's shoulder. "Stay in touch with me on this, Sam." He glanced toward Frank Tubbe, who was disappearing down the hall. "Don't let yourself get dragged into anything stupid. That guy strikes me as a ringed-tail tooter. And remember the drill. Night or day, I expect to hear from you."

Chitto nodded, not needing further explanation as to Black-fox's personal concerns. Official concerns were another matter.

"Tuskahoma's outside my district, Dan. Could be stepping on Ed's toes."

"Ed's coming off medical leave, needs time to catch up on paperwork. But I'd have sent you anyway. My gut tells me you're the right man for this assignment." He grinned. "Besides, you been wanting a change from the grind. Maybe this'll scratch that itch."

CHAPTER FIVE

Chitto drove northeast on U.S. 271 into the Ouachitas, which he categorized as a twisted old sister of a mountain range. Sired by cataclysm, it had been belched up out of fiery depths and folded into stony ridges like a giant staircase.

Which is how the Winding Stair Mountains got their name . . .

Like a dark ribbon, the highway threaded its way through valleys that rose sharply on either side, thick with oak, hickory, shortleaf and loblolly pine. Red-tailed hawks and turkey vultures flew close to ground level, disappearing like phantoms in heat waves rising off the pavement. As hot as it was, Chitto knew he would smell pine pitch if he rolled down the windows. There were few other vehicles on the road now that tourist season was over, and he was glad for that. With ninety miles to cover he pushed the speed limit, wanting to get to Tuskahoma and the crime scene as quickly as possible. Though he would've preferred looking at the picture-postcard scenery, he put his attention on flying road hazards—birds the size of boat motors.

But Chitto didn't need a visual to know this land, and as he drove, he turned introspective. As a student, he'd spent long days in these hills. Gathering shards. Chipping fragments. Studying crystals. Once as high and rugged as the Rockies, the Ouachitas had been ground down over millennia to something more akin to hills. One day, if the Earth survived threats from outer space, internal combustion or a manmade Armageddon, it would cease to be a mountain range at all. But in its lifespan, it had witnessed more change than could be imagined.

If only stones could talk, he reflected, thoughts wandering to Sonny Boy Munro. As much as the lawman in him wanted to attribute the old man's story about angry stones to age or alcohol, another part of him refused to purchase it. The old Mystery Man had been stone cold sober that morning. Chitto was convinced he was remembering something real. If there was smoke, there was fire.

Glancing through the rearview mirror, he turned his attention to the land behind and the humans that occupied it. The Arbuckles, a stepsister to the Ouachitas, dipped steeply, near vertical in orientation. That range ran contrary to the adjacent country and formed the southern border of the Chickasaw Nation. And though not visible to the naked eye, he knew that under the grasslands further west laid a shelf of Permian rock. Kiowa and Comanche, Cheyenne and Arapahoe country. Dry prairie underpinned with marine rocks. Fossiliferous shales, limestones and dolomites. Briny sediment that, over time, oxidized and turned the surrounding rock red. Broken, bruised and bleeding, the rocks told the story of the Indian people. Broken, bruised and bleeding. The rocks told the story of the Indian lands. That much was fact, no mystery involved.

A dark SUV cozied up behind him. Tubbe was hugging his bumper like he was being towed. Tapping the brake or slowing a smidgeon and he'd plow into him like a tank. Just like the land that birthed him, the man's nature tended toward vertical. The arrogant grin spoke to that. In a pinch, could he depend on him?

Chitto turned in to the Tuskahoma council house grounds, a five-acre tract resembling a county fairground: ball fields, open grounds for festivals, an arts and crafts pavilion. Spotting yellow crime-scene tape at the pow-wow grounds in front of the capitol building, he drove towards it, Tubbe close behind.

The imposing red brick building, built in 1838 as the first seat of government in the new lands, was now a museum. At the first session held there, the elders decided the capitol would be known as *Nanih Waya*, meaning "mountain that produces." These two words held special meaning for the Choctaw. The sacred mound left behind in Mississippi was also called *Nanih Waya*. Children of the forest, the Choctaw, both the first People and those born in the removed land, held deep reverence for nature.

Opening his car door, Chitto was stunned at the noise. Cicadas, what locals called heat bugs, droned incessantly. Grasshoppers' raspy chirping added to the racket. The heat-loving insects had decimated the leaves on the trees, leaving behind skeletal remains. An unnatural cycle had lead to systems devouring other systems.

Chitto studied the ground as he and Tubbe approached the others. The Bermuda grass was dry and lifeless, in part due to the dry summer and ravenous insects, but mostly because at-tendees had trampled it the previous weekend. Packed hard as cement, footprints would be hard to identify. Traces of human-ity would be copious, remnants from crowds numbering in the hundreds. The best hope lay in evidence left on the body.

Without fanfare, he introduced Tubbe to Everett Mullins, the squat, bald medical examiner for Pushmataha County, and Tony Cargill, aka Seven, the District 7 officer, a man in his mid-twenties. The third man, named Hawkins, was there to assist Mullins.

"What's the verdict, Everett?" Chitto studied the body of a heavily built, nude man lying spread-eagle in the center of the pow-wow grounds.

"Well, you prob'ly noticed his head's been cut off." Mullins's drawl spoke to his west Texas roots; his macabre candor, to forty years of dissecting spiritless remains. "Near as I can tell, severed on the spot." He pointed to a dark area beneath the victim's neck. "Figure it happened 'bout daybreak."

Daybreak. When the Earth was at its darkest. That in-between time when night creatures gave up the hunt and day creatures had not yet begun theirs. A desolate time to die.

"Rub marks on his wrists and ankles indicate he was tied down," Mullins added. "Holes in the ground where stakes were driven in. All of it removed, nothin' left behind."

"Jesus holy moly—" Tubbe squatted on his heels near the corpse. "Pissed someone off, didn't he?"

Chitto studied the man's face, noting the mass of light, curly hair and empty blue eyes. Not surprisingly, blowflies were at work.

"Doesn't appear to have struggled much." Chitto picked up one of the dead man's hands. Nails were clean—very clean. He frowned, noting the muscular arms, calloused palm and finger pads. Too clean for a working man.

"You saying he just laid there and waited for his head to be lopped off?" Seven looked between the investigators and medical examiners.

"Prob'ly drugged," Tubbe said. "Could've slowed his movements, reactions."

"That'd be my guess, too," Mullins said. "Know more once I run tests."

It wouldn't have mattered if he hadn't been drugged. He would've been killed anyway.

Chitto glanced around the remote site. Few homes nearby, grounds wouldn't be highly scrutinized. Easy to overlook something when you're accustomed to ignoring it.

"Wound made with a sharp instrument," Mullins said, moving around the body to take pictures.

"Ax?" Chitto shot pictures of his own.

"Can't say for sure. I'd' have expected more tissue damage from an ax." Mullins rubbed his face. "Not so easy to cut off a person's head as you'd think. Weapon was razor sharp, like a giant scalpel. Prob'ly put something under his neck that would resist the impact. Whatever it was, took it with 'em. That's just speculation, but notice the pattern on the ground where his neck was. Not so much blood."

Chitto snapped a picture of the ground beneath the victim's head.

"Could've been a machete," Tubbe said.

Machete? Chitto glanced at the scar in Tubbe's hair. Gut instinct told him the Chickasaw would be a formidable opponent, or a good man to have on his side.

He turned to the field officer. "Who found him?"

Seven laughed softly. "Would you believe a couple of the council members? *Lady* council members. Guess there was a meeting today." He pointed his chin toward a building left of the capitol. "Over there at the council house. Got their names, 'case you wanna talk to 'em."

Chitto nodded, idly wondering if his mother might have been one of the two that found the dead man. He quickly dismissed that idea, knowing the officer would have recognized her name. Besides, his mother would've called him right away. She always called with issues dealing with law enforcement on tribal lands.

But she didn't call . . .

Chitto picked up a stone, working it between his fingers as he looked at the council house. No cars in the parking lot. Windows dark. The meeting was over. He wondered if his mother had missed the meeting. If she was sick. If something was wrong with his grandmother.

He flicked the stone away. Even if she had been absent, he would hear from the others. The entire council would ride his back until he got this business cleared up—even after Blackfox brought in the FBI. Regardless of jurisdictional issues, the council held the tribal police accountable.

He pointed to the pile of clothes on the ground. "Anything in his garments? Besides his wallet, I mean."

"Couple pennies." Seven handed Chitto the man's wallet, sealed in a plastic bag.

"Car keys?"

"No sir, not even car keys—" Abruptly, he looked at Chitto. "Know another funny thing? Clothes just taken off the clothesline. Got those little pinch marks clothespins leave."

Tubbe threw his head back, laughing. "Pinch marks, huh?"

Seven colored. "Wife line dries the clothes."

"Go on." Chitto looked at the officer. "You were gonna say something else."

"Oh. The, uh, the shoes were clean, too."

"Shoes," Chitto repeated, noting the flush on Seven's face.

"Yeah. That's, uh, that's gonna make it a hard go to find any trace evidence."

Tubbe grunted.

Chitto looked at him. "What's your thinking?"

"I'm thinking," Tubbe said, talking slow, "the killers knew something about forensics."

Killers . . .

Tubbe was right. It would take more than one person to transport a big man and stake him out, even one that was drugged. Two or three, maybe more. And one of them strong enough to lop off a man's head.

"Hell," Mullins snorted. "With all them damned crime-scene shows, everyone knows 'bout forensics these days. CSI Las Vegas. CSI Miami. CSI New York. Maybe I oughta start one called CSI Indian Nation."

That idea brought a snicker from the others.

"Okay I take the body now?" Mullins asked.

Chitto looked at Tubbe. "Want to look at this dead naked guy some more?"

"Hell, *no.* Kind of bothers me, the way he's laid out in all his glory like that."

Nodding, Chitto looked at Mullins. "Bag him. You find anything at the autopsy, let me know. Maybe his stomach will provide some leads."

"Unless he was starved a couple of days," Mullins drawled. "Or given a purgative."

Chitto didn't say anything to that, but the comment prodded another question. How long since the dead man went missing?

"Think I'll have a walk around." Tubbe looked at Chitto, grinning. "You feel the need to accompany me?"

Chitto couldn't help but smile. Tubbe was following protocol, but not without using the spurs.

"Go ahead," he said, knowing nothing would be found. "I'll look through his things."

Chitto pondered the incongruities as he sorted the clothing. The victim's wallet left behind, so someone wanted others to know of his end. Yet the rest of his humanity eliminated.

"Here go, Hawkins." Mullins handed his assistant a sack. "Bag up that head."

Watching the head disappear, Chitto was glad no newspaper reporters had gotten wind of the crime. Beheading of any kind would get lots of publicity. And a white man killed on Indian land would definitely attract the FBI.

Examining the clothing, he noted the clothespin pinch marks Seven had called out. He handled each piece gingerly before he let it go. Once the FBI got their hands on the clothes, he wouldn't see them again.

Tubbe joined him, a headshake indicating he found nothing worth mentioning on his walk around the grounds.

As the examiner and his assistant loaded the body bag, Chitto's thinking continued to churn. A Chickasaw killed on Choctaw grounds smacked of blood revenge. Choctaw men killing a Chickasaw? Possible. But washing and drying his clothes? Premeditation didn't fit with a revenge killing.

After the physical remains and clothing were safely stowed in the ME's van, Chitto walked with Tubbe toward their vehicles.

"Like to talk to Wilcox's widow right away," he said. "What say we head on over."

"Wilcox lived in Sasakwa, just north of Ada. How well you know Chickasaw land?"

The Chickasaw Nation, like all the nations, was as chopped up as the Choctaw. For that matter, the entire state of Oklahoma was nothing more than a giant checkerboard made up of smaller checkerboards.

"Lead off." Chitto grinned. "I'll follow you . . . this time."

CHAPTER SIX

Rocky uplifts, hardwood and pine trees gave way to rolling grasslands, stands of oak and hickory strung with mistletoe. Indian paintbrush was fading, but come spring, its pink and red plumes would daub the grasslands.

As he drove, Chitto checked in with Wanda. "Anything need tending before Monday?"

"You expecting something?"

"Rona Guthrie's sending me a report on that rape case this morning, but doubt she's done it yet. Anything on the perp?"

"Tomlinson? Was let go 'bout half hour ago."

Chitto swore under his breath. Tomlinson had nailed this one on the head. Not one night in the slammer. Another example of the convoluted justice system in the checkerboard working to the criminal's best interest. Even lowlifes with the morals of a pissant.

"Where you at?"

"Driving. So, my mother didn't call?"

"I'd have told you that right off, Sam."

Chitto heard the snap in Wanda's voice and wondered if he should provide an explanation. His mother and Wanda had known each other since public school and rekindled the friendship after they lost their husbands. Widowed on the same day.

The memory caused a pain like a knife scraping against a rib. Wanda's husband, Bert Gilly, and his father had gone out on a call. A routine investigation involving a land dispute near the

Arkansas River in LeFlore County. The caller refused to identify himself, not an uncommon occurrence in the Nation. Both patrolmen died with their hands laced behind their backs with their belts and a single bullet behind their right ears. A professional hit. Anyone who looked at the pictures could tell that. According to protocol, Dan Blackfox called in the FBI. It had been a cold case for ten years now and a thorn in both their sides.

"Mattie all right? You want, I can give her a buzz."

"Yeah, I'm in the middle of something here. Just expected to hear from her today and didn't. Tell her I'll be out to the house tomorrow. Something's not right, call me back ASAP."

"You're supposed to let me know your whereabouts at all times."

Chitto swore under his breath again. Sometimes Wanda made him feel like a dog on a chain. But he knew it wasn't her doing. Since losing Bert Gilly and Will Chitto, Dan Blackfox kept close tabs on all the officers.

"I'm on State Highway 1, heading east."

"What're you doin' way up there?"

"Not important, Wanda. Go on home and enjoy the weekend." He looked at the clock on the dash. "No, wait up. Would you contact Betty Tomlinson before you leave? She's the aunt of that girl that got raped this morning. See if she'll swear out a restraining order."

"You think this Tomlinson will do it again?"

"Wouldn't put it past him."

Her silence was long enough to be noticeable, as was her sarcasm. "You think a restraining order would do any good?"

"Prob'ly not." He pulled a breath, let it out slowly. "Would give us more clout, he tries anything again."

"If it'll make you feel better."

Make you feel better . . . Whatever righteous intent he might have had flown out the window with those words.

"It's all I can do, Wanda."

What did she expect, he wondered. She wasn't the one in the trenches, trying to oust the bad guys in this lopsided checker game.

Hearing a click in his ear, Chitto hit the OFF button on his cell. Pulling a piece of gum from his shirt pocket, he put his mind on State Highway 1, a twisting snake of a road. At McAlester where the state penitentiary—euphemistically called Big Mac—was housed, he followed Tubbe west on U.S. 270 and soon after that, the bypass around Ada. He checked his odometer. A hundred twenty-five miles from Tuskahoma, and Sasakwa was further yet.

The blackjack cast long shadows before Tubbe's turn signal came on. Chitto followed him down a dirt track leading to a white box of a house sitting in a bare yard. A brindle dog on a chain announced their arrival.

Chitto looked over the place as he joined Tubbe. A clothesline in the backyard, stretched between two metal uprights looking like rusty crosses, caught his eye.

"Half the Chickasaw Nation hang their clothes out to dry," Tubbe commented.

Chitto nodded. "Same with the Choctaw."

The front door opened and a girl's face appeared.

"Tribal police," Tubbe called out over the barking dog. He showed his badge. "You wanna shut that dog up so we can talk?"

She let the dog bark.

"*Sit.*" Chitto held his hand out to the dog, flattened like a stop sign, then lowered it to the ground. When the dog dropped to its haunches, Tubbe gave him an eye.

"Worked with dogs some. Most know the basic commands."

Chitto didn't bother with further comment about being the K-9 officer when he started in the department.

"Your mother home?" Tubbe stepped onto the front porch.

"No." The girl talked through a partially opened door, a chain lock stretched tight. "I thought you was her."

"When you expect her?" Chitto could hear a TV show playing in the background, one of the cartoon shows that come on in the afternoon. Recalling Tubbe had called the house earlier and found the girl at home, he wondered why she wasn't in school.

She shrugged. "Gets off work 'bout four. Sometimes she stops at the grocery store first."

"We'd like to ask you a few questions," Tubbe said.

" 'Bout what?"

"Maybe we could come inside," Chitto said. "Pretty hot out here."

The crack in the door narrowed. "Not supposed to let anyone in the house."

"Never mind; it's okay." Chitto took a step backwards. "We'll wait out here."

No sooner had the door closed than an older model, maroon Buick pulled down the drive.

"Looks like Mama didn't need groceries," Tubbe said.

The woman in the driver's seat eyed them suspiciously. Chitto listened as Tubbe explained to Emma Love Wilcox that the visit was official. She paused briefly, then walked to the house without comment.

Suffocating heat hit Chitto as he walked through the door. In spite of hundred-degree temperatures, the house was closed up tight. A small fan in the front room barely stirred the air. A stained plaid sofa, brown, imitation leather recliner, TV, and a table and lamp crammed the room. In the attached dining area was a small wooden table and four chairs, the kind donated to the Salvation Army or Goodwill. He couldn't help but wonder why the family did not fare better. Emma would be on the Chickasaw roll, and she held down a job. Delbert's hands indicated he was a working man.

"Turn off the TV, Nanny," the woman said to the girl. "Go to your room."

Chitto watched the girl called Nanny walk toward the TV. She was older than he originally thought. Twelve or thirteen, sixth grade or thereabouts, and pregnant. Maybe four, five months.

"You don't mind, ma'am, I'd like it if the girl stayed," he said. "She might be able to shed some light on this situation."

"What situation?" The woman took a seat on the sofa, motioning the girl to her side.

Tubbe sat down and opened his notebook. "Your, uh, your husband was found dead today. Over in the Choctaw Nation."

Chitto stood to one side, watching mother and daughter. The widow's face remained fixed. Neither mother nor daughter seemed surprised to learn of Wilcox's death. Or distraught. In his peripheral vision, he observed Tubbe watching the pair, too. Watching and waiting.

"How'd he die?" the widow asked.

"Suspicious means. What can you tell us about him being found over there?"

Chitto watched Tubbe sit quiet, waiting for a response. The Chickasaw's time in the Colorado wilderness had left him a little raw, but Chitto gave him credit for withholding the gritty details.

"Don't know nothin'. He hasn't lived here in a long time."

Chitto looked for changes in her respiratory pattern, eye movements. She was blinking some, as though mulling things over, but nothing abnormal given the circumstances. Either she didn't know anything, or she was a hell of a liar.

"How long would that be . . . exactly?" Tubbe asked.

" 'Bout two, three months now." The woman shrugged. "I don't know nothin'," she repeated, and glanced at her daughter. "She don't either."

"And you haven't seen or talked with him since he left?" Tubbe asked.

She hesitated. "Maybe once or twice on the phone. He wanted the rest of his things. You know, tools and stuff."

"What about you, Nanny?" Chitto looked at the girl, deciding it was time to test the water. "When's the last time you saw or talked to your daddy—"

"He wasn't her daddy—Nanny's by my first husband."

The sharpness in the woman's voice, the flush on her cheeks, indicated the parting had not been amicable. A second marriage would also explain the girl's dark coloring, nothing like the murdered man's.

"Where'd he work?" Tubbe said. "You know where he was staying? Had to be living somewhere."

"Worked at a towing company there in Ada—Reynolds' Towing. Don't know where he was staying. I packed up his clothes and set them out on the road."

Tubbe jotted down more notes. "What kind of car he drive?"

"Red pickup—Ford, but I don't know what year."

"Did you file for divorce, Mrs. Wilcox?" Chitto asked.

She shifted in her seat. "My, uh, my religion won't let me. I'm Catholic."

Chitto concluded the first husband must have died, as devout Catholics did not believe in divorce. If they were in a bad marriage, they stuck it out. Except Emma had thrown out Husband Number Two.

Not as devout as she used to be?

Tubbe looked at Chitto. "I know where that towing company is."

59

Chitto nodded, then looked at the mother. "Have to say you don't seem too upset about Delbert's death, Emma."

"It's the answer to a prayer."

"What do you mean?"

She looked at her hands. "Means he won't be buggin' me anymore for the rest of his stuff." Standing, she faced her daughter. "Go to your room now, Nanny. These men are done here."

"All right then." Tubbe pulled a business card from his shirt pocket. "You think of anything else, give me a call."

Following Tubbe outside, Chitto watched the door close. He waited, listening for the sound of the chain lock sliding into place. It didn't.

"We might be able to catch the owner of the towing company," Tubbe said.

"We're this close," Chitto said, pushing fatigue into the background. Though he returned Tubbe's grin, he would've given an eyetooth for a nicotine fix.

En route to the towing company, Chitto mentally rehearsed what they had learned. Clearly, Delbert Wilcox's death was the answer to the widow's prayer, for it allowed an end to a bad marriage that her religion had prohibited her from leaving. The real question dealt with whether the prayer's answer came as a result of coincidence or fate.

"Fate," he grunted, mind going back in time. Two years had passed since he took Mary to see the healer. She had talked about fate, too.

It was her time to leave, the elderly Choctaw said. *A person's end is fated from birth. It's in the stars.*

"Bullshit," Chitto mumbled. "We just didn't catch it in time."

He rubbed his mouth, thinking again of the two reasons he'd come up with to account for Wilcox's death.

Then there was that third option . . .

"Delbert's *dead.*" Rex Reynolds sat down quickly. "Well, hell, that would explain why he ain't been to work since . . ." He pulled a time card from a file box on his desktop. "Since Tuesday."

"Three days ago," Tubbe said.

Chitto calculated days since the festival at Tuskahoma. Four days. The victim had gone missing the day after the festival ended.

"Yes, sir, that'd be right. What was it? Car accident? Sonofabitch got drunk agin, didn't he?" Reynolds shook his head. "I told him and told him, he was gonna have to give up that drink, he expected to work for me. I mean, how's it look to have a drunkard hauling in other people's wrecked cars 'cause *they* got drunk."

The widow's living situation cleared up for Chitto. Wilcox drank his paycheck, maybe part of hers. He wondered if that was what led to the separation. The girl's condition. His thinking went to the earlier incident with Teresa Walker. Alcohol involved there, too. And two girls the real victims.

"His death was by suspicious means," Tubbe said.

"Well, I'll swan. You mean, like he was kill't?"

"Too early to tell," Chitto said. "You have an address for Mr. Wilcox? I mean, since he and his wife separated."

Reynolds's eyebrows hitched. "Him and Emma split the blanket? No one told me that." Another headshake. "Can't help you there, but most guys like 'at put up at the motel on the old highway." He looked at Tubbe. "You know the one. That cheap, sleazy rat hole."

"We'll check it out," Tubbe said. "He have any enemies? Owe

61

anyone money?"

Reynolds rubbed the back of his neck. "Not I know of, least none I can think of right off."

Tubbe dispensed his second business card within an hour. "Give me a call, anything else comes to mind."

Outside, Chitto faced Tubbe. "We were told to move fast. Maybe we better check out the motel now, before the FBI gets wind of things."

"Follow me," Tubbe said, grinning.

The motel manager let them into Delbert Wilcox's room. Red shag carpet, worn thin. Red-flocked wallpaper, rubbed shiny. Exposed bedding, dirty. Bathroom tiles looking as though they hadn't been scrubbed in a decade. The smell of stale beer.

"So you haven't seen him since . . . when?" Tubbe asked.

The motel manager was a small, dark man of indeterminate ethnicity who spoke with clipped speech. "Pays by the week. Rent is due tomorrow."

"Wouldn't be too quick renting out this room. What can you tell us about his habits?"

"He comes, he goes." The man lifted his shoulders in a detached manner. "Spent more time at the bar around the corner than here. The Double-Aught, that's what it's called."

Bar . . .

Chitto sighed. He hadn't made it by the Red River Tavern to follow up on the Munro mugging. He noticed a grinning Frank Tubbe looking his way.

"What?"

"You look like a cowpoke that's been thrown and stirrup-drug. Sure you're up for this, professor?"

Chitto laughed quietly. "How about we hoof it to the tavern. I could use some air."

★ ★ ★ ★ ★

"Been wonderin' what happened to him." The bartender at the Double-Aught swiped a dirty rag across the bar top. "Damn truck's been parked in the lot for days now."

Tubbe looked at Chitto, then at the barman. "How many days?"

"Lemme think." He dipped his head, looking at the floor. "Tuesday night. Last time he was in here was Tuesday night."

"He leave with anyone?"

"Can't say. I get tipped not to notice things like 'at. When's he gonna come move that pickup? This ain't no public parking lot."

"I'll send a tow truck out."

"Let's take a look at that pickup," Chitto said as they exited the bar. They found the red Ford locked, nothing out of the ordinary inside from what they could see.

"So, he was picked up at his favorite bar," Tubbe said as they walked back to their vehicles. "That means, whoever it was followed this dude long enough to know his habits. Then they held him from Tuesday night through Thursday, killed him at sunup on Friday." He looked at Chitto. "That add up to you?"

"Four days if you do the math," Chitto said. "Other than that, no." He wrote his cell-phone number on the back of a business card. "Appreciate it, Frank, you let me know anything else you learn. I'll do the same. Day or night, doesn't matter. I'm sittin' on this one."

"Will do. I'll check on past incidents of domestic violence, any drunk-and-disorderly complaints." Tubbe wrote a cell-phone number on the card he gave to Chitto. "Maybe question the neighbors, see if they saw the husband around since he was thrown out—*reportedly* thrown out."

So, Tubbe thought Emma Love Wilcox looked like the best suspect, too.

"Girl's not going to school, she might spot you around the neighborhood. They get spooked, they'll run. Innocent or not."

"They would at that." Tubbe paused, looking thoughtful. "Have to work this weekend, fall festivals in Tishamingo. We keep a high profile to make sure the no-drinking rule's enforced. First thing Monday, I'll give child and family services a call. See about getting that girl back in school. Too young to have her life taken away because of an unwanted pregnancy."

"Maybe check if Emma's father's alive, if she has brothers. Uncles. You know, men in the family that might take care of a problem."

"Yeah . . ." Tubbe tipped his hat and walked off.

Chitto studied the Chickasaw in his rearview mirror, reassessing his initial impression. Looked like the part in his scalp had done him some good. He wasn't so full of himself anymore.

CHAPTER SEVEN

Chitto rolled down the window of his Chevy Dually, glad for cooler air. Overnight, the humidity dropped ten percent and the forecast called for temperatures in the eighties. Threadbare jeans and a cotton tee helped, too. He thought about turning on the radio but decided against it. He liked it quiet. Setting the cruise control to sixty-five, he settled into himself.

Through the back glass, he glimpsed hay and alfalfa remnants swirling out of the pickup's bed. He'd spent the morning at the stable where he boarded his horse, Blue. He brushed the big gray gelding and checked its hooves. Finding one shoe loose, he considered pulling all four, letting the horse go barefoot. But he preferred using his own horse for mounted patrols, as when he worked the Tuskahoma festival. That meant Blue needed new shoes.

He considered his schedule, how it was taking him out of his own district, even the Choctaw Nation. His non-existent weekends. While he preferred shoeing Blue, his schedule was unpredictable. And Blue couldn't wait. Retrieving his cell phone, Chitto pulled up the number for a farrier. After three unsuccessful attempts and a lot of swearing about cell-phone reception, he got through.

"Hey, Shorty. Sam Chitto here. Can you work Blue in next week?"

He listened to what sounded like pages in a daytimer being turned, picturing the six-foot-two farrier on the other end and thinking about the nickname. People had a weird sense of humor.

The naked corpse of Delbert Wilcox came to mind. Pasty, pink skin. Hairy body, bushy hair and brows. Eyes open like they were staring at the ax dropping overhead. Was the dead man's appearance meant to be a joke? Someone saying, *Yuk, yuk, who's got the last laugh now?* as the ax fell. Shorty's voice broke up the grisly vision.

"Next Wednesday, 'bout four o'clock. How's 'at sound?"

"I'll set it up at the barn. You know where to send the bill."

Ending the connection, Chitto dialed the stable, then continued north on U.S. 69. The reverse route he traveled the day before on the way to Ada to question Wilcox's widow.

I'm going in circles, getting nowhere.

Before he went to bed the night before, Chitto called the two women who discovered Wilcox's body. With identical results. Both the councilwoman for District 7 and for District 10 used the same words to describe what they saw. *A big, hairy, naked guy with his head cut off.* Neither saw a vehicle in the pow-wow area nor anyone walking around the complex. And neither expressed any concern about a crime being committed on council grounds.

The calls left him dissatisfied. The two women had reputations for being steamrollers. Why hadn't they expressed outrage? Pressed him for answers? Chitto cautioned them not to discuss the matter before he let them go and finished the evening with a call to Dan Blackfox.

"You tell the ME to make us a copy of the autopsy report?" Blackfox asked. "FBI will prob'ly drag their feet."

"Yeah. Tubbe wants a copy, too. He's planning to follow up with neighbors, look at family members that might've held a grudge."

"Why'd they be holding a grudge?"

Chitto hesitated, debating whether to bother Blackfox with the pregnant girl, Nanny Love. "Just a hunch right now. Something more substantial surfaces, I'll let you know."

"Sounds like we got everything we can get. I'll fill the Bureau in first thing Monday."

"Hold up, Dan. I'm not ready to turn loose of this one."

"Didn't expect you would; just keep your head down. I'll play it up as an Indian matter with the FBI, not worth their time. Of course, they'll want a briefing on what we found. You need to be handy for that."

An image of Ramon Rodriquez popped into Chitto's mind. "Why? Haven't learned anything more than what'll be in the ME's report."

"Doesn't matter a hill of beans, you know that. I'll let you know when they'll be here. Meanwhile, work around your other duties and update me regular." Another pause had come on the line. "You think you'll be working outside our jurisdiction, give me a whistle. I'll see what I can do to clear the road."

Chitto was glad he had free rein on the case, but the questions he had pondered the day before still festered. Though he often woke with answers, this morning he had none.

"Maybe some downtime will help clear out the lint," he said half aloud.

Traffic was light. Now and then, Chitto caught sight of a beat-up pickup and older sedan in the rearview mirror, tag teaming each other. Other vehicles passed him up or turned down side roads. He glanced beyond the hard lines of the highway to the country beyond.

Prolonged heat had taken its toll, causing crops to ripen early or die in the effort, trees to change color prematurely or go straight from green to dead. In spite of dryness, the foothills of the Ouachitas showed speckles of red and gold, and the rivers and creeks, though lower than normal, ran freely. Opting for natural air rather than artificially cooled, Chitto lowered his window to smell the new-cut hay in the fields and the smoke from burning irrigation ditches, feel the wind blow his hair and the sun warm his face. Content to let his senses soak it up, he put his mind on cruise control and let eighty miles roll beneath his wheels.

Chitto exited Highway 69 onto Highway 1 and within minutes reached Krebs. His hometown once thrived as a coal-mining center. Now it domiciled two thousand souls, most of which worked in McAlester, the county seat and location of the state penitentiary. Big Mac.

McAlester was home base for the District 11 tribal offices. When Chitto decided to work for the Nation, his mother had wanted him to apply for the District 11 position, the one his father's death left vacant. He opted for headquarters at Durant, thinking it would put him in a better position to solve his father's and Bert Gilly's murders. Because he hadn't succeeded didn't mean he wasn't tuned in. Time had a way of making people careless.

Leaving Krebs behind, Chitto drove down a road skirting low, wooded hills. Ten minutes later, he turned onto a graveled track leading through a narrow tunnel of hickory trees at the end of which sat a brick, ranch-style home. His mother's house. A fold-up clothesline slumped in the backyard, unused since his mother purchased a clothes dryer. To one side, a good-sized fenced area filled with ragweed was going to seed. He remembered when corn stalks danced in the breeze. Right now, it was a weed patch.

At the front door, he turned the handle, testing to see if it was locked. It wasn't. He shook his head, thinking how people tended to overlook the obvious. To locals, a maximum-security prison was just another building they drove past on their way from here to there. The more familiar something was, the less the perceived threat.

"Mama?" Chitto's first order of business was to ask his mother about the council meeting the day before.

"She's in the kitchen," a woman's voice answered.

He walked into a large living room filled with overstuffed furniture and a flat-screen TV, volume turned up. A quilting frame occupied the middle of the room where a stoop-shouldered woman worked, white hair twisted into a bun on her neck. His grandmother, Rhody Pitchlynn. He walked to her side and gave her a hug.

"New quilt, Grandma?"

"No. Old fingers don't work too fast." She nodded toward the television. "That man there say a big rock going to blow up, turn us to stardust." She looked at him with cloudy eyes. "You a rock man. What you think about that?"

He glanced at the TV, listening to a narrator on the science channel talk about Gliese 710. The orange dwarf's approach could scatter sections of the Oort Cloud, causing meteor showers to bombard Earth. The timeframe numbered in thousands of years.

He laid a hand on her shoulder. "Good chance it won't happen in your lifetime, Grandma, so don't worry about it."

"I don't worry about it." She pointed to the quilt stretched before her. "This tells the stories of our People. I make it for you so you don't forget." She looked at him. "When that rock blows up, you take it with you to the stars so our stories don't die."

Chitto made no attempt to correct his grandmother's thinking, deciding a scientific explanation would sound as far-fetched as her own. He nodded respectfully and admired the colorful blocks that recalled old folktales.

The spider with a red spot on her back was Grandmother

Spider, who stole fire from the white man, carrying the hot coal on her back to get it to the People. The gray, mouse-looking creature with a large mouth was Possum, who tricked Deer and laughed so hard its mouth stretched permanently. The one she worked on now was unfamiliar to him, a green plant surrounded with snakes and insects.

"You say Mama's in the kitchen?" He glanced toward the hallway.

"Blabbin' on the phone—always blabbin' on the phone. Politickin' instead of plantin' corn." She looked at him. "When winter is done, you plant me a Tom Fuller patch."

Tom Fuller. An Anglo corruption of *tafula,* the Choctaw word for corn soup. In early days, a corn patch was the first thing red people planted come spring. Since ancient times, corn helped the People survive winter. The starving time. Settlers quickly adopted the ritual, but that was long ago, and the last thing Chitto wanted to think about was planting corn.

"No need for that, Grandma. Neighbors give you all the fresh corn you can eat. When that runs out, I'll buy some at the Safeway. They got all kinds. Yellow corn. White corn. Hominy corn. Corn with peppers in it. You name it, I'll get it for you."

Chitto did not understand his grandmother's next utterance, but perhaps that was a good thing. Leaving her to her quilting, he walked into a kitchen smelling of roasted chicken. He noticed a platter of corn fritters and a dish of berry-corn cobbler on the table, place settings for three.

Mattie Chitto, a dark slender woman with short, graying hair, sat at a kitchen bar, ear to the phone. "You planning to stay for dinner?" she said, covering the receiver with her free hand.

He looked at the three place settings again.

"Dr. Anderson's coming. Set another place if you're planning to eat."

"Dr. Anderson—you sick?"

"P-H-D doctor," she whispered, tapping her head. "Not M-D."

An academic. Chitto tried to pull up a face to go with the name. None came to mind.

After setting another place, Chitto pulled a fritter off the platter. He shook his head as he listened to his mother's conversation, which involved a meeting of some kind. She was not following the path he envisioned when his father's murder made her a widow. She ran for the District 11 council position instead and won, becoming a member of more committees than he could shake a stick at.

Would she have taken a more traditional path if Mary and I'd had children . . . ?

The doorbell interrupting his train of thought, Chitto glanced toward his mother. She jabbed a finger at the front door.

Chitto stared at an auburn-haired woman with green eyes. Maybe thirty, tall and angular in frame. Not what he would call attractive, but she had a natural quality that made her striking. He noted the casual dress. Wrinkled Dockers, short-sleeved camp shirt, walking shoes.

So different from my Mary. So small, round and soft . . .

"Um, hi."

"Oh—sorry. Mama's on the phone." He stepped aside so she could enter. "I'm Sam, Sam Chitto. Her son." Looking past her, he saw an older model, half-ton Suburban that appeared packed for a long trip.

"Leslie Anderson." Observing his interest in the Suburban, she answered his unspoken question. "Been staying with a friend up at Tahlequah. Since I'll be working with the Choctaw, I'm moving my stuff down here."

"Oh?"

"I'm a cultural anthropologist. You know, old lifeways and

71

values. Rituals. Stories. But my real focus is on the causes and consequences of social and cultural variation. You know, adaptations? I got acquainted with your mother a few years ago. She's interested in the old ways and reestablishing cultural values. Lot of people are."

The wrinkled clothes became clear. Field research didn't allow for conveniences such as laundry service or steam irons.

"You said you'd be working with Choctaw now. That mean you've been working with some of the other nations?"

"The Creek and Seminole year before last and the Cherokee this last year. After the Choctaw, I'm planning to move on to the Chickasaw. Those are the ones that formed the original Four Mothers' Society. Mattie's going to introduce me to some people down here."

Leading the anthropologist to the living room, Chitto introduced her to his grandmother.

"Yes, we've met," Leslie said. "Your grandmother's highly respected across the nations—and very influential." She walked over to look at the quilt. "This is beautiful, Rhody."

She looked at Chitto. "You're a lucky man to be getting this, it's one of a kind. Why, it's probably worth . . ." She looked at the quilt again. "I don't know, hundreds of dollars. Maybe even thousands."

Chitto eyed the quilt with new eyes.

"Is that a double-headed drum?" She walked toward a drum in the corner of the room. "It is, and it's *old.*" Kneeling, she traced her fingers across the worn drumhead.

"My father's," Rhody said. "He used it at many sings."

Hearing his mother call out from the kitchen, Chitto helped his grandmother to her feet and pointed Leslie toward the kitchen. "I don't remember hearing about that society you mentioned."

"The Four Mothers' Society?" She laughed. "For good

reason. Started way back in the early 1800s, before the Removal. The Choctaw-Chickasaw Heritage Committee is a spinoff of it, and that was just started in the 1970s." She looked at him. "You *do* know that Mattie and Rhody belong to the heritage committee."

He shrugged, thinking of the committees his mother and grandmother got involved in over the years.

"Well," she continued, "other tribes have similar things to the old society. Only today, the meanings behind the old traditions have been transformed into more social purposes. Like the Green Corn Ceremony is now a social dance." She arched her eyebrows. "Not taken nearly as seriously as in the old days."

"My mother's the one into those old customs. Not me."

She paused. "Well, I don't know if you could say I'm *into* them. I come at them more as a scientist." She looked at him. "I hear you do geology on the side, so pretty much the same mindset. Only I deal with people instead of rocks—and I do it full-time."

Geology? Chitto wondered how she would know that—and that his grandmother was making him a quilt. He was bothered when strangers knew things about him he had not disclosed.

"So, where are you setting up base?"

She looked at him, blinking. "Why, *here*. When I saw Mattie at the Choctaw sing this last weekend, she insisted I stay with her."

"*Leslie*," Mattie said as they walked into the kitchen. "Welcome to my home. Dinner's about ready. And don't worry, there's plenty for all of us."

Leslie hesitated, looking toward Chitto. "Did I get the wrong day?" She pulled a dog-eared daytimer from a large bag slung over her shoulder.

"No, it was Sam. He's the one got the wrong day."

"*Me?*" Chitto stared at his mother. "Didn't Wanda call yesterday? She was going to call, let you know I was coming."

Mattie tossed her hand dismissively. "She prob'ly mentioned it, but we got to talking about other things. I just expected you tomorrow. Sundays are when you usually come."

"Oh. Well, I needed to talk to you about . . ." Chitto hesitated, thinking about his reason for being there. "But it can wait 'til later."

"Don't matter. I always cook for a crowd." Mattie looked at Leslie. "You can move your things into the spare bedroom later. Let's eat while it's hot."

"Oh—I almost forgot." Leslie pulled a brown paper bag from her satchel. "I picked up some ice cream for dessert. Thought vanilla would be a safe bet. It's probably starting to melt."

"Ice cream—you bring ice cream?" Rhody's face clouded. "That is made with *milk*."

"Yes . . ."

"*Pish.*" Rhody shook her head. "Thought you knew something 'bout Indians. Milk and likker is bad business for us. One makes us bloat, the other makes us crazy."

"Bloat—*oh* . . ." Leslie's face flushed. "Seems not everything's covered in a textbook."

Chitto squelched an urge to laugh.

Mattie took the sack from the anthropologist's hand. "Don't pay her no mind. She don't want to eat it, she don't have to. Just leaves more for the rest of us. I'll put this in the icebox." She looked at Chitto. "Well, don't just sit there. Start the food 'round the table."

Chitto didn't need to be prodded. As soon as everyone was seated, he started passing dishes. He ate hungrily and noticed Leslie, unlike most white women he encountered, didn't pick at her plate either.

"So, who're you working for?" he asked, his curiosity meter

74

running. "Government office? College?"

She met his eyes. "I'm on a grant, an independent grant funded by the American University in D.C. The program solicits research proposals in cultural anthropology, both substantive and theoretical subfields."

"And your research grant's on this Four Mothers' Society—"

"You're being rude, Sam. Leslie's come a long way to get here. Besides, this stuff's boring to you."

"Boring?" Leslie looked at Chitto, her eyebrows raised.

"Well, not really—I mean, not *all* of it."

Chitto noticed she was grinning. The anthropologist had a sense of humor. Returning the smile, he said, "Back to your research. Substantive or theoretical?"

As Mattie started to protest again, Leslie spoke up.

"It's okay, Mattie. I'm pleased when people show an interest in my studies." She faced Chitto. "Both, actually. I'm working with the documented material gathered from groups in Mississippi, Tennessee and western Alabama prior to the Removal, exploring how it's adapted and changed." She looked at Mattie. "I'm anxious to see what you have for me."

"Well, if everyone's had their fill . . ." Mattie retrieved a paper from the corner desk. "Here's that list of people you wanted me to put together. Want me to tell you how to find them?"

"Oh, yes. Please."

Chitto grew restless as the women began to talk among themselves. He found his mother's deference to the anthropologist irritating. The talk, boring. His plans for a quiet weekend, a puff of smoke. Then, the conversation at the table caught his attention.

". . . and you're sure they'll talk to me, even though I'm a stranger?" Leslie said to Mattie.

"Told them you were coming. Some of them don't like talking to a machine, so you'll have to write down their stories."

Mattie pointed out certain ones on the list. "These get a little nervous 'round tape recorders, but they'll talk to anybody who'll listen."

The last comment struck a chord with Chitto. Frank Tubbe was scheduled to work this weekend at their fall celebration, a good chance to talk to him about anything new on the Wilcox case. Barring that, maybe he could get people talking, see if they would leak something to a stranger.

"Another thing . . ." Leslie looked between Mattie and Rhody. "Would either of you know if anyone's doing healing ceremonies down here? Maybe cleansing rituals? I ask because I've been hearing about them in other nations. There was a cleansing ritual for some men last night up in the Cherokee Nation, and Wade—he's a colleague of mine who's working on that kind of thing—invited me to attend with him and . . ."

As Leslie continued to talk, Chitto's thinking digressed to the number of anthropologists and sociologists invading the state. Unlike archaeologists, they did not dig in the ground for bones that would identify a community of people. The Peoples in Indian territory were displaced from their origins and had no boneyards. At least not ancient ones. These scientists dug through minds, the collective unconscious, attempting to identify a community of humankind. A culture. Looking at mythology and religion. Social development. How a person related to another and to the whole. Observing the woman's enthusiasm, he turned his attention back to the conversation.

". . . Wade's the one who mentioned healing ceremonies for women being held down this way. And some more are scheduled soon. Can you help me find out who's doing that?"

"Not sure." Mattie pointed out a name on the list. "But you might check with him."

"Mr. Munro in Bryan County? That's near the Red River, isn't it?" She cocked her head, then grinned. "Oh, I remember him now. He's a singer."

Munro? Chitto glanced toward his mother, frowning.

"Who wants ice cream on their cobbler?" Mattie rose from the table and walked to the refrigerator.

"Me," Rhody said.

"What?" Mattie stared at her mother. "After what you said to Leslie?"

"So? No skin off my nose. And she will learn a lesson." Rhody looked at Leslie. "Next time, bring chocolate."

A grin played at the corners of Chitto's mouth. "Yeah, I'll have ice cream."

"Me, too," Leslie said, smiling at him as though they shared a joke.

Chitto picked up the list from the table. A lot of the names were familiar. Old timers in the Nation, one of which he had just spent time with.

"Wait up, Mama." Chitto laid a hand on his mother's arm as she rounded the table. "How is it you know Sonny Boy Munro? Bryan County's District 9, way outside your territory."

"What—?" Mattie removed his hand from her arm. "You forget it's my business to know the people in the Nation—no matter where they live. Now give Leslie back *her* list."

He handed the list to a red-faced Leslie Anderson.

She accepted it silently. Clearly, she had been caught by surprise, too.

"Need to get back to Durant." Chitto stood, said his farewells to his grandmother, and turned to the anthropologist. "Nice to meet you, Mrs. Anderson."

"Call me Leslie. And it's *Miss* Anderson. My job's all-consuming, I'm afraid."

A contradiction. A woman interested in the old ways of doing things who didn't follow tradition herself.

Chitto looked at his mother. "Walk me to the door, Mama."

It was not a request.

"Didn't mean to snap at you, Sam. You surprised me, that's all. I'm not used to my son interrogating me and my guests like we're criminals—and in my home." She glanced at him. "You know how your father felt about these things."

"Yeah, it's just . . ."

Reconsidering his mother's familiarity with Sonny Boy, Chitto did not finish the thought. This was not the place to divulge information about people he encountered on the job, especially when it dealt with an honored man who had fallen from honor.

"It's early yet," Mattie said when they reached the front porch. "Why don't you stay? Leslie's a nice girl—and smart. *College* smart, like you. I was hoping you and Rona would hit it off." She shrugged. "But you haven't, so I thought maybe . . ."

Chitto tensed, knowing what was coming.

"Sam, it's high time you thought about finding someone. I still want grandchildren, you know."

"Don't start on me, Mama. I told you, I'm not ready."

"You think I don't know that? You don't even put flowers on Mary's grave on Memorial Day. It's because you won't let her go. Her *Shilombish* won't leave if it thinks things aren't right with you."

"You know I don't buy that old stuff about inner and outer shadows." He rubbed a tight circle on his forehead with his fingers. "Besides, I had a reason for wanting you to walk me to the door."

"Then . . . what?" She lifted her shoulders, let them drop.

"Pertains to the murder there at the old capitol. Were you at the council meeting yesterday?"

"Haven't missed one in ten years."

"I figured you'd call me soon as you heard about it."

"Well, Esther and Wynona already called the police by the time I got there."

"Yeah, I know, but I figured I'd hear from you anyway." He paused, waiting. "So, did the council have anything to say about it?"

"No . . ." She glanced to the side, blinking. "We had a lot of other business to cover."

"And you didn't see anything out of the ordinary? I mean, you're more in touch with law enforcement than the others. Anything strike you as unusual?"

She shrugged again. "Just a big, hairy, naked guy with his head cut off."

"Just a . . ." The exact words the two councilwomen who found the body used. Chitto didn't know whether to laugh or swear and decided either response would take too much effort. "Thanks for dinner," he said, turning to leave.

"Wait up, Sam." Her forehead wrinkled. "You're investigating that killing, aren't you? Why isn't the FBI doing it? It's out of your jurisdiction."

Chitto sighed. His own mother had treed him. "I'm not assigned to the case, Mama. Just curious because of where it happened." He headed for his truck.

"You know that old saying about the curious cat," she called out.

He turned. "Meaning what?"

"Don't go sticking your nose where it don't belong. That's what I mean." Her voice softened. "Look what happened to your daddy."

He smiled at her. "I'm not in any danger, Mama. Call you later in the week."

Before leaving, Chitto took a quick look inside Leslie's Suburban. An office on wheels was a better description. File boxes, tape recorder, laptop computer, portable printer, camera. He noticed a bedroll and pillow on the back seat, a small camp stove on the floor. Apparently, the Suburban served as sleeping quarters from time to time.

Suddenly, Chitto felt envious. If he'd pursued geology seriously instead of "on the side," his life would be a lot less restrictive, too. Pushing aside feelings of regret, he climbed into his truck, reminding himself that he had an ulterior motive for the decision to go into law enforcement. Ten years now, he'd been looking for his father's killer. And found nothing.

But he did find Mary . . .

The moment Chitto met Mary Folsom, he wanted to hold her close, protect her. She wasn't much taller than her fifth-grade students.

She'd invited a member of the tribal police to visit her class to talk of its role in the judicial system. Blackfox sent Chitto, a rookie investigator with a college education. He wasn't expecting the small, delicate girl-woman, eyes tilted slightly, giving her the seductive look of a geisha. He became so tongue-tied, she had to come to his rescue during his talk, gently asking questions to keep him on track.

Afterwards, she read the desire in his eyes, felt the fire in his touch and asked him to take her to dinner. She led him to her bed that same night. A month later, he asked her to marry him, four weeks to the day, and accepted his wedding vow as a lawman accepted a vow to protect the weak and defenseless.

I take you, Mary Bernadette Folsom, to be my partner, loving what I know of you and trusting what I do not yet know. I eagerly anticipate the chance to grow together, getting to know the woman you will become, and falling in love a little more every day. I promise to protect you through whatever life may bring.

It *was* the vow of a lawman, he realized now. A pledge to keep someone treasured from becoming a phantom figure in a magic shadow-show.

But he hadn't protected her.

CHAPTER EIGHT

Chitto spent Sunday morning on domestic duties. Cleaning. Laundry. Garbage removal. He planned to drive to Tishamingo later, the location of the Chickasaw celebration, hoping to get a bead on Wilcox's killer.

Finding a half-eaten microwave dinner in the kitchen, he decided to donate it to his neighbor's dog. Hattie George was the only neighbor who'd befriended him since he'd lived there, a fact he attributed to being in law enforcement. For the general populace, a cop was someone to be avoided, on or off duty. But Hattie was not a member of the general populace.

He raked the leftovers into a tin pie pan and walked next door. As he set the pan on her front porch, Hattie walked outside. Legs, bowed from straddling a saddle before bones calcified, made for a waddling gait. Short, peppered hair on end. She wore her usual attire, a blue chambray shirt and suede Chukka boots.

A mongrel pup hound, long in the leg and square in the jaw, pushed past her and stuck his nose in the pan.

"*Boycott*," she scolded. "You got the manners of a Texas warthog."

Hattie named the dog after Cesar Chavez's dog, which led him to question the right of humans to eat other sentient beings. She experienced a similar awakening some thirty years before, causing her to swear off meat. Her vegan habits were still not well accepted in her pioneer ranching family.

"I swear," she said, scratching the dog's head, "I'm gonna feed you to that big alley cat one of these days."

Grinning at the threat, Chitto picked up the empty pan and sailed it like a Frisbee to his front porch.

"Wish someone would take this little greaser off my hands, Sam. I cain't keep up with him."

"Wouldn't be fair to the dog, Hattie. What with my job and all."

"You think he lucked out finding my back stoop, hobbled like I am? He's gonna make a good watchdog, hears ever' little thing. Smart, too, for all his ugly. Much as you're gone, you need a dog to watch out for your place. Better 'n Neighborhood Watch."

"Don't need Neighborhood Watch or a dog. I've got you."

She bristled. "Got better things to do than watch out for the likes of you."

"Like what?"

"*Sam . . . Sam.*" Aggravation flavored her tone.

"Well, if things change." He let it go at that.

"Heard your vacuum running earlier. Got a cleaning lady helps me out from time to time. Fixin' to call her myself. You want, I can mention you need help. Name's Angelina Something-or-Other." She looked him in the eye. "Only thing is, you'll have to pay her in cash."

Chitto nodded, saying nothing. Payment in cash meant Angelina Something-or-Other was an illegal.

"Honest as the day's long, if that's your worry. Ain't found nothin' missin' yet, lessen you count some eggs and canned goods, loaf of bread. Got two little boys she's raisin' by herself. My philosophy tells me a person don't steal food lessen they're hungry . . ." She looked away, staring at some distant place on the horizon. "Ever notice how many girls are raisin' their babies alone these days?"

Figuring she didn't expect a reply, he said nothing.

She looked at him. "Does a good job, tackle anything you want her to. Not the fussy kind."

He shook his head.

"All right then," she said. "Give a whistle when you're ready."

Chitto helped Hattie wrestle the hound pup back into the house. As he drove away, he considered the housekeeper idea. He didn't refuse Hattie's offer because the housecleaner was illegal but because he couldn't stand the thought of another woman in Mary's house. Handling her things, moving them, eliminating her scent. Things he didn't feel comfortable expressing.

Chitto took State Highway 78 to Tishamingo. Fall festivals made for a busy time in all the nations. Stomp dances. Stickball demonstrations. Singings. The four-day events were to celebrate the end of the old year and the beginning of the new. Custom dictated the length of the celebration, but four was a special number. A link to nature. The four seasons. Four primary directions. Heritage committees and cultural societies were responsible for the resurgence of the interest in the past.

He rolled down the window and breathed deep, thankful for another cool day. Cumulus clouds floating in from the Gulf held promise of rain. He slowed to scrutinize leaves on trees along the highway, remembering an old saying of his grandmother's. *Leaves that turn their bellies to the sky is a sign of rain.* To his regret, he saw no leaf bellies showing, so he sped up again.

He was glad for an excuse to get out of the house. Weekends were times when he could almost believe in things his mother talked about. Like shadows, which some of the People referred to as ghosts. Just one of the things the Mississippi teachers taught those forced out of the old homeland as part of the

Removal—and one that both his mother and grandmother had bought into.

In olden times, the Choctaw did not believe in Christian concepts like the soul. Instead, the person possessed an inner shadow, the *Shiliup*, and an outer one, the *Shilombish*. After death, the inner shadow began the long journey to the west, but the outer shadow remained until the funeral ceremonies were completed. But, as his mother pointed out the day before, sometimes the outer shadow would not fade away until it felt everything was all right with its family.

"Bullshit," he mumbled. It was only natural he would think of Mary when he was at the house. The woman was the center of the home.

Unless you're a cultural anthropologist.

Made of quarried gray stone, the Chickasaw's old capitol was similar in architecture to the Choctaw's. People scurried about and parking places were at a premium. Chitto watched for tail-lights that signaled a space being vacated. On his second sweep, two teenage girls carrying folding lawn chairs walked in front of him. One of them caught his eye. Slender. Long, dark hair. And a face that looked like nine miles of bad road.

Teresa-with-no-H?

He drove to the end of the row and turned up the next, hoping for a closer look. He glimpsed the girls disappearing in a crowd heading for the dance grounds.

Couldn't be, he thought. It's only been a couple of days.

Pulling into a parking place, he reminded himself he was there to be a fly on the wall. Listen to strangers talk up the latest gossip. See if any let something slip about the recent murder. Barring that, he would search out Tubbe to see if he had learned anything new.

★　★　★　★　★

A half hour later, Chitto had learned nothing. People were wary. Young mothers watching over broods eyed him warily. Groups of older people sitting in the shade stopped talking when he neared. Clusters of men seemed as intent on watching him as he was watching them. Had news about the beheading after the Choctaw sing made the circuit?

He happened on a man riding horseback wearing a Chickasaw Nation police uniform. "Frank Tubbe around?" He showed his ID.

"Somewhere . . ." The officer stood in the saddle for a better view. "Want me to run him to ground?"

"Naw, I'll probably run into him. You got your hands full."

Chitto bought a soda at one of the food booths and walked toward the dance grounds. The large, grassy area was crowded. Anglos, blacks, Indians. Children and adults. Sitting on the grass, in lawn chairs, watching a dozen-or-so dancers in ceremonial dress. Feather headdresses. Rattles. Robes. Some dancing feverously. Others, meditatively. He recognized the dress of the Choctaw, the Chickasaw and Cherokee. Others he could make an educated guess on. Celebration schedules were advertised in newspapers, posted on tribal web sites, attracting dancers from across the country. Many were at the Choctaw festival the weekend before. Like rodeos, the pow-wow circuit attracted repeat performers.

A red-headed woman caught his eye. Leslie Anderson had traded Dockers and walking shoes for a short-sleeved blouse, long loose skirt and strap sandals. Her hair, tied back on her neck, was knotted with a green scarf. Bent over a tape recorder, she did not see him.

He frowned. She was supposed to work with the Chickasaw after she worked with the Choctaw. What was she doing here? He watched to see what she was recording.

In front of her, a half-dozen singers pounded a large drumhead and chanted. Honored men from around the nations. Their dress was not as elaborate as the dancers'. T-shirts and faded jeans. Khakis and cotton shirts. He gave the singers a brief look, then paused, looking at one in particular. An old man wearing a plaid shirt and jeans, worn canvas loafers. Sonny Boy Munro. He watched for several minutes. Observing the old man's movements. Listening to his voice rise and fall.

Chitto frowned again. Sonny Boy said he turned to drink because he was an honored man, yet here he was a few days after falling off the wagon performing with other honored men. Somehow, that didn't stack.

Caught up in his chant, the singer did not look his way. Someone else did.

"Hey there." Leslie grinned as she approached him. "Thought you weren't into this kind of thing."

"Official business." The quick up-and-down look she gave him made him uncomfortable. He realized he was in casual clothes. "Oh, *unofficial* official business."

"Undercover, huh? Yeah, your mom said you lived and breathed your job." She hesitated. "Don't interpret that as criticism. My work takes over my life, too."

He shook his head slightly. He'd been the topic of conversation again.

"My mother come with you?"

"No—yes. I mean, I followed her over. She had something else to take care of, didn't want to stay all day." She hesitated, the smile disappearing. "What is it? You're looking at me like you're dissecting a frog."

"Didn't expect to see you here. Thought you were working with the Chickasaw *after* the Choctaw, and . . ." He pointed with his chin toward the dance area. "Surprised you're being allowed to record the singing."

"*Ah,* that." She glanced to where her tape recorder sat running. "Mattie arranged it. I heard about the celebration today and she knew just who to call." She glanced toward her tape recorder again. "Look, I need to see how my tape's holding out, but maybe we can grab a bite later. People are talking about the fry bread and corn soup; we should check it out."

"Yeah, maybe." Watching her walk away, Chitto felt two-faced. He had no intention of eating with her.

Chitto spotted the two teenage girls he'd seen earlier, sitting to one side of the singers. Circling to get a closer look, he saw the battered girl was, in fact, Teresa Walker. He was glad to see the bruises on her face mottling, a sign of healing. Sidling up to them, he squatted on his heels next to her.

When she noticed him, her face displayed surprise, but she said nothing.

"Good to see you, Teresa." Chitto spoke quietly. "You feeling better, then?"

"Yeah, pretty good." She sat up straighter. "She thought it would do me good, you know, to come."

Rona Guthrie, Chitto thought, putting a name to "she."

He nodded at the girl sitting beside her. "Name's Chitto. I'm with the Choctaw tribal police." The girl made no comment. Indian women were not forthright by nature, but getting these girls to talk was like pulling teeth. "Didn't get your name," he pressed.

"Letty," the girl said softly. "Letty Munro."

Munro. The old man's granddaughter? The one who was supposed to call him?

"We go to the same school," Teresa said.

Chitto looked at Letty again. "Looks like your grandpa's feeling better." Noting the girl's confusion, he said, "I gave him a ride home couple days ago."

"Oh, you're *that* cop." She grinned. "Yeah, he likes you. He said you make good PBJs."

He smiled at that. "Gave your grandfather my card, told him to have you call me."

She held his eyes, not blinking. "He didn't give me no card."

Chitto nodded. More times than not, cards ended up in waste cans.

"Okay, then. You girls drive safe when you head back home. Be a lot of people on the roads."

Mumbling, "Yes sir," they went back to watching the dancing.

"Huh," Chitto grunted as he walked away. This mission seemed to be a bust.

"Huh . . . what?"

Startled, Chitto turned to face an Indian wearing a pearl-snap shirt with the tail out, faded jeans, and a purple-and-black Colorado Rockies ball cap. Trucker sunglasses hid most of his face.

"*Damn*, Tubbe. Why'd you sneak up on me like that?"

Tubbe chuckled. "Seemed like a good day to be indigenous." The smile faded. "To repeat my question, " 'Huh—*what*'?"

Chitto rubbed a hand across his mouth. "I, uh, just ran into a person involved in another case I'm working."

"That battered girl you were talking to? Or that redhead?"

Chitto laughed, deciding Tubbe was pretty good at the indigenous thing. "The girl. Her grandpa's one of the singers."

"Should've let me know you were coming. I'd have put you to work."

"Impromptu," Chitto said. "Had some time on my hands, thought I'd see if you learned any more about Wilcox."

Tubbe shook his head. "Went by that fleabag where he was staying again. Talked with the cleaning staff, but they didn't know anything."

No one seemed to know anything.

"How 'bout you?" Tubbe asked.

"Pretty much the same. Two councilwomen that discovered the body didn't see anything out of the ordinary."

Just a big, naked guy with his head cut off.

"Gonna pick it up again tomorrow," Tubbe said. "Festival starts winding down then, so I'll be back in my office. I'll follow up with the wife's relatives first thing."

Tubbe's radio gave a squawk. Pulling it from his hip pocket, he talked a half minute, then turned to Chitto. "Need to stop a pushing match before it ends up a brawl. Let you know if anything new develops."

"Same here. Expecting the full autopsy report this week. See you get a copy."

As Tubbe jogged away, Chitto assessed what his drive to Tishamingo bought him. Zip, he decided. Finding Teresa there *and* Sonny Boy was unexpected. Letty Munro, too, but the link between the girls made sense. Sonny Boy being the girl's grand-father was also a coincidence he could accept. But the crowd's behavior? No two ways about it: someone had spilled the beans about Wilcox. A man found dead on Indian grounds after a sing was enough to make anyone jumpy.

"Hell," he mumbled. "From the looks of things, must've broadcast it on national news."

He pitched his empty soda can into a recycle bin and angled toward the parking lot, planning to return to Durant. But not to the house. Empty houses could make a person jumpy, too. Maybe the stable—

"Ready to grab a bite?"

Turning quickly, Chitto found Leslie behind him. Twice in one day, he'd been caught unawares. He swore under his breath, thinking how Choctaws of old were renowned hunters and war-riors. Sneaky devils. According to his grandmother, he came from a long line of those sneaky devils. His skills that day would not have made any of his ancestors proud.

"Uh, sure. Guess I could eat."

She smiled. "My nose says the fry bread's this way."

Chitto fell into step with the tall redhead, who matched him stride for stride. When he and Mary walked together, he had to shorten his step so she could keep up.

You going to a fire? she would say, her eyes laughing.

Chitto sat across from Leslie at a table under a large oak. Even though the temperature was high, shade and a light breeze made the middle of the day bearable.

"Pretty damn good." Tearing fry bread into chunks, Leslie dunked it in the soup.

Chitto nodded. The soup was thick, a mix of fresh corn cut off the cob and diced pork, tender to the fork and seasoned with crushed red chili pepper. Sonny Boy knew a thing or two about raising pigs.

"Where's your tape recorder?" He realized the cultural anthropologist didn't have it with her.

"Member of the local Heritage Committee's watching it. It'll be all right for thirty, forty minutes." She gave him the infectious smile again. "My stomach was about to eat me from the inside out, so thought I'd better feed it."

He grinned at that. As much as he didn't want to like this unfettered woman, he did.

"Saw you talking to those two girls with Mr. Munro," she said. "You know, the name on my list you were curious about? Is that how you know him, because he's a singer?"

"No, just in passing." He eyed her. "Why?"

She made a short grunt. "He attends a lot of these ceremonies. People say his prayers are very powerful."

"Prayers? Oh, the chants." Chitto shrugged. "Wouldn't know

anything about that. Is your plan to translate them into English?"

She looked up from her soup bowl. "Not translatable. Only the Creator knows what the singer's saying. I'm just capturing them for posterity, documenting the particulars. You know, like how the chants are actually prayers and, four days later, the Creator might grant what the singer asks for. All depends on the seriousness of the singer."

Chitto sighed. She knew more about Indian customs than he did.

"So . . ." She glanced at the sneakers on his feet. "Looks like you wore your dancing shoes. I'm told bystanders will be invited to join in soon."

"Didn't come to dance." White women's brazenness never ceased to surprise him. "Just had some free time so thought I'd have a look-see."

"Be a shame to come all this way and not dance. Sometimes non-natives aren't invited to participate, but the woman on the heritage committee thought it would be okay." She gave him a questioning look. "Shouldn't pass up an opportunity. Only live once, you know."

And for some, that life was all too short . . .

Before he knew it, he was remembering the day that Mary called him. Between sobs, she told him the results of tests doctors ran. The diagnosis: pancreatic cancer, advanced stage. More doctor visits came after the initial diagnosis. A second opinion. Then, specialists. Finally, the native healer. Not because Mary wanted it, but because he did. *Some things I cannot fix, Sam,* the healer told him. Six months later, a funeral.

He gave up smoking two years before the diagnosis because of Mary. The Surgeon General's warning scared her so bad, she begged him to quit. The irony? She was the one who died. Where was the justice in that?

"*Hello.*" Leslie grinned. "Did I lose you? I said, you ready to dance?"

"Oh, sorry." He shook his head. "Dance impaired."

She flashed the contagious grin again. "Nothing to it. Just bounce a little on the balls of your feet and shuffle. Even the dance-impaired can handle that."

"Can't." He looked at his watch. "Need to get back to Durant. Lots to take care of."

"Okay, but you don't know what you're missing out on." As they threw their trash into a waste container, she looked at him. "Driving back tonight. I'll tell Mattie I ran into you."

Chitto nodded and watched her walk away. Her inquisitiveness bothered him. The scientist in him said it was normal, but too many of her questions dealt with unscientific matters. Maybe it was time to contact an inspector he knew up-country, see what he knew about her. Swindlers and scam artists excelled at getting on the good side of innocent people, then fleecing them.

Taking a circular path to the parking lot, Chitto stopped where he could see the dance ground. Clusters of men and women watched from the sidelines. The two teenage girls sat in their lawn chairs. Sonny Boy continued to cast his prayer skyward to the Creator. And Leslie, a red shawl over her shoulders, joined others in the center area moving in a slow circle. The anthropologist lifted her arms skyward like a bird in flight, her body swaying slightly as she moved. An educated white woman more Indian than some Indians.

And freer, a voice inside his head whispered.

Chitto turned from the dancing and found his pickup. The road busy, he focused on traffic. But now and then, the scene of the redbird soaring with wings spread flicked through his mind's eye, and he found himself hoping Dr. Leslie Anderson was on the up and up.

CHAPTER NINE

Early Monday morning, Chitto took Highway 70 east, stopping at the Red River Tavern. Red paint chipped and peeling, the single-story building looked like it suffered a bad sunburn. The sign was faded, too, but the images still identifiable. A winding red stream denoted how the Red River was the state line for Oklahoma and Texas, before civilization started messing with the natural order of things. Earthen dams—hundreds of them—had created artificial lakes for sport, most of them silting up now. Indian land turned into giant mud puddles.

White man's resourcefulness, red man's despair.

Chitto tempered these thoughts with nature's destructive habits. The Black Mesa, the Wichita, Arbuckle and Ouachita Mountains, as well as the Ozark Plateau, were all examples of destructive geologic processes. Through weathering, the rocks that constituted these landforms were continually being broken into smaller particles. Rainwater filling fissures and cracks in rocks, then freezing and expanding, acted as a wedge forcing pieces of rock apart. Sometimes the water mixed with carbon dioxide from the atmosphere, combining to make a weak acid that slowly dissolved other types of rock. Like limestone. Erosion, the weathering and movement of soil and rock, constantly changed the landscape. Destructive, but different.

The natural way of things.

He pushed open the door to the tavern. Because it was early, the place was empty except for a swamper.

"Hey, I just clean the joint," a muscular man about forty said to Chitto's questions about the Munro mugging. "Owner called me to come in early today to clean up a mess 'fore he opened up. He's the one you need to talk to."

Wondering why a man in his prime looking healthy and strong would be doing this kind of work, Chitto asked for I.D.

"Why you need to card me?" The man pulled his license from his billfold. "I'm working, not buying."

"Just need to be sure who I'm talking to." Chitto noted the man's address and phone number in his notebook and returned the license. "This what you do for a living? Clean bars?"

"Hell, no. I work there at the Walmart, in the warehouse. You know, unloading trucks, handling shipments. Hours got cut so I fill in here."

"How 'bout nights? You work late, maybe help clear out the place when it's closing time?"

"Sometimes, but the owner's the one closes down. I'm usually long gone by then."

"You work last Thursday night when that old man got mugged?"

The swamper took time to think about the question. "Yeah, left 'bout eleven. Not too many still here when I took off. Remember seeing a couple of young bucks talkin' to an old man. Guy was looped pretty good, crying in his whiskey about somethin'." He gave Chitto a straight look. "Look, man, that's the gospel truth. All I take out of this place is a paycheck and a damn measly one at that. But I got kids and Christmas is comin'. My wife, she put things on layaway. Can't disappoint my kids."

"Okay. I'll just have a look 'round before I go. Any more questions, I'll be in touch."

Chitto checked licenses posted on the wall, noting they were current, then walked to the kitchen. He smelled the grease traps before he hit the light switch. As light flooded the room, cockroaches the size of horned lizards ran for cover.

"Hell fire—" From the doorway, he considered next steps. Maybe it was time to pull an Elliot Ness.

Leaving the tavern, he placed a call to a friend in the health department, then proceeded to work. He wanted to pursue the Wilcox murder, but Blackfox told him to work around his regular duties. Today, that included an interrogation.

As soon as he pulled into the parking lot at the Choctaw complex, Chitto knew something had been added to his agenda. A black SUV with a distinctive license plate was parked in one of the spaces. The FBI was in the house.

Walking to the back steps, he saw Wanda standing at the top, talking to two men wearing construction helmets. One had a tape measure clipped to his belt. The other tied long hair back on his neck and carried a ball-peen hammer. She waved them aside as Chitto climbed the steps. He shouldered past them and fell into step with her.

"How's the new construction coming?" He glanced over his shoulder, saw the men walking toward the new building. "Everything on track?"

"Few hitches," she said, shrugging. "Nothing serious."

"Who belongs to that black wagon out there?"

She grinned. "Your favorite Fed."

Rodriquez.

"Dan's been waiting for you to show up," she added.

He followed her upstairs, mind in overdrive.

"Sam—need you in here." Blackfox stood in front of his office door. From the look he gave Chitto, he was not a happy man.

Chitto joined him.

"Thought I told you to keep this on the QT," Blackfox said.

"You didn't call them?" He got a look of surprise, a slight shake of the head.

Rodriquez was waiting in Blackfox's office. A dark slender-built man in his early forties, he sat with one leg crossed over his knee, rotating Ray Ban Aviator sunglasses. The movement was mesmerizing, almost hypnotic. He didn't extend a hand to Chitto or bother to rise from his chair.

Macho.

Chitto resisted the urge to jerk up Rodriquez's pant leg to confirm the rumor about a Mexican dipstick. Boots were favorite places for gang members to hide a switchblade. Instead, he sat down opposite him.

"Nifty glasses, Raymond," he said, grinning.

"It's Ramon." Continuing to spin the glasses, Rodriquez trilled the *R* so it vibrated off his tongue.

Chitto lost the grin. "Those are nifty glasses, *Ramon.*" His attempt to trill the *R* sounded like he was gargling mouthwash.

Blackfox gave Chitto a look as he took his seat. "Told Agent Rodriquez all you told me, Sam. Also told him we figured it was an Indian problem." He paused. "Anything new to add?"

Chitto shook his head. "Not one damned thing."

"Any other theories?" Rodriquez's voice was even, controlled.

Watching the sunglasses rotate another turn, Chitto hunched his shoulders. "What's your theory, Raymond? Gang related? Drugs, maybe? Terrorism? Something . . ." He stared out a window, as if searching for words. "Something more important than finding out who killed two of our men ten years ago?"

The sunglasses stopped turning. Slipping them into an inside pocket, Rodriquez stood and faced Blackfox. "You said the ME's report would be ready when?"

Blackfox looked to Chitto for a response.

"Soon as he gets it done, I reckon."

Rodriquez eyed him. "Of course, it will come directly to me."

97

"And of course, you'll get us a copy for our files," Blackfox said, standing to face the agent.

Rodriquez laid two business cards on his desk. "Call me, anything new surfaces."

"Thanks, but we keep the FBI's number on speed dial," Chitto said, reaching for the cards.

"I'll take those." Blackfox retrieved the cards and walked Rodriquez to the door. "Wanda will see you out. We'll, uh, we'll be in touch."

Watching Blackfox return to his desk, Chitto waited for the explosion.

"Nifty glasses? Speed dial? What the hell was that comedy act about?" Blackfox slapped Rodriquez's cards on his desk. "Doesn't pay to get too cocky, Sam. Might need that guy one of these days."

Chitto pulled his phone from his pocket, entered the FBI agent's number, and held it up so Blackfox could see it. "Said it's in my speed dial and it is. How you suppose he heard?"

"Damned if I know. You tell everyone at the scene to keep their mouths shut?"

"Yes, sir, and those councilwomen that discovered the body."

"Well, someone's gone deaf." Blackfox rubbed his face. "Maybe that Chickasaw. He didn't strike me as someone that runs by the book."

Not if it's a good day to be indigenous.

"Wasn't him; bet my life on it. Guy's ex-military, the kind of service where you put your life in the hands of the men you're serving with. You could pull all his teeth and threaten parts elsewhere, he wouldn't talk." Chitto paused. "Want me to give Everett the news? About the medical report, I mean."

"No. I'll give him a call after I get out of my budget meeting. Keep me posted on anything else you learn and—"

"Yeah, I know," Chitto said. "Steer clear of the FBI."

Blackfox sighed. "I was gonna say, keep your head up out of your ass. Can't afford to lose your perspective in this business, Sam. It's a short walk to the edge, damn long drop down."

CHAPTER TEN

Chitto sat at his desk, reviewing the list of questions the polygraph examiner used on the subject. He had been an advocate for polygraph exams with all the district field officers, encouraging their use as an investigative tool. Seven must have bought the pitch, because he'd showed up bright and early that morning, subject in hand. And since Chitto was filling in for Seven's field lieutenant, he was tagged to assist with the interrogation.

"Perp might not've been directly involved in the robberies," Seven told Chitto, "but my gut says he knows who is. I told him he was my primary suspect and if he wanted to get off my shit list, he might wanna take this test."

Chitto laughed at that. He relied a lot on his gut, too. But he was dead serious about polygraph exams and made sure the examiner followed standard procedures to the letter. He wanted to ensure the district officers as much success as he could. All that was left to do with this one was review the results and do the follow-up.

He glanced at the clock. Just enough time to grab a sandwich at one of the burger joints. The phone rang before he could get to his feet.

"Mullins here, Sam. Hey, just finished up the autopsy on that dead naked guy up at the dance ground and found something kind of unusual."

Like having your head cut off while you're buck naked isn't unusual?

"What's that, Everett?"

"Piece of scalp's missing, 'bout an inch and a half square. His hair was somewhat long, curly, too, so I didn't spot it at the scene. What'd'ya make of that?"

Chitto rubbed his face, remembering Sonny Boy Munro's reported talk of scalped men.

"What part of his head?"

"Smack dab on top," Mullins drawled. "Like a miniature scalp lock. You think some young bucks have taken to the warpath?"

Chitto rubbed his face again. If he could have predicted something relevant showing up at the autopsy, it wouldn't have been this.

"Too early to tell. Anything on stomach contents?"

"Hardly nothin' in his stomach. It's like that Chickasaw guy Tuber said—Naw, that's not right. A tuber's a potato. Aw hell, I got his name writ down here somewhere . . ."

"Tubbe," Chitto said. "Frank Tubbe."

"Yeah, Tubbe. Well, anyways, he nailed this one. Victim didn't eat for a good while, probably not since he was abducted. Large intestine pretty much evacuated. Results not back on the blood, but he was drugged out of his mind. On an empty stomach, could be as simple as alcohol."

Wilcox went missing on Tuesday night, and his body not discovered until Friday morning. And alcohol was mostly sugar, which meant it burned up fast—frying grey matter in the process. A possible reason the guy didn't resist.

"Find anything else, let me know," Chitto said.

"Have my full autopsy report to you by end of the week."

"Hold up, Everett. Dan ran this case by the Feds this morning, so the original report's supposed to go to them. He'll call later to make it official, but I'd sure like a copy . . ." He let his words hang, hoping Mullins got the message.

"You'll get everything the FBI gets."

"In duplicate. Tuber Guy wants a copy, too."

Chitto sat a while after hanging up the phone. Unconsciously, he picked up a piece of rock, one of many worry stones he kept on his desk, and rolled it between his fingers. On days when he needed help sorting out a mystery, he turned to one of them. Though they didn't talk like Sonny Boy's stones apparently did, sometimes they came close.

His collection was varied. An igneous rock called rhyolite that he'd picked up in the Wichita Mountains in southwest Oklahoma. A piece of basalt found on the top of Black Mesa at the northwest tip of the Oklahoma panhandle; gypsum and dolomite rocks in the panhandle were left from the Permian geologic period, over 200 million years ago. Erosion left caps of gypsum and dolomite on the mesas, from a distance looking like giant, capped mushrooms. He also had a piece of granite, formed within the Earth as magma slowly cooled, that he'd picked up northwest of Tishomingo. Rocks in that part of the checkerboard were believed to be over a billion years old. And each one of them with a story to tell.

This day, Chitto chose a chunk of metamorphic rock to act as his worry stone. A piece of parent rock, a rock that could change from one type of rock to another under certain conditions. If the right mixture of heat, pressure, and chemically active fluids and gases was present, the original rock could become a parent for another kind of rock. Metamorphic rock was not common on the surface of Oklahoma's landscape, but if one knew where to look, it could be found. He had stumbled onto his sample at Beavers Bend State Park in southeast Oklahoma. His own stomping ground.

He rubbed the stone between his fingers now, contemplating Wilcox's murder. Though a non-native, Wilcox married an Indian woman, a citizen of the Chickasaw Nation, and became father to an Indian girl. A parent. Then he'd been murdered in a sacrificial way on sacred native ground. What caused the natural order of things to alter?

Abruptly, Chitto looked at the clock. Thirty minutes until the interrogation. The snack machines in the break room seemed his best bet for lunch. Hurriedly, he pulled his wallet from his pocket and walked to Wanda's desk to see if she could make change.

"Still at lunch," he mumbled, looking at the deserted desk. "Or outside, burning one." The department had a no-smoking policy. A chain smoker, Wanda spent a lot of time on the back steps.

Recalling Wanda kept change in her desk drawer, Chitto took a chance. He grunted in satisfaction at a stash of quarters, dimes and nickels, and quickly exchanged two dollars worth. As he shut the drawer, he recognized handwriting on a yellow sticky note stuck to a manila envelope. Rona Guthrie's scrawl. He pulled the envelope from the drawer.

He'd worked with Rona off and on over the last ten years and liked the attractive, if sharp-tongued, victim's advocate. Rona's marriage ended in divorce after a year, with her as the initiator. On nights when he lay awake, feeling the emptiness in the bed next to him, the thought entered his head that he should probably ask her out, even enter into a casual relationship. Rona had given off vibes that she was receptive, but the thought never survived the light of day.

The sticky note said, *Please get this to Sam Chitto ASAP.* Turning the envelope over to unseal it, Chitto hesitated. The clasp was not secured.

Hell. Wanda probably reads Blackfox's mail . . .

He pulled out enough of the envelope to identify its contents. The medical report for Teresa Walker. He carried the envelope with him to the break room and returned to his desk a few minutes later, package of corn chips and soda in hand. He slipped the Walker medical report out of its envelope and skimmed it as he munched corn chips.

NAME: Teresa Inez Walker. AGE: 15. PLACE OF RESIDENCE: 15903 OK HWY 70. NAME OF PARENTS: Deceased. GUARDIAN: Betty Tomlinson.

He skipped the rest of the demographic information and went to the medical exam. *Contusions to the face and body, severe bruising to upper thighs and pelvic area caused by forced entry—*

Chitto closed the report and sat back in his chair. Having seen the girl just the day before at Tishamingo, attempting to pick up the pieces of her life, made him admire her even more. Another part of him ached to even the score with her rapist uncle.

Outside my jurisdiction.

Recalling he had asked Wanda to call the aunt about a restraining order, he wondered about the outcome. Replacing the report in the envelope, he locked it in a desk drawer and concentrated on another medical exam. The autopsy on Delbert Wilcox. Rocking back in his chair again, he laced his hands behind his head.

Scalp lock. A token of some kind? Symbolic of something maybe?

Abruptly, Chitto's thinking about the missing piece of skin went down another path. A memento. A serial killer's signature. He dismissed the idea, realizing several people were involved in the Wilcox murder. The victim was a big man. It would have taken two, maybe three or more to subdue him, even if he was drunk, and hold him down while someone with muscle in his arm lopped off his head.

All signs led to someone involved in tribal customs. Like Sonny Boy Munro. A singer who participated in native rituals around the state and who—according to the incident report—referred to dead *men*. *Scalped* dead men. The problem was, there was only one victim.

Chitto sighed. Out of options, he decided to put the word out on his tribal telegraph, a list of lawmen in other nations that he stayed in touch with, to see if some young bucks *were* causing trouble. If maybe Wilcox wasn't the first.

Chitto finished downing his soda as Seven appeared at his desk.

"Got the kid downstairs, Sam. He's ready to split, sweatin' like a weenie on a barbecue grill. You ready?"

"Let's do it." Chitto closed up his desk and followed the officer down the hall, interrogation materials under one arm. They met Wanda on the stairs, gasping for breath with each step she took.

"Maybe it's time to give up smokes, Wanda," Seven said. "You know, like Sam did. Those things can kill you."

"Want your advice," she snapped, "I'll ask for it." She looked at Chitto. "Some of us prefer to go out in a blaze of glory."

Taking in her mood, Chitto opted not to comment.

"Suppose you're out of commission the rest of the day," she said, continuing up the stairs.

"Pretty much. Want to get this interview finished up before Seven's subject bails on him." He turned on the landing, looking up at her. "Oh, and I found the case report Rona sent over, so don't be surprised when you find it gone. She calls, tell her I'll get back to her with any questions."

"You were in my desk—"

"Swapping dollar bills for change. You know, for the pop machine. You got a problem with that?"

"Would you have a problem with someone rummaging

around in *your* desk?" She resumed her climb.

"Wait up, Wanda," he called to her. "Not a good idea to leave that kind of information unsecured. Next time, get it to me right away—even if I am involved with something else."

"Sure thing," she said over her shoulder.

"One more thing," Chitto called to her. "What happened with Betty Tomlinson and that restraining order?"

Wanda looked down at him from the top of the stairs. "No deal. Be like putting a burr under his blanket." She walked away, disappearing by degrees from sight.

Damn. That meant Teresa-with-no-H was still a target.

"Must be one of Wanda's ball-busting days," Seven said, grinning.

Chitto grinned, too, then put his mind on the results of the lie detection test. As always, he would focus his attention on making an accurate comparison of the relevant questions with the control questions, a key indicator of dishonesty. If the subject responded more strongly to the control than the relevant questions, he was telling the truth. But if he responded more strongly to the relevant than the control, he was lying. You sweat the trivial stuff, chill on the important. An oversimplification, but basically that's how lie detection worked. Which is why people who knew how it worked could lie through their teeth and not get caught.

"Hey, answer me a question, Sam." Seven paused outside the door to the interview room. "Why *do* you keep those smokes in the glove box? You used to be a pack-a-day man. Doesn't it bother you, knowing they're just a reach away?"

"Every damn minute of every damn day." He looked at Seven. "Speaking of questions, that day at the pow-wow grounds, you picked up on something other than pinch marks on the clothes . . . and it wasn't shoes."

Seven flushed slightly. "Fabric softener. Clothes smelled the

106

same as what my wife uses." He grinned. "Stupid, huh?"

Chitto wasn't smiling. "No such thing as stupid in law enforcement, Seven. Next time, don't let others influence you. Just do your job."

"Yes, sir."

"You know what softener your wife uses?"

Seven rubbed his mouth. "For a fact, I don't. Want me to check?"

"Wouldn't hurt."

"Will do," Seven said, grinning again. "Now, let's cook this weenie."

CHAPTER ELEVEN

The call came through on Chitto's cell phone Friday morning while he was frying eggs in a skillet he'd just cooked bacon in. He shoved the pan to a back burner.

Grabbing the phone, he growled, "This better be important."

Frank Tubbe's mouth started to rattle like a machine gun.

"Another guy with no head, found on the Tishamingo dance ground. Cleaning crew found him 'bout half hour ago. Name's Charlie Carter. Wife's a member of the Muskogee Nation. One of their inspectors is driving down for the follow-up. You want in?"

"You had to ask?"

A chuckle came over the line. "I'm working on my interpersonal skills. Some folks think I'm short in that department. See you in my office."

"Wait up—" Chitto spent the week working on cases and striking out on the Wilcox investigation. And now another body, identical to the first, had shown up.

Or was it?

"Anything . . . unusual about the body?" He listened to a half minute of dead air.

"Like what?"

Chitto hesitated. He didn't have the official autopsy report yet, so hadn't shared the information about Wilcox missing a piece of his scalp.

"Like with his head." Hearing a grunt on the line, Chitto

didn't wait for Tubbe to hone his interpersonal skills. "If you can hold the body, I'd like a look while it's fresh. Running with lights, can be there in 'bout an hour."

"Well, turn 'em on. Now that two stiffs have been found on Indian lands, FBI's bound to flex muscle."

"Already did. Visited us last Monday. Got wind of it before Blackfox called them."

Another grunt came over the line. "They're gonna be all over this one, too."

"Have your boss call mine, work both ends against the middle."

Hanging up, Chitto poured his coffee into a travel mug, slipped three slices of bacon and a fried egg between slices of white bread, and headed for the garage.

On the way, Chitto left a message for Dan Blackfox, informing him of the new finding and to expect a call from Ada. Next, he called Wanda Gilly's machine, letting her know his whereabouts. He'd covered twenty of the eighty miles between his house and Tishamingo when his cell phone rang.

"Fill me in," Blackfox said.

"Sounds like the same MO. No answers yet, but some interesting similarities."

"Why do you think I put you on the case, Sam? Let's hear what's rattling around in that over-educated skull of yours."

Turning over the facts as he knew them, Chitto began to talk. "Okay. Two white men killed on Indian ceremonial grounds. Both naked. Beheaded. Scalped, at least symbolically. And both found on a Friday, less than a week after a festival. Four days after a festival, to be exact."

His mind stumbled, trying to bring up a comment Leslie Anderson made when they lunched together at Tishamingo. Something about the Creator granting a prayer four days after a ceremony if the singer was deemed sincere. Something else about Sonny Boy's prayers being considered powerful. And Sonny Boy was a singer at the Choctaw festival *and* the one at Tishamingo.

Chitto replayed his encounter with the old man. Something drove him to fall off the wagon. What would make an honored man pick up the bottle again? He shook his head, failing to see how an old man long in the tooth could be involved in anything more than pigs and prayers.

Another thought pushed that one aside. Emma Love Wilcox looked upon her husband's death as the answer to a prayer. Two festivals, two prayers, two dead men.

"You saying the time frame had something to do with a symbolic rite?" Blackfox said.

"I think it does." Chitto thought about Leslie again. "But don't ask me how. Haven't figured out that piece yet."

"Well, what *do* you have figured out?"

"Well, neither victim lived where their bodies were found, which means both were strangers with few, if any, connections to the location. And different jurisdictions brings in a different set of players."

"So, multiple jurisdictional areas inject more squirm into the bucket of worms," Blackfox said, talking slow. "And you think that's part of the plan?"

"Yes, sir. I sure as hell do."

"Anything else?"

"No, sir. You'll be the first to know, I learn something else."

After he disconnected, Chitto thought again about the symbolism aspect of the murders. Leslie knew more than anyone else about symbolism, and she was at both festivals. He still had questions about her sudden appearance and her probing for information. More troubling, she was living right in the house with his mother and grandmother, walking compendiums of

110

information, eager to share what they knew.

He shook his head. Someone out there knew more than he did, and he didn't like being the blind person holding the scale. At times like this, he wished he'd pursued geology rather than law enforcement. Rocks were easy to read.

Sometimes, they even talked.

This day, Chitto had no trouble finding a parking place at the old Chickasaw capitol. He retraced his steps to the dance ground, part of which was marked off with crime-scene tape. He nodded at a group of men standing on the sidelines, surmising they were the cleaning crew that found the body.

"You boys been told not to create any chatter 'bout this?" He got thumbs up all around.

Chitto experienced a sense of *déjà vu* as he neared the group standing around a body. He nodded at Tubbe when he walked up, who introduced Fred Bunyan, the Johnston County medical examiner, and a Chickasaw Lighthorse policeman named Waters.

"Looks pretty much the same," Chitto commented, looking at the sprawled body. "Except this one's got less hair on his head."

He squatted on his heels next to the decapitated body of a Caucasian man, forty to fifty years of age. Calluses on the palm pads. Clean fingernails. Looking around, he did not see the man's clothes and assumed they'd been bagged and loaded into the ME's van.

"You wanna tell me what's going on with his head?" Tubbe squatted on the other side of the body.

Chitto studied a raw-looking square on top of the victim's head. "Damned if I know. All I can figure, it has some symbolic meaning."

"Like a signature?"

Chitto shook his head. "Doesn't fit the profile for a serial killer. Too many people involved."

"What can you tell about the way this scalp was cut away," Tubbe asked, looking at the ME.

"Not much right now. Clean cut. Sharp instrument."

Chitto recalled Everett Mullins's description of the first victim. "Razor sharp, like a scalpel," he commented.

"Naw, hunting knife could've done that," Waters said.

"You think?" Chitto looked at the field officer, a seasoned man, about forty. "That's pretty fine carving."

"Hunters round here keep their knives sharp as razors." He let out a snort. "Have to, if you're gonna field dress a buck."

Chitto nodded. "So what you're saying is, it wouldn't take that much skill to pop off a piece of scalp, or cut off a man's head."

"Not if you're any kind of hunter."

"Well, that narrows the field." Tubbe grinned as he got to his feet. "Just what is the population of Oklahoma now? I've been gone a while."

That brought a laugh from Bunyan and Waters. Chitto grinned, too, but he was thinking Tubbe's point was a good one. How would they narrow the field?

He leaned over the torso for a closer look. "See these slight indentations?" He pointed at the place where the victim's neck would have been. "Similar marks at the Choctaw ceremonial grounds. And there's no blood spatter in that spot, which means it was shielded. Just like the other one."

"Yeah." Tubbe looked on from the other side. "Block of wood maybe. Whatever it was, they took it with them so they could get rid of it."

"Or maybe use it again." Waters shrugged when Chitto glanced up at him. "I do that, keep stuff for butchering game so I don't have to go looking for something new all the time."

Butchering. Remembering a block and tackle hanging from a tree at Sonny Boy's place, Chitto had a sudden urge to visit the old man. To find out what kind of "stuff" he kept around so he wouldn't have to start new every time he slaughtered a pig.

"You heard of anything like this in other counties?" Tubbe looked at Bunyan. "Other nations?"

Chitto rubbed his face, recalling he hadn't put out the message on the tribal telegraph yet. He looked at the remains of Charlie Carter, wondering if he could have saved his life, and decided it wouldn't have done any good. The man's end was already sealed.

"Nope," Bunyan replied. "But then, I don't get outside this county too much."

Of course he doesn't, Chitto thought. MEs didn't wander far from home. Which meant they were dealing with identical murders involving different law-enforcement agencies, different counties, different nations, different medical examiners. All of which confirmed what he'd just told Blackfox.

Tubbe laughed without humor. "Water keeps getting muddier and muddier, doesn't it? Whoever the son-of-a-buck is that's running this craps table, he's playing with loaded dice."

"You through with the body now?" Bunyan asked. "Gonna ripen fast in this heat."

Tubbe looked at Chitto. "You wanna look at this dead naked guy some more?"

The same question Chitto asked him at the Wilcox murder scene. "Nope. But I'd sure like a look at his clothes."

"Can save you the trouble. Same pinch marks clothespins leave."

"That's not what I had in mind." Chitto pulled Tubbe aside and briefed him on the fabric-softener lead. "Smell's going to degrade fast, especially exposed to a dead body."

"You think somebody's yanking our chain?" Tubbe's eyes

were slits. "Burns me to think we're the butt end of a bad joke."

"Guess that's possible." Chitto looked away for a half minute, then back at Tubbe. "Like you said, whoever's running this crapshoot knows what he's doing. Maybe he didn't worry about it because he knew it wouldn't be traceable."

"Not traceable? Hell, man, they can trace anything these days." Tubbe turned to the ME. "Fred—how quick can you determine what kind of fabric softener was used on Carter's clothes?"

Bunyan let out a snort. "My job's to determine cause of death, and with our funding, I barely got the wherewithal to do that." He jabbed a finger at Tubbe. "But I'll tell you what. Even the most sophisticated lab would have a hard go isolating one trace substance in something like clothes and comparing it to a known substance in a control sample. You want something that sophisticated, call the FBI." He jabbed the finger again. "But I guarantee, you do something like 'at, they'll think you're crazier than a bedbug."

"Well, then, doesn't leave us much choice," Tubbe said. "You're gonna have to unseal that bag of clothes, Fred."

The briefing at the Chickasaw Nation headquarters in Ada was a repeat of the one in Durant the week before, with different players.

"Okay, boys," said Wylie Hartshorne, the Chickasaw law enforcement director. "Just like Blackfox, I'm treating this as an Indian matter. Feds are busy staking out meth labs this week, which makes the job easier. But they'll get an agent involved soon as they hear about it. Within a couple days, would be my guess." The corners of his mouth turned up slightly. "But we're not going to wait around for them to bless us with their presence."

He looked around the conference table. "Tubbe here's in

charge of the investigation on our end." He looked at Chitto. "I understand you're handling the first one?"

Chitto nodded, then looked toward Eli Sunday, the inspector who had driven down from Okmulgee. A tall man, with muscles strung together like jerky. "I figure you're here because the victim was connected to the Muskogee-Creek Nation. That be by marriage?"

"Married to a Creek woman," Sunday replied, his expression noncommittal.

"Same with the first," Chitto said, answering the question in the Creek's eyes. "Only he was married to a Chickasaw."

"A Chickasaw's husband found dead on Choctaw ground," Sunday said, more a comment than a question. "And now, a Creek's husband found dead on Chickasaw land."

"That would be right."

"Beheaded," Tubbe interjected. "Both of them."

The comment brought no reaction from Sunday. Chitto studied the Creek investigator's broad, dark-skinned face. It was not unlike those he saw in his own jurisdiction, or for that matter, in the Chickasaw Nation. For good reason. They all had roots in the Muskogean family. Even their native languages had the same roots. The Creek-Seminole were from further east in the old country, known as Alabama these days, while the Choctaws and Chickasaws lived west of them, in Mississippi mostly. Right now, the Creek's face appeared chiseled in stone, not even a glimmer showing in his eyes.

"Any plausible explanation for Wilcox being in the Choctaw Nation?" Hartshorne looked between Chitto and Tubbe.

"Not so far," Tubbe said.

Sunday's foot tapped the floor lightly. Chitto observed the foot dance quietly. He liked this inspector. The Creek didn't say much, but that didn't mean the engine under the hood was idle.

Hartshorne looked at Chitto. "Sunday's new to the game. You kick off. What you got on the first victim?"

Chitto shook his head. "Slim pickings. Expecting the full autopsy report today, but I don't expect much from it. Our ME indicated there wasn't enough stomach contents to do us any good. He's doing a blood workup, figures the victim was drugged."

He glanced at Tubbe, then back at Hartshorne. "He called earlier in the week to report an *unusual* finding, something he missed when he first looked at the body. Wilcox had considerable more hair than Carter. Once he got him back to the lab, he found a piece of scalp removed. He described it as a miniature scalp lock."

"And our man's missing a piece of his scalp, too," Tubbe said.

"*Damn.*" Hartshorne ran a hand through thick, salt-and-pepper hair. "First thing people are gonna think is some deranged Indians have reverted to the old way of handling things." He sighed, shaking his head. "But I'm more inclined to think it's a way to put a spin on things, throw people off track. Wouldn't be the first time." He turned to Tubbe. "Anything new on Wilcox? Would make my day if there was a connection between these guys."

"Too soon to tell. Have to do more checking to see if the two knew each other. Wilcox was pretty much a loner. Hung out at local bars, drank most of his paycheck. Probably wouldn't have taken too much to get the guy stoned out of his head."

Tubbe gave Chitto a quick look. "I questioned the neighbors and they confirmed what the widow said. Wilcox moved out 'bout four months ago. Haven't seen hide nor hair of him since."

"You learn why the guy moved out?" Chitto said.

"Not clear. Wife didn't file for divorce because of religion. I checked with her priest, but . . ."

But priests don't divulge what's said in confidence, Chitto thought, finishing Tubbe's sentence.

Chitto was not an advocate of organized religions of any flavor, not even his own People's. Too many used religion as an excuse to take extreme measures. Like terrorism. Revenge. Murder. He wondered now how many illicit acts confessionals had protected—*were* protecting.

He looked at Tubbe. "What'd you find out about male members of the family? Emma have a bunch of brothers? Maybe some uncles?"

Tubbe flashed a grin. "Hell, yes—and every one of them with an alibi."

Chitto looked between Hartshorne and Sunday. "Wilcox's widow has a daughter from her first marriage. Girl's pregnant, maybe four, five months along."

The Creek inspector raised his eyebrows.

"Oh, this just keeps getting better and better." Hartshorne handed out photocopies of Charlie Carter's driver's license. "Look this over, anything else comes to mind, ask it now." He leaned back in his chair, continuing to talk. "Let's keep a lid on both these cases long as possible—especially the part about the missing scalp lock. It's the unique piece to this puzzle."

Without warning, he leaned forward, looking around the table. "I don't like the way these murders are pointing to the nations. Don't have to tell you men how hard it is to get the other agencies to cooperate with us *now*. All they need is the hint of an excuse to drop us like a hot potato. So work fast."

Chitto walked out of the office with the other two inspectors. Sunday stopped in the hallway, looking at Tubbe.

"Thought I'd run by the scene of the crime on my way back to Okmulgee. Like it if you'd accompany me."

"Meet up with you out front." He looked at Chitto. "And I'll be looking for that autopsy report."

Chitto nodded, then fell into step with Sunday en route to the parking lot. "Mind if I go with you to interview the Carter widow? Sometimes an extra pair of ears is helpful."

"There's some truth to that." Sunday's eyes blinked, indicating he was giving the matter thought. "Don't want to spook the gal. Let me check the lay of the land and I'll give you a jingle."

"One more thing," Chitto said before they parted company. "You have any celebrations, festivals coming up?"

"Matter of fact, we do."

"Appreciate it if you'd get me that information. Might take a run up that way, check it out."

Sunday stopped at his cruiser, looking at Chitto. "You on to something?"

"Nothing I'm ready to take to the bank."

"Uh-huh," Sunday said, half aloud. "Like a copy of that medical report on the first victim, too."

"Goes without saying."

CHAPTER TWELVE

Chitto took the stairs at the Tribal complex two at a time. He wanted to update Blackfox on the latest murder ASAP. He was not expecting to run into Rona Guthrie coming down the steps and wondered if he had missed an appointment with the victim's advocate.

"You here on one of my cases?"

She shook her head. "Domestic violence. Wanda gave me what I needed." She paused. "Got time for a bite? Haven't had lunch yet."

Rona stood close enough for Chitto to smell her scent. A sweet, pungent fragrance not unlike the scented oil Mary used to wear. He hesitated, feeling the emptiness in his gut, but though his stomach said yes, his head argued otherwise.

"Sorry. Things I need to check on. New case that might have a connection with an old one."

"One of mine?"

Chitto noticed the hopeful look. "No connection. Sorry 'bout lunch."

"Another time then." She continued down the steps.

Chitto turned on the stairway. "Saw the Walker girl at the Tishamingo festival last weekend. Said your counseling did her some good."

Rona's forehead wrinkled. "Well, thanks, but afraid I can't take the credit. Didn't spend much time with her. Maybe ten, fifteen minutes at best. After I got her to the clinic, I filled out the paperwork and left." She hesitated, her eyes showing concern. "How'd she look—did she look okay?"

"Far as I could tell."

"Surprised she'd venture out this soon."

Chitto replayed the conversation with Teresa. *She thought it would do me good.* Who was the "she" referenced if not Rona?

"Could she have talked to another counselor? Maybe someone else at your office?"

"Possibly. Gave her one of my cards, so she had the office number. But, typically, the office doesn't switch us around. An advocate usually sticks with a case."

And because of her Indian blood, Rona was assigned cases dealing with Indian women and girls. Which was why he saw her so often.

"So, you didn't take her home then?" he asked.

She shook her head. "First thing she did when we got to the clinic was make a phone call. Told me someone would be picking her up." Rona raised her eyebrows. "What's the verdict on that dickhead you took in?"

Chitto stared at Rona. "Turned it over to the U.S. attorney's office, just the way regulations require. Suggested to the girl's aunt that she take out a restraining order. She refused."

Rona made a guttural sound.

"That's how the system works," Chitto said, his neck turning warm. "You know that."

She shook her head again. "Justice system's broke, Sam. Maybe it's time someone fixed it."

"Like who?"

Shrugging, Rona resumed her trek down the stairs.

Chitto continued up the steps, wondering who had advised Teresa to go to the Tishomingo festival.

Maybe her mother?

Something pulled at Chitto's memory, something he couldn't put his finger on. He'd overlooked something.

As he neared his office, Chitto heard laughter, smelled food and remembered it was potluck day. He walked to the break room and searched out a face he knew would be there. Today, that face looked drawn. Tired.

"What's the chance of a hungry man getting a handout, Wanda?"

"Bet we can put a plate together. Want me to bring it to you?"

"That'd work," he said, glad to see Wanda in a better frame of mind. "Need to check in with Dan and get an e-mail out. Also looking for something from Everett Mullins."

"Put an envelope on your desk. Couple phone messages for you, too."

Chitto stopped en route to his cubicle to give Blackfox a briefing on the latest murder, then picked up the message slips Wanda mentioned. One from his mother said, *Come out for Sunday dinner.* Another from the Hugo clinic read, *Call ASAP.* Chitto slipped his mother's message into his shirt pocket and hurried to his desk.

Putting his phone on speaker, he dialed the clinic. Opening his case folder, he laid the copy of Charlie Carter's driver's license on the desktop, again wondering if he could have altered the outcome of the man's death. No more delays. He needed to alert his contacts in other nations about both the Wilcox and the Carter murders—and to be on the lookout for suspicious activities after celebrations. Four days after celebrations, to be exact. Gut instinct told him the latest victim wasn't the only one they would find staked out on Indian ceremonial ground.

"Emergency Ward," a voice on the phone said.

"Lieutenant Chitto, Choctaw tribal police. You left a message."

"You say your name's Chitto?"

"That's right." He heard a long sigh.

"A man here waiting for you. Found passed out this morning, leaning against a dumpster. Refused a ride home with one of the county officers. Had your card in his pocket, told us to call you. Something about pigs and peanut butter?"

Chitto rubbed a spot between his eyes that began to throb. "Be right over."

As he hung up, Chitto decided Friday wasn't just potluck day. It was also the day that Sonny Boy fell off the wagon. Four days after a festival, like clockwork.

Wanda walked into his cubicle, a paper plate piled high with lasagna in one hand, a steaming Styrofoam cup in the other. "Didn't know what you wanted to drink, figured coffee was a safe bet." She pushed paperwork aside to make space.

"Sorry, change of plans." He picked up the cup of coffee. "I'll take this with me though."

"Where you going?"

"On a call. Just leave the food on the desk."

"You coming right back?"

He recalled the last time he took Sonny Boy home. "Not sure how long I'll be."

"You're not sure, I'll wrap it up. You can take it home, nuke it in the microwave for supper."

He hesitated, looking at the papers strewn across his desk. It would definitely be late when he got back. And if the last time was any indication, smelling like a pigpen.

"Don't worry about this." Wanda indicated the desk. "I'll straighten it up for you."

"No, I'll get back to it. Some things I need to handle today."

"Oh? I got time. What needs doing?"

He paused, looking at dark circles under her eyes. "Sure you're up to it?"

"Up to it?" Her cheeks spotted with color. "You callin' me old? Why, I'll have you know I work circles 'round those other girls—"

"Okay, *okay.*" He retrieved the report Everett sent over, the business cards for Frank Tubbe and Eli Sunday. "Send copies to these men."

"That's it?" She glanced at the two cards. "Shoot, this'll take all of five minutes."

Chitto hesitated, considering the time he would be losing that afternoon and the latest finding on the fourth-day murders.

"All right then, pull together a list of the festivals and celebrations scheduled this season."

Wanda raised an eyebrow. "Fall festival was at Tuskahoma weekend 'fore last."

"Not just our celebrations, the other nations', too. Whatever's going on, *wherever* it is, I want to know about it."

"Okay," she said, eyes round. "I'll see what I can find out. Anything else?"

Chitto rubbed his chin. "Can you dig up some of those colored stick-on slips you use for files?"

"Post-it flags? Got a drawer full."

"Need some, two or three different colors. And have one of those maps showing the boundaries for the different nations blown up—the *big* checkerboard map." He looked at the wall next to his desk. " 'Bout this big." He outlined a square on the wall.

She nodded, but the look on her face said she was rethinking her offer to help.

"You know how to reach me." He headed for the stairs, coffee in hand.

"Wait a minute," Wanda called out. "Want me to call Mattie, let her know about Sunday? She said your last visit didn't go too good."

"Yeah," he sighed. "Tell her I'll be out."

On the way to his SUV, Chitto thought about Sonny Boy's latest bout with alcohol. He knew he should be aggravated with the old man. Expecting him to be a taxi service. Pig waterer. Cook. But he would never have a better opportunity to see what kind of butchering implements he owned—*and* see if his memory had improved. Especially those involving scalped men. He couldn't shake the feeling Sonny Boy was somehow involved.

"I am better this time," Sonny Boy flashed a toothless grin.

"Glad for that." Chitto *was* pleased to see the old man sitting in a chair instead of propped up in a hospital bed. "Wait here."

Chitto searched out the same doctor he talked with the week before. "Where was he picked up?"

The doctor glanced at a clipboard. "Same place. Red River Tavern." He pulled a manila envelope from a drawer containing Sonny Boy's wallet. "Just like last time with this, too. Money's still inside."

Chitto swore under his breath. Obviously, what worked for Eliot Ness hadn't worked for him. "He good to go?"

The doctor snorted. "Could've left hours ago; insisted you were coming to get him."

"Need any medicine?"

Another snort. "Probably be good if Mr. Munro left off *all* drugs, if you get my drift."

Chitto did. He walked to where the old man sat.

"Okay, Sonny Boy. Let's get you home."

"Yeah. Pigs gonna be real thirsty."

★ ★ ★ ★ ★

Five minutes later, Chitto headed east on U.S. 70 toward Bokchito, the old man buckled in the seat next to him.

Sonny Boy patted his shirt pocket. "I am out of smokes."

Chitto pointed his chin at the glove box. "Help yourself."

The old man removed a cigarette and held the pack out to Chitto.

"No, thanks. Gave it up some time back."

Sonny Boy studied the pack, full except for the cigarette he removed. "Why?"

"It's a long story."

Sonny Boy stared at him. "I got time."

Chitto considered how to deflect the question without seeming rude to an Elder. "Another time, Grandfather."

Sonny Boy made a move to replace the pack in the glove box.

"Keep it," Chitto said. "Time I bought a new one."

Sonny Boy grunted softly. "I will send up a prayer for you." He lit up with a stick match, cupping the flame in his hands, and inhaled deeply.

Cold fingers slid up Chitto's spine. In olden days, lighting tobacco was the same as saying a prayer.

"I think I blacked out again," Sonny Boy said a few minutes later. He took a last draw, pinched the fire from the stub, and dropped it in the car's ashtray.

Chitto rolled his window down, letting air circulate through the Tahoe. "Why wouldn't you ride home with the other officer, Sonny Boy?"

"That boy's nose said he didn't like the way I smelled."

Chitto curbed an urge to laugh. "Didn't those people at the AA give you a call? They were supposed to get you back in the program."

"Yeah."

Chitto waited a respectful minute. "Yeah, what?"

"Yeah, they called. My granddaughter is taking me to my drunk meetings on Wednesdays."

Wednesdays. And by Friday, he was back drinking.

"Why'd you go back to the bottle this time?"

Sonny Boy laid a hand on his chest. "My heart is filled with sadness."

Chitto frowned. "What's making you sad?"

He wondered if the old man was feeling remorseful about something. If that something had to do with two murdered men. Two *scalped*, murdered men.

"Because the daughters cry," Sonny Boy said.

Chitto just sighed.

At the house with a pyramid roof, Chitto ran the Sonny Boy–Munro drill. First, a shower and clean clothes. Then, pigs. While hauling buckets of water, he noted there weren't as many to tend.

"What happened to the other pigs?" he asked.

"Those men came got them. The ones that buy them."

"Where were they going?"

Sonny Boy paused. "Don't think I asked that."

Chitto shook his head. Talking with Sonny Boy was like scraping dried paint off a windowpane. A trait his granddaughter inherited. Thinking about Letty Munro brought the Walker girl to mind.

"Say, Sonny Boy," he said, refilling the water bucket. "What do you know about Teresa Walker, your granddaughter's friend that went to the sing this last Sunday? She fell on some hard times here recently."

The old man eyes turned liquid. "The hurt will go away."

"Yeah, I hope it does, too."

As he finished watering the last pig, Chitto's mind worked overtime trying to figure out how to find out the information he needed without showing disrespect. But with two unsolved murders on his hands, he didn't have time for conventions.

He faced the old man. "I need the names of those guys who picked up those pigs, Sonny Boy. It's police business."

"Don't know that." He replaced the lid on the barrel holding pig food. "They call on the phone, tell me how many they want."

"What about a bill of sale? Cancelled check?"

"Cash on the barrel head." Sonny Boy smacked a fist into the palm of the other hand. "Only way to do business."

Right. Easy to spend, impossible to trace.

Deciding it was time to move on, Chitto walked to the barn area to take a quick look around. Tools hung from the walls. Saws, rakes, shovels. And knives. He walked closer. Rusted knives. He ran one of the blades across his thumb. Rusted knives too dull to cut butter. No butchering had been done in that shed in a long time.

"I am hungry now."

Chitto spun around, swearing silently. Even Sonny Boy could steal up on him.

"Got peanut butter? Jelly?"

"You bet."

As they walked to the back door, Chitto noticed new tracks leading toward the rough structure a half mile back in the woods. "Somebody come out to hunt last week?"

"Not I know of." Sonny Boy leaned on Chitto's arm as they climbed the steps.

Chitto felt bony arms through his cotton shirt. One thing for sure, the old man wasn't the one doing the killing.

Sonny Boy turned on the TV in the front room and settled into his chair.

A few minutes later, Chitto set a plate on the table next to the old man. He rocked back on his heels watching Sonny Boy eat, glad the old alcoholic's appetite was good. Most drunks

127

relied on the sugar in the bottle to keep them going.

"If you're good, I need to get going."

"Yeah, I'm in good shape," Sonny Boy said.

Chitto paused, wondering if it would do any good to ask the remaining question that begged an answer. He opted to try.

"You singing at any more celebrations, Sonny Boy?"

"I will sing until the fires have all gone out."

Chitto shook his head. "Stay out of the bars, Sonny Boy."

Chitto's cell phone rang as he climbed into his Tahoe. The clock on the dash read 5:30. His regular assignment was Monday through Friday, eight to five. Officially, he was off duty. Unofficially, he was on call 24/7.

"Lieutenant Chitto," he said.

"Where are you?" Wanda snapped.

"Just finishing up for the day. Why are you working late?"

"Why am I—Why do you think I'm working late?"

Chitto sighed, remembering the list of things he'd given her to do.

"What about this food?" she asked.

Damn.

"Hey look, just take it home with you. I, uh, I've got something else I need to take care of."

Such as take a hot shower to remove pig stink.

"Like what?"

He gave his head a shake. "It's personal, Wanda." He listened to a half minute of silence.

"Enjoy your evening," she snapped.

"Sure thing," he said to dead air.

En route back to Durant, Chitto picked up the smell of burnt tobacco. He pulled the cigarette butt from the ashtray where Sonny Boy deposited it and held it to his nose. Pitching the butt out the window, he wondered if the old man said a prayer as he lit up. And if he did, what he prayed for.

Stopping at a Walgreen's on the outskirts of town, Chitto purchased a pack of Marlboro Reds. Tearing a square out of the top, he lingered before placing it in the glove box, breathing deep. The smell of fresh tobacco was perfume to his nose.

No, he reflected. More like incense.

CHAPTER THIRTEEN

Eli Sunday, the Muskogee-Creek inspector, called at eleven that night.

"Charlie Carter's widow can meet up with us at her place in Checotah," he said. "Does shift work over to Muskogee, gets home 'bout noon. You make it?"

"I can make it. You tell her about her husband?"

"Briefed her on his death. Told her it wasn't by natural means. Not the details."

Thinking about Emma Love Wilcox's dispassionate reaction to Delbert's death, Chitto asked how the Carter woman had taken the news.

"Not much of a reaction t'all," Sunday said.

Chitto wrote down the address of a truck stop in Checotah, which was south of Muskogee and east of Okmulgee where the Muskogee-Creek police department was located. Since Highway 69 passed right through the town, the stone-faced lieutenant told Chitto he would meet up with him there.

Chitto lay awake after Sunday's call, staring at the ceiling fan, feeling the emptiness on the other side of the bed. When the alarm went off, he felt groggy from lack of sleep but forced himself to get up and begin household duties. Things he and Mary used to do together so they could go to a movie later. Maybe out to dinner. Even better were those times they stayed home and ordered in. She was a patsy for movies that featured Native Americans—*real* Native Americans. Good flicks—not melodramas where the Indian was played by an Italian actor and a blonde chick hooked up with him. *Smoke Signals* was her favorite movie. *Shows the bad stuff,* she would say, *but it's the real deal.* Ironically, her favorite food was Italian. How many times, Chitto reflected, had they spent Saturday evening watching that movie and ordering in pizza.

Not enough . . .

Working alone, Chitto didn't complete all the tasks. In spite of that, he stopped at nine o'clock to clean up. The hundred-and-twenty-mile drive to Checotah would eat up a lot of time.

Light rain started to fall as Chitto drove north on Highway 69. Trees, shrubs and grasses melted into that shade of wet nature assumes when it receives a long-awaited reprieve. Seeing other headlights reflecting off the puddled highway, he made sure his were on, too.

He rolled down the window to feel the rain on his face. On the chance he might encounter someone from the bureau—someone by the name of Ramon Rodriquez—he opted to drive his truck and dress casual. He checked his rearview mirror often, looking for a black SUV dogging his tracks. The only vehicle dogging him was a beat-up Ford pickup looking like it had been rescued from a junk yard. The right lamp on the truck wobbled like a bobble-head doll. Two people were visible in the cab.

Deciding Rodriquez wouldn't be caught dead in the wreck, he gave the Ford a last glance.

Chitto reproached himself for being paranoid. The FBI might not like him running his own investigation but it didn't have resources to put a tail on him. Still, he considered, Rodriquez wasn't your five-and-dime FBI agent. If he *had* been a member of a gang down on the Rio, his temperament might make him act unpredictably.

Like hassle a smart-aleck tribal cop who dissed him.

Sighing, Chitto turned his attention to the day he had planned before Sunday rearranged his schedule. Wanda had pulled together the things he requested. All of it was on his desk now, waiting for him to put together pieces to the puzzle that had taken over his life.

A crack of thunder and darkening sky caused him to roll up his glass. He wiped his face dry with the sleeve of his shirt, thinking the advance preparation would go to waste unless the interview with the Carter woman didn't take that long. The following day was definitely out because he was expected at his mother's house. He had already pissed Wanda off, maybe Rona. He didn't need his mother mad at him, too.

Should have gone by the office and picked up that food, he thought now. He would apologize on Monday morning. Old and set in her ways as she was, Wanda was going out of her way to help him.

Pelting rain and disappearing highway lines driving all else from his mind, he focused on the tail lights of the car ahead of him.

The clouds rained themselves dry as Lake Eufaula came into view. Stretching like a lazy snake between Krebs and Muskogee, six hundred miles of shoreline traced the banks of the hundred-thousand-acre lake.

As a boy, Chitto's father had taken him to fish on Eufaula. On Sunday mornings, they hauled his dad's fourteen-foot aluminum boat behind a pickup truck, listening to it rattle as they drove to the marina. His father never failed to comment on the bass boat he would buy once he retired. A twenty-one footer with a center console. That dream ended up in a cold-case file.

Chitto checked his rearview mirror again and saw the junk-yard truck. He straightened in his seat, growing wary. He began to check the mirror often. At Checotah, he pulled into the place Sunday gave as a landmark and waited. The truck continued northward, disappearing from sight.

Paranoia . . .

A sedan sporting a Muskogee tribal police shield pulled into the parking lot. Chitto glanced at the clock. A quarter to twelve. Barely enough time to reach the new widow's place.

He lifted a hand to Sunday and pulled behind the cruiser. They traveled a few miles down a gravel road parallel to Highway 69, low wooded hills in the background, then pulled into a trailer park lined with single- and double-wide trailer homes. Chitto noticed a cinderblock building, obviously meant for the residents' use, and wondered as to its purpose. As they drove past, he saw it was a washateria, and his thoughts went to fabric softener.

He took note of backyard clotheslines strung with worker's clothes. Saturday was obviously wash day. Blue jeans and khakis, tees and denim shirts, all twisted in the breeze like ghosts of decapitated men. Briefly, the thought entered his head that Delbert Wilcox and Charlie Carter had returned from the dead, that their *Shilombish* was hanging around to see if he found their killers. Shaking off an uncomfortable feeling, he parked in front of one of the trailers and followed Sunday to the porch.

Seeing Carter's widow waited behind the screen door, he thought of Emma Love Wilcox. The two widows didn't look that different. But then, why would they? Dark hair and black eyes were common among those with Indian blood. As he got closer, he noted one difference between the two. This widow's face looked like it had encountered too many swinging doors.

"What do you know about the wife?" Chitto asked as he and Sunday neared the front stoop.

"Not much. Hooked up with Carter 'bout four years ago,

after she divorced her first old man. His name was Harjo." He glanced at Chitto. "He's doing time down in Texas. Armed robbery. Drug dealing. Seemed to fare better with husband number two. One speeding ticket on Carter. Real clean rap sheet."

Chitto nodded, his mind racing. If the first husband was in jail, he couldn't be the murderer unless he had a network outside doing his dirty work. He realized he was considering a conspiracy theory for the murders. It wouldn't be the first time an inmate remotely spearheaded a plot carried out by a group on the outside. But in this case, there were a couple of flies in the ointment: the ex-husband was doing time for crimes that didn't add up to a need for revenge, and a connection with the first victim seemed remote.

"How you want to play this?" Sunday asked as they neared the door.

"Your jurisdiction, your lead."

Chitto took a seat in a kitchen chair, watching Sunday and the new widow settle on opposite ends of a worn sectional sofa.

While he waited for the questioning to begin, Chitto read the room. Large-screened TV, a pillow and light cotton blanket folded on one of the end tables, a corner table that served as a catchall. A bookshelf alongside the TV filled to overflowing with children's books and games. Several dolls and other toys shoved underneath a tweed sofa.

Chitto listened for the sound of children's voices. Hearing none, he glanced through the window off the dining area. He saw two girls playing at a swing set, the expensive kind with a slide and playhouse attached. Next to the playhouse was a clothesline, the collapsible type that worked well in a small yard that doubled as a children's play area. The clothesline was opened and strung with clothes. As the questioning began, he turned to listen.

"Sorry for your loss," Sunday said, opening his notebook. "Doing our best to get to the bottom of this thing. Anything you can tell us will help. For starters, what was your husband doing in the Chickasaw Nation?"

"He didn't come home; that's all I know."

Sunday recorded the information, then looked at her. Waiting. She returned the look.

Cool customer, Chitto thought. Not unlike Emma Love Wilcox.

"When was that exactly?" Sunday pressed.

She glanced to one side, blinking. "Tuesday night; he didn't come home Tuesday night."

Same night of the week Delbert Wilcox went missing.

Sunday wrote down the information, then looked at the widow again. "When did you call in the missing person's report, ma'am?"

She blinked several times, then swallowed. Chitto wondered if she was going to break down, begin to weep, but he saw no moisture in her eyes.

"Just figured he was fishin'."

Sunday hesitated slightly. "Are you saying you didn't file a report?"

She nodded. "Didn't see no reason."

Sunday recorded another note, then asked about Carter's line of work. She reached for a piece of paper lying on the table beside the sofa.

"Warehouse in Muskogee. I wrote that down." She handed the paper to Sunday.

Chitto felt an unprofessional urge to laugh, thinking this interview could be a tape recording of the one with Emma Love Wilcox.

Sunday looked over the paper and faced her again. "What about fishing buddies? Where are their favorite fishing holes?"

She shrugged. "Went by hisself mostly. Might've met up with guys there on the lake, but don't know for sure. Maybe those people where he used to work would know."

Used to work. She had already severed connections with Carter.

"Who's he had problems with lately?" asked Sunday. "Anyone who might've held a grudge?"

She hunched her shoulders, which Chitto interpreted as an emphatic, *I don't know nothin'*.

"You in touch with your ex-husband?" Sunday asked next.

"No."

Sunday paused. "What kind of vehicle your husband drive?"

"Truck. Chevy truck. Blue."

Sunday glanced across the room to the corner table on which lay a jumble of papers. "License number would be helpful. Copy of the registration."

She shook her head. "He kept that kind of stuff in the truck."

Looking at Chitto, Sunday closed his notebook.

Chitto glanced out the window at the clothes on the clothesline. Children's clothes. Women's clothes. No men's. The women's clothes definitely for two women, one larger than the other. A week's worth of washing. Then he looked again at the little girls swinging at the play set.

Chitto turned to face her. "Those girls out back yours, Mrs. Carter?"

She nodded.

"I figure they're what, nine or ten?"

"Nine and eleven."

"They'd be by your first husband then."

She nodded again.

"Your second husband adopt them legally?"

"Their last name's Harjo, like their dad."

"He ever write to them? Call them?" He glanced at the toys

136

scattered around the room. "Maybe send them presents?"

She glanced at the toys, too. "We bought them those things."

"That would be you and your second husband, their step-father."

A slow nod.

"Who's watching the girls at night now? While you're work-ing, I mean. Believe you work third shift. What hours would that be? Two in the morning until when? Ten or eleven? Maybe noon?"

She hesitated. "My mother's been watching them."

Chitto looked at the blanket and pillow on the end table, the women's dresses on the clothesline, at her again. "Your mother move in with you 'bout a week ago, Mrs. Carter?"

She shifted around in her seat. "I think maybe she did," she said, staring at folded hands.

Chitto looked at Sunday. Sunday stood to leave.

"You do your wash at that laundry there in the middle of the courtyard?" Chitto said, pausing at the doorway.

She nodded, brow wrinkled.

"Buy your laundry detergent there, too? Maybe fabric soft-ener?"

"I buy that stuff at the grocery store unless . . ."

Chitto waited.

"Unless I run out. Cost too much in them machines. I only buy it there when I run out."

"Okay. Again, we're sorry for your loss."

Outside, Sunday stood next to his patrol car, staring across a strip of native prairie. A pair of scissortail flycatchers picked off grasshoppers in brome grass; a meadowlark sat perched on a cluster of stiff goldenrod. Beyond the prairie was Highway 69. "You wanna tell me what that line of questioning was about?" he asked, not breaking his gaze.

Chitto stared across the prairie, too, listening to the call of birds, the whine of semis on the road. "Just fishing, I guess. Sensed some contradictions in that house. You know, things that didn't add up."

Sunday nodded. "Yeah, for a guy that spoiled her kids rotten, she doesn't act too grieved. And I'd like to know if those scars on her face are mementos from her first old man, or this last one." He opened his car door. "I'll see what else I can find out at that place where he worked. Check the lake to see if we can find the truck."

"Helluva big lake, Eli."

"It is at that. Let you know what we learn. You do the same?"

Chitto nodded. "While you're at it, might see if Emma has family other than her mother. You know, brothers, uncles, cousins who might've taken off a few days from work last week?"

Sunday looked thoughtful, then nodded again. He left without further discussion, but Chitto noticed his eyes looked sharp as obsidian points. If there was anything to be ferreted out, that man would find it.

Chitto walked to a bank of dispensers on the back wall of the washateria, next to a soft-drink machine. He saw packets of soap. Bleach. Stain remover. Fabric softener.

Dropping coins into the soft-drink machine, he found a chair that gave him a view of the dispensers. Other occupants were women, most with children sitting nearby. He focused on those that bought supplies, noting what they chose to purchase. Detergent, bleach and fabric softener were top picks. A few bought stain remover. Sniffing the air inside the building, he decided the whole world used fabric softener.

As he was about to leave, a lone man walked in. Young. Shirtless. Grungy ball cap pulled low over his face. Settling into his chair again, Chitto flipped the pages of an outdated *National*

Geographic, watching him sort laundry. A load of dark clothes. Plaid and chambray shirts, jean jacket, dark socks, some oily looking rags. A load of whites. T-shirts and underwear, a couple of ragged-looking towels.

When done sorting, the man walked up to the dispensers, nodding at Chitto in passing. Glad he'd come in plain clothes, Chitto watched to see which knobs the man pulled. Two packets of soap. A packet of stain remover. One of bleach.

Just what he would've done. Stain remover for the work clothes. Bleach for the whites. No fabric softener.

Chitto got up from his seat, assessing the information he'd gleaned so far. He'd seen the signs before. Battered woman. Pregnant girls. Children silenced with threats or bought off with expensive presents, sometimes hard cash. Red flags signaling abuse. He knew that both the Wilcox and Carter women were somehow involved in the murders, and, more than likely, their daughters were victims of abuse, but he also knew the guy that was running things wouldn't implicate them. He was too smart. And he liked to complicate things.

Pulling some bills from his wallet, Chitto fed them into the dispenser. He left with packages of Tide powdered detergent, Bounce dryer sheets and Downy fabric softener in a box.

Outside, a steamy fog hugged the ground. Chitto's shirt was clinging to his shoulder blades by the time he reached his pickup. He would be running the AC on the drive back to Durant.

The mix of floral scents from softener and detergent assaulted Chitto's nose, causing his head to throb. Turning off the air conditioner, he rolled down the windows to allow hot air to scour the truck's cab.

He glanced in the rearview mirror out of habit. Seeing no black SUV, he relaxed. Then he looked again.

Coincidence.

Twenty miles down the road, he checked again.

Thirty, again.

He checked his mirror often after that. Increasing his speed, decreasing his speed. The truck with the bobble-head light kept perfect pace. Chitto never carried his duty gun when he was off duty. Now, he rethought that decision.

The hundred-twenty-mile drive between Checotah and Durant seemed like twelve hundred. The truck pulled off the highway just before Chitto reached the Durant city limits. It kept just enough distance to prevent him from reading the plate and exited the highway at a place where he couldn't turn around and follow.

"Huh," he grunted, after the truck disappeared. He had someone's attention. The question was, whose?

Debating whether to report the incident to the state patrol, he laughed. The first question asked would be, *Why would someone be following you, Lieutenant Chitto?* And, of course, he would say, *Because I'm investigating a double homicide, but I can't talk about it because I'm working undercover and don't want FBI Agent Ramon Rodriquez to catch me at it.*

Oh, yeah, a surefire way to keep his head out of his ass.

Chitto's mood turned dark as he parked at the Choctaw nation complex. No two ways about it, he was on his own on this case. A lone duck on a big, open pond.

Entering the building, an old saying came to mind: *The perils of duck hunting are great, especially for the duck.*

CHAPTER FOURTEEN

Chitto's desk looked like a supply cabinet had been dumped on it. He stowed the laundry packets from the washateria on top of his four-drawer file and examined the pile. An oversize version of the *Tribal Jurisdictions in Oklahoma* map. Pads of peel-off sticky notes. Scotch tape. A stack of computer printouts showing pow-wows, celebrations and festivals scheduled across the checkerboard. Wanda hadn't overlooked a thing.

Taping the map to the wall, he sat down, staring at it. Much of Oklahoma had been dissected into various colored shapes. Seven large blocks stood out. The Cheyenne-Arapaho Nation, in a red sandstone color, and the Kiowa-Comanche-Apache, in coral, dominated the southwestern section. In the south-central section was a turquoise block, the Chickasaw Nation. The Choctaw Nation, the color of desert sand, filled the entire southeastern corner. Above the Choctaw was the Muskogee-Creek Nation, shown in a pale chestnut. In the northeast corner was the Cherokee, colored pumpkin gold. West of the Cherokee and bordering the Muskogee Nation was the Osage, a yellow-green on the map. Smaller colored squares made up the rest, representing the remaining nations. Thirty-eight federally recognized tribes in all.

He looked through the stack of scheduled events next. Some were one-day long, others two or three. Fewer in number, those that lasted four days. He sat awhile, considering common denominators of the puzzle he was piecing together.

Celebrations lasting four days.

Ones that would attract enough traffic to erase any signs of traceable evidence.

Those held in remote locations where unusual activity would not be noticed.

Those occurring in late summer and fall, celebrating the end of the old year and beginning of the new.

An hour later, the large stack was sorted into several smaller ones, but only one stack interested him. Picking up the pad of yellow Post-its, he wrote down the dates of the four-day celebrations and their locations.

July 22–25 . . . Cherokee Nation . . . Tahlequah
July 29–August 1 . . . Red Earth Festival . . . Oklahoma City
August 5–8 . . . Oklahoma Indian Nation Festival . . . Concho
August 12–15 . . . Ottawa Nation . . . Miami
August 19–22 . . . Southern Plains Festival . . . Apache
August 26–29 . . . Ponca Nation . . . Ponca City
September 2–5 . . . Choctaw Nation . . . Tuskahoma
September 9–12 . . . Chickasaw Nation . . . Tishamingo
September 16–19 . . . Wyandotte Nation . . . Wyandotte
September 23–26 . . . Muskogee-Creek Nation . . . Okmulgee

Chitto placed the yellow stickers on the map, noting the Choctaw and Chickasaw Nations had already been hit. The Wyandotte festival was taking place that weekend, and the Muskogee-Creek, the following one.

Broad strokes in place, it was time to narrow the field. Picking up the green sticky pad, he printed DW on two of them, representing Delbert Wilcox, the first victim. He placed one flag at Tuskahoma, where the man was found dead, the other north of Ada, where he lived. He selected orange for Charlie Carter, victim number two. He flagged Tishamingo, the place of Carter's death, and another in Checotah where he lived.

Rocking back in his chair, he picked up one of his worry stones and studied the stickers. Looking for what was missing. Thinking about two men getting on with life who met a sudden and brutal ending. He needed a link between the victims.

None surfaced.

Grudgingly, he peeled off another green flag, wrote *DW* on it and stuck it on the side of the map. A *Pending* space. He followed up with an orange one labeled *CC*.

He began to worry the stone again, pausing when his fingers became raw. The stone was a piece of conglomerate, rough as sandpaper. Miscellaneous small rocks held together with a natural glue, forging them into one larger stone.

Glue . . .

Chitto returned the stone to its place on his desk. Punching the *On* switch to his computer, he addressed an email to a list he created over the years. Not contacts from all thirty-eight nations, but at least half. People who could help him identify the missing pieces, identify a bonding agent that held the pieces together.

Typing hurriedly, he outlined the two fourth-day murders, providing information on Delbert Wilcox and Charlie Carter, and alerting his counterparts to be on watch. Asking if they knew of similar incidents, could provide links that would lead to the murderers.

Links? He leaned back in his chair again, wondering what kind of clues he should advise them to look for.

White men married to Indian women?

Hundreds fit that description. He considered other similarities. Both victims were found on ceremonial grounds. Naked. Beheaded. Scalped.

Sacrificial? Something to do with a rite?

Leslie came to mind. She would know all about rites and

rituals, religion and mythology, and she worked in the different nations for several years.

He read aloud as he typed. "What do you know about a cultural anthropologist named Dr. Leslie Anderson? Would like information on her whereabouts in your area and what her activities included. Also provide word on ceremonies or rituals held in your jurisdiction." Reviewing the email, he decided to add one last comment. "The sooner the better."

Chitto glanced out the window as he hit the *Send* button. Shadows were lengthening. Days getting shorter. Autumn celebrations would be over soon. Would he solve this mystery before the new year began? If not, would the FBI find the cases worthy enough to pursue?

Leaving the building, he heard the call of crows overhead. He watched them gathering from the four directions, heading to a single tall cottonwood at the rear of the complex. Breeding season was over. Winter was approaching, the time for roosting together at night. His presence disturbed the reunion, and they cawed their disapproval.

He had parked in the back parking lot, near the new construction site. Approaching his SUV, he noticed a manila envelope in the fading light, stuck under a wiper blade. He looked around quickly, then pulled the envelope free. Undoing the clasp, he shook an object into his hands. A small lock of curly hair.

"Sonofabitch—"

Thump.

Hoklonote'she . . . ?

Silence became screams as Chitto drifted from one state of darkness to another. He opened his eyes to the night sky, identified the screams as the caws of crows. Rolling to his knees, he stumbled to his feet. Instinctively, he felt for his service revolver, then remembered it was locked in a cabinet at his house. That memory was followed by another one: two men in a truck with a bad headlight. Did they know where he worked? Had they skirted him, followed him to the office? Turning in a dizzying circle, he looked for his assailants. Crows were his only companions.

He felt the back of his head. No blood, but he could expect a helluva headache come morning. Remembering the envelope, he picked it up off the ground. Apparently, he surprised whoever was delivering it.

Pulling a flashlight from his glove box, he examined the envelope's contents. Delbert Wilcox's scalp lock. Returning the leathery remnant to the envelope, he pitched it onto the passenger seat.

Why didn't I see them? Hear them?

Chitto scanned the area with his flashlight on high beam. Nothing. With so much construction equipment around, his assailants had their pick of hidey-holes. And the crows were making enough noise to wake the dead, so he wouldn't have heard them.

As he drove toward his house, he wondered what message the grisly gift was meant to convey.

A warning?

Another memory slowly surfaced, something he thought of as he gained consciousness. *Hoklonote'she.*

An old story his grandmother told him as a boy, *Hoklonote'she* was a telepathic shape-changer that stalked hunters. Could the memory be a remnant image of his attacker? Someone coming out of the shadows?

But why would *he,* whoever his assailant was, consider him a hunter?

He sighed, recalling something else. *Hoklonote'she* could also assume the form of various birds and animals.

Crows, he decided. It had to be the crows. It was the only thing that made sense.

At least in his current state of darkness.

CHAPTER FIFTEEN

Traffic was light on Oklahoma 69, which Chitto attributed to it being Sunday. He had grazed on toast and black coffee for breakfast—accompanied by aspirin in large quantity. A thumping headache and Delbert Wilcox's scalp lock curbed his appetite. He considered taking the scrap of skin and hair to Everett Mullins to confirm its owner, but decided against involving the ME. Or Dan Blackfox, for that matter, who would pull him off the case faster than a knife fight in a phone booth. Besides, there was no real doubt whose head the memento came from. Or why it was left for him.

Scare tactic. He was getting close to something.

Picking up the lingering scent of laundry packets, he made a mental note to retrieve them from the office. In his hurry to leave the night before, he'd left them on the file cabinet. Blackfox had the nose of a hound dog and would want an explanation. Something he wasn't prepared to do, especially now. This thing had become personal.

Rainfall the previous week had energized the countryside. Angus cattle in cornfields glinted like black glass. Leaves on oaks and hickories mustered one last hurrah before winter, their leaves reflecting sunlight like precious stones.

Sipping coffee from his travel mug, Chitto checked his rearview mirror often. This time, the truck with a bad headlight was not part of the drive. A battered, white Toyota, the right front fender painted brown, was. Pacing him speed for speed, mile for mile. He turned wary again. Exiting on the access road that led to Krebs, he pulled to the shoulder. The Toyota continued north. He watched until it disappeared from sight.

Paranoia again?

Parking in front of his mother's house, Chitto noted Leslie's gray Suburban was absent. The sense of satisfaction was followed with an almost equal feeling of disappointment. A part of him found the woman's forthrightness refreshing, her down-to-earth manner, enjoyable. She talked easily, just as Mary used to do. She laughed easily, too, just as Mary had. More than that, she made *him* want to laugh again.

Another part of Chitto found Leslie's presence in the checkerboard disturbing. Her appearance coincided with the recent murders. Happenstance? Perhaps, but his background in law made him a believer in causal chains, not chance. An event caused an effect, and, in turn, the first effect became an event on its own—a cause, creating another effect. No two ways about it, the woman was a question mark. Until he had more answers, it was better their paths did not cross.

Especially if he had stirred up a hornet's nest.

"Hello the house," Chitto called as he walked inside. He'd acquired the habit as a boy growing up in a part of the country where loaded shotguns leaned behind front doors. The practice was so old, he didn't know where it originated. But he could make a guess. After Indian territory was created, it quickly became known as outlaw territory because if was free of most legal jurisdictions. Which meant criminals flocked to the area. Ruthless bands of outlaw gangs. Vigilantes, too. Homesteaders, no matter their skin color, needed protection within easy reach. Reliable protection. And it was hard to miss with a shotgun.

Hell, has so much changed . . . ?

"You think I am gone deaf?" his grandmother said from the

front room.

Chitto walked to the quilting frame where she worked. "Didn't want to surprise you, *Sapokni*." My grandmother.

"No big surprise some freeloader was gonna show up." Rhody Pitchlynn wore a short-sleeved, cotton shirt over a lightweight denim skirt, her white hair pulled back in a tight bun. The air conditioner rumpled edges of the quilt she worked on. "Mattie has been cooking all day."

He grinned at the rebuff. His grandmother was in one of her moods. Contrary. Quarrelsome.

"Sewing on Sunday," he said, faking concern. "Isn't that breaking the Sabbath? Supposed to rest from work on Sunday."

"*Pish*. Tried the notions of them tithe takers. Paying taxes to pray to God." She bent her neck so she could see him better. "Did you learn nothing from me? Old ways are better for us, *Sappoknakni*." My grandson.

He knelt so she could look at him more easily. "I learned many things from you." He fingered the quilt stretched out before her. "And this will be my teacher after you are gone."

Her dark face softened. "Foolish to waste time on those notions anyway. Pretty soon, everything gonna be stardust."

Chitto smiled at that, remembering their previous discussion about a meteor demolishing the planet.

"I'll go let the cook know the freeloader is here," he said.

"Dinner's almost ready. Talk to me while I finish the potatoes." Mattie had dressed casually, too. A patterned, blue blouse topped lightweight chambray slacks, closed-toed sandals flopped softly as she walked between counter and stove.

She watched as he sat down at the counter. "Tell me what you learned about the killing at Tuskahoma."

Chitto raised an eyebrow. Her request was a-hundred-eighty degrees from the one on the last visit.

"Nothing new," he shrugged. "Why? You getting pressure about it?"

"No one's pressuring me about anything." She looked at him. "Someone pressuring you?"

"No pressure. Just don't want to talk about work today."

She stuck a fork in the potatoes, testing doneness. "You don't want to talk about the Nation's business, we'll talk about other things."

As the minutes passed, Chitto came to a realization. His mother and he did not have a lot to talk about *other* than the Nation's business.

"You seen Rona lately?" she asked, glancing sideways at him.

Chitto sighed. She had brought the conversation around to another thing he did not want to discuss. He paused, considering how to deflect the line of questioning.

"Run into her couple of times a week. You know, when she comes into the office to check on stuff."

"Stuff." She looked up from the pot on the stove. "You mean, like Indian women getting beat up and raped?"

Chitto hesitated, frowning. "That's her job as a victim's advocate."

"And if you did your job . . ." Her voice went up an octave. "She wouldn't have to deal with such things."

"Hey look," he sighed. "Let's start over again. I don't want to get into anything today."

"Well, maybe I do."

He stared at her. His grandmother wasn't the only one with a short fuse.

"Someone needs to do something about this problem," she said. "I talked with Rona this week. She said her caseload doubles every year."

Chitto lifted his hands, palms up. "We're doing all we can, but you'd know that. You helped with that grant to help battered women."

"So I did," she said, taking a masher to the potatoes. "And what did the tribal police do with that money? Set up *classes* for women to take."

He hesitated, wondering where this was going. "That's right, rape prevention training, educating women and girls on how to protect themselves from being abused."

"Well, has it worked? Rona's caseload is growing, which means it was the wrong answer." She raised her hands in the air. "A waste of money and time and—and people are getting frustrated."

Chitto looked away, staring past the backyard to low hills covered in yellowing trees and russet-colored brush. "So, what *is* the right answer?" he asked, facing her again.

"Stop these men from committing those crimes!" She beat butter and cream into the potatoes with a heavy spoon that she wielded like a war club. "There are those who think you have become too much like those government policemen. You need to act more . . . more *Indian.*"

He flinched. Was she comparing him to the FBI?

"Who thinks that way?"

She waved a hand dismissively. "Talk is you are not a justice man."

He flinched again. "I agree with you about stopping the crimes." He chose his words carefully. "Classes seemed like the right approach. What do you think we should've done? Set up classes for rapists? Guys who bounce their wives off walls? You think *they're* going to voluntarily come in asking for help—"

"You sound like squalling cats!"

Mattie turned toward the kitchen doorway.

Chitto turned, too, looking to where his grandmother stood doing her old-person's dance. Shifting her weight from one leg to the other, a mannerism common in old people whose hip sockets had worn down to bone.

Rhody marched to where Mattie stood. Talking in her native tongue, she spoke so softly Chitto could not make out the words. His mother stood for a minute, her mouth a straight line, then turned to face him.

"Okay, we start over. Set the table. I am done with the potatoes."

Chitto walked to the cabinet that held dinnerware and took out three plates.

"Four," she said. "Leslie will be here any minute." She set a platter of fried chicken and bowl of green beans on the table.

Chitto closed his eyes, breathing deep. His quiet day had not only turned into a battleground but also an unwanted match-making exercise.

Before he could object, he heard the front door open and a voice call out, "I'm here."

A smiling Leslie Anderson walked into the kitchen. The brown bag she carried triggered an immediate grunt from Rhody.

"No," Leslie said quickly. "It's chocolates—I brought choco-lates."

Rhody opened the bag, examining the box of chocolates. *"Pish—"* She looked at Leslie. "Next time, no nuts. Nuts too hard on old gums."

"Oh, sorry. You bet, no nuts." She looked at Chitto, eyes wide.

Chitto grinned. "Not everything's in a textbook . . ."

She returned the grin, then looked at Mattie. "I'm a little late. Hope that didn't cause problems."

"You're just in time. Dinner's ready to go on the table."

"Oh, *good*. I could eat a horse. It's a long drive from El Reno."

As the talk in the kitchen turned to Leslie's work, Chitto's thoughts drifted. He was more interested in coming up with a polite way to leave early than hearing about Leslie's exploits—or enduring more criticism from his family. If an occasion rose, he would take advantage of it. Then, he became aware of something in his subconscious, nagging him for an answer. Something Leslie had said.

"Isn't El Reno in Canadian County?" he asked.

"What?" Leslie glanced at him. "Oh, I couldn't say for sure."

Chitto *was* sure. El Reno was in Canadian County and Canadian County was in Cheyenne Arapaho country, due west of the Chickasaw Nation. Not far from where the last decapitated victim was found. Becoming aware of the silence in the room, he wondered how to talk work without talking work.

"Thought you were working with Choctaws now." He lifted his shoulders in a dismissive way.

The smile returned. "Ward Schmidt, that friend I mentioned, invited me to go to a cleansing ceremony last night outside El Reno."

"So, this cleansing ceremony was for someone from one of the nations over there?"

"Arapahoe." She took the bowl of potatoes Mattie handed her and placed it on the table.

"Who was it needed a cleansing?" He took a seat across from her. "What was it? Rite of passage for girls?"

Leslie shook her head, looking amused. "Cleansing ceremonies are for men, although women have a role to play in them, too—"

"No talking 'bout work things," Mattie said abruptly.

Chitto looked at his mother. To interrupt someone, especially a guest in your home, was a rudeness the Choctaw did not permit. She had done it twice recently.

"Sam wants to talk about *other* things." Mattie passed the platter of chicken around the table.

Chitto shook his head. His mother was not done being angry with him.

"This is different," he said. "Leslie's talking about Indian customs. Like you said, maybe it's time I became more Indian." He was not being entirely truthful. If the cleansing ceremony was for men, the participants had done something serious. Perhaps serious enough to fall under his jurisdiction.

Mattie sat back in her chair, staring at him with arms crossed. He had turned the tables on her, and she didn't like it.

Her eyes darting between the two, Leslie spoke hesitantly. "Well, I haven't been to many of these ceremonies myself, so I'm not the expert. Ward's the one to talk to, not me."

"Think I could attend one of them?" he asked.

"Oh, I can't pull that off. Outsiders are rarely allowed. Ward had trouble getting me in." She hesitated. "If you want, I can set up a meeting with Ward. Maybe he can."

"First of the week would work best." Chitto pulled a business card from his shirt pocket and wrote his cell number on the back.

"Okay, I'll give him a call later."

When Mattie made a grunting sound, Chitto braced himself.

"These things are out of your jurisdiction, Sam. Shouldn't go messing in things that don't concern you—"

"No more talk—" Rhody picked up the box of candy and motioned Leslie to take a piece. Next, she handed the box to Mattie. "Time for sweet things."

Mattie removed a piece from the box and passed it to Chitto. After he took a piece, Rhody indicated they should eat their candy.

"Now, I tell you a story," she said. "One I learned from those who came to teach us. The story of how poison came into the world.

"A long time ago, when the world was new, a plant grew in

the waters where the Choctaw people went to wash themselves. If one of the people touched this vine, he would get sick and sometimes, die.

"The vine liked the Choctaw people and felt sad that it caused them pain. So, it decided to give away its poison. It called together the chiefs of the small people of the waters—the wasps, bees and snakes—and told them it wanted to give them its poison.

"The small people held a council to talk about the plant's offer. All of them had been stepped on by the big people and had no way to defend themselves. They did not want to cause harm to others, but they agreed to take the poison and use it wisely.

"Bee told the plant, 'I will take a small part of your poison and only use it to defend my hive. I will warn people away before I poison them. Even if I have to use my poison, it will kill me, so I will use it very carefully.'

"Next, Wasp said, 'I will take a small part of your poison, too. For then I will be able to protect my nest. I will keep my poison in my tail, but I will buzz close to them as a warning before I poison them.'

"Water Moccasin spoke then, saying, 'I will also take some and use it only if people step on me. I will hold it in my mouth and when I open it, people will see how white it is and know to stay away from me.'

"Rattlesnake spoke to the plant last, saying, 'I will take all that is left and hold it in my mouth, too. But before I strike someone, I will shake rattles on my tail to warn them, to let them know that they are too close.' "

Rhody looked around the table, coming to rest on Chitto. "You see, *Sappoknakni.* The little people use poison to protect themselves, but if the big people listen to their warning, they will not die."

"I see," he murmured though, in fact, he did not.

Rhody turned to Leslie. "Write that down. I will not say it again."

Nodding vigorously, Leslie mumbled, "Yes ma'am."

"Good," Rhody said, picking up a bowl from the table. "Now we eat potatoes."

The meal went quickly as Leslie was eager to record the story about poison, which gave Chitto a reason to excuse himself early. But on the drive back to Durant, his mind refused to turn loose of the words spoken that day. He replayed the scene with his mother, trying to figure out why she had reacted as she did. From the time he walked in the door, both she and his grandmother had displayed irritation with him. Anger. Even hostility.

Systematically, he pieced together the events that brought the situation around. His mother wanted an update on the murder at the old Choctaw capitol grounds. She mentioned Rona Guthrie talking about her caseload. The grant money being used for rape prevention training. Him acting like a white police-man.

He turned to his grandmother's story about the poison vine, the way her eyes searched him out at the end. She chose that story for him; that much was clear. Why?

A warning? Did they know he was already mixed up in the fourth-day murders?

One thing was clear. His mother and grandmother were disappointed in him, wanted him to be something more than he was. Something . . . different. He wondered what that would look like.

The miles slipped past, but Chitto continued to fight the bit, not wanting to accept that those most important to him felt he had failed. What would it take to appease them?

Glancing in the rearview mirror, he did a double take. The

white Toyota with a brown front fender was back, far enough away he couldn't read the plate. And behind it, a truck with a headlight that wobbled.

Damn . . .

Lone Duck was being double-teamed.

The vehicles following Chitto exited the highway on the outskirts of Durant, taking an access road that made it impossible for him to pursue them.

Making a quick stop at the office to pick up the packets of laundry products, he was relieved to see a Tahoe in the parking lot. Weekends, an automated service transferred emergency calls to other agency offices with full-time staff on duty. But today, one of the other tribal officers was at the office.

Chitto walked past Sergeant Junior Wharton, the Evidence/K-9 officer, who punched computer keys with thickened fingers, knobs for knuckles. A black German shepherd named Jake lay beside his desk, ears alert.

"How's it going, Junior?"

"Livin' the dream," Wharton muttered. A former football player, he was a beefy man with thick neck and slope shoulders, the type agencies searched out for Hummer ads.

Laughing quietly, Chitto went to retrieve the laundry packets. His smile faded as he eyed the top of the file cabinet. The packets were gone.

Retracing his movements the day before, he was positive he placed them on the tall, four-drawer cabinet in the corner. Looking over his area, he found everything else as he left it. The map on the wall with its colored flags. The tape and sticky notes. Even the half-filled coffee cup on his desk.

"Hey, Junior," he called. "You take those packets of soap and fabric softener off the top of my file cabinet?"

Wharton looked up from the report he was working on. "Is

that what I've been smelling?" He grinned. "Thought Wanda got tired of this place reeking like a locker room." He shook his head, the smile disappearing. "Didn't touch 'em, Sam."

"Anyone else around when you got here?"

Wharton leaned back in his chair, causing it to squeal in protest. "Nope. Me and Jake's been here by our lonesome for 'bout an hour now, doing some cleanup work."

Cleanup work . . .

Chitto glanced at his wastebasket. Empty. The cleaning crew had come and gone. He wondered if one of the workers pocketed the laundry packets.

"You need soap, I got some at home." Junior grinned. "Can't help you out on the fabric softener though."

"Thanks, but it's not a problem."

You think? came the taunt in his head.

CHAPTER SIXTEEN

By Monday morning, the scent from the missing laundry packets had faded at the office. While their disappearance still bothered Chitto, he focused on more immediate issues. Blackfox had assigned a field officer to check into a drunk and disorderly call that put two young bucks in the county jail. But when Chitto heard which bar was involved, he asked to look into the incident himself. He spent his morning talking to Ernest and Bennie, who'd got into it the night before at the Red River Tavern.

Chitto took a liking to the two from the beginning. Auto mechanics, Bennie wore a grease-smeared ball cap, and Ernest wore long hair slicked back from his face. Both had fists like wrecking balls.

Talking to the men separately, he heard the same story. Too much alcohol led to too much sharing, where they learned they were dating the same girl. No, *sleeping* with the same girl. Male testosterone had kicked in, a natural anabolic that boosts the metabolism, increases the volume of muscle, making a man more aggressive. Two healthy, young, aggressive men could do a lot of damage. The Red River Tavern was closed for repairs.

That fact caused Chitto to laugh. The two feuding friends had done what he could not. Temporarily. On the spot, he decided now was the time to shut the Red River Tavern down permanently.

"Find anything interesting when you examined the premises?" Chitto asked the county officer at the jail. "Maybe something we can use to shut the joint down?"

The officer lowered his voice. "Lots of checks in the till, mostly from old men on the Choctaw dole. Pension checks, too. Even Social Security. Seems the owner of the joint has the old men sign the checks over to him as collateral for bar tabs. Neat little side business. Very lucrative, seeing the old men prob'ly passed out from rotgut whiskey after a few drinks and wouldn't remember where they spent their money. I'd bet a dollar to a donut, he shortchanged them."

Chitto thought about Sonny Boy. Twice mugged. Twice left with a full wallet.

"You think he might be responsible for old men getting mugged out back?"

The officer looked interested.

"I followed up on a couple of muggings recently," Chitto went on. "Happened out back of the Red River. Old man had a knot on his head the size of a baseball."

"Damn good possibility. I'll add your case to the list—make ours stronger."

"Enough to shut the place down for good?"

The officer grinned.

Chitto pled for the release of Ernest and Bennie. He managed to get them absolved from paying property damage, given the bar in question was in the process of being closed down. Both were charged with drunk and disorderly and given a short jail sentence. They would be out of commission long enough to sober up. In the meantime, they would hear from someone on the outside that *their* girl had hooked up with someone new. When their time was done, they would leave together, best friends again.

Domino effect, Chitto thought as he left the lockup. He was thinking now about Sonny Boy. With the old man's liquor source gone, he would not be a problem anymore. No more quick runs to the emergency room. No more pigs and peanut-butter sandwiches. Just the way a causal chain was supposed to work.

Some days were golden.

Chitto wolfed down a burger and fries on the drive to the office, thinking about the rest of his day. What should have been a short job ended up taking hours. On the way to his desk, Blackfox intercepted him.

"Anything new on these murders?"

Chitto rubbed the back of his neck, debating whether to mention the vehicles tailing him, the missing laundry products, the scalp lock on his kitchen table. The lump on his head that still required aspirin to dull.

"Nothing concrete, but I was out all morning on that drunk and disorderly." He pointed his chin toward his desk. "Expecting to hear from Tubbe and Sunday today. If not, I'll follow up with them."

Blackfox nodded, looking thoughtful. "You still want to pursue this?" He indicated the map on the wall Chitto put up.

Chitto glanced toward it, too. In the reflective light coming through the window, the green, orange and yellow flags looked like blinking traffic signals. "Yeah, this thing's got under my skin."

"Uh-huh." Blackfox nodded slowly. "You do know that a day might come when you've got no choice but to back off, let the Feds have their way with it. If we need to have a sit-down to discuss that eventuality, let me know."

Chitto knew what bothered Blackfox. He thought he was hanging on to this case because he hadn't been successful finding his dad's and Bert's killers.

"If and when that day comes," Chitto said, "I'll know it."

"Keep your head down then. Don't want unnecessary

problems on my back."

Chitto laughed to himself. He didn't want unnecessary problems on his back, either.

Or his neck.

Chitto checked for a phone message from Tubbe and Sunday, found nothing. Pulling up his e-mail, he looked for responses to the message he'd put out on the tribal telegraph. Nothing there either.

A washout, he thought. As if on cue, the phone rang.

"Chitto," he said, reaching for his coffee cup. He took a sip, realized it was leftover from the day before, set it down. A woman's voice answered, but it was a bad connection.

"Can you hear me?" she said. "How does tonight sound?"

"Tonight?" He paused, trying to place the voice.

"Ward can meet us over at Sulphur for dinner. There's a café there he knows about. It has a back booth that's quiet where he can tell you about cleansing rituals. Will that work?"

Things clicked. Leslie had followed through with her colleague. Chitto fumbled through his desk drawer, looking for a pencil.

"Yeah. Yeah, I can make it. What's the name of the place? I'll meet up with you there."

"Thought we could drive over together. I'm doing some interviews down your way, so I can pick you up."

Chitto hesitated, considering how to handle the situation. He would be off the clock, so he would need to take a personal vehicle. That meant they could drive his pickup that smelled of alfalfa and horse manure or go in Leslie's gas-guzzling Suburban, which at top speed probably did fifty an hour.

"I'll need to change," he said. "How 'bout I pick you up."

"Well, that would be good except I'd rather not leave my 'burban at someone's house. You know, the last place where I'll be interviewing someone? It'll be late when we get back. What's your address? I could leave it there. Would five, five thirty work? It's a good hour's drive to Sulphur."

What would Mary think? Chitto laughed quietly. She would tell him to make sure the toilet seat was down, that there were no dirty dishes in the sink. *Make the house ready for guests. As soon as they get in the door, they'll either want a glass of water or need to pee.*

"Yeah, guess that's the best way to handle it."

After he hung up, he glanced at the clock. Two o'clock, three hours before he met with Leslie. Two hours if he allowed time to straighten up the house, shower and change. Glancing again at the message slips Wanda left him, he saw nothing of a critical nature.

Locating Tubbe's business card, he called the cell-phone number. Tubbe answered on the first ring.

"What have you got for me?" Chitto asked.

"Nothing good. Widow wanted possession of Wilcox's pickup. Needs to sell it to pay off his bills. Sounds like he was flat-ass broke. Even owed a bar tab at The Double-Aught. Since my boss hasn't called in the FBI yet, not clear how to proceed . . ."

A wrinkle Chitto hadn't counted on. Working cases off-line was messing up people's lives. Emma and her daughter, Nanny, didn't need extra debt. Especially now the girl was pregnant.

"So, I'm stalling," Tubbe said. "I got Emma hooked up with tribal services over here. She's agreed to get her daughter back into school—but not the public one she went to. I found one of our people who home-schools her kids. She's gonna teach Nanny, too."

"Those kids get diplomas, just like regular schools."

"Yeah. Emma's considering keeping Nanny in a home-school program all the way through high school. She's very protective of that girl."

Chitto hesitated. "What about the baby?"

A pause came on the line. "Not sure 'bout that."

"You thinking what I am?" Chitto asked. "Adoption makes sense—given the age of the mother and the expense of baby stuff."

An adoption would also eliminate a living, breathing reminder of a bad experience. Of course, that hinged on who the father was. Something told Chitto the baby would have a new home soon after it was born.

"Makes sense," Tubbe said.

"You find out if Wilcox had any close friends? Belonged to any men's clubs? You know, Moose Lodge? Masonic?"

"Loner from the sounds of it. Hear anything from Sunday?"

"Plan to call him soon as I hang up. I'll let you know if anything relevant surfaces."

Chitto left a message for Eli Sunday next, then felt a need for caffeine. Fresh caffeine.

On the way to the break room, Chitto estimated the number of cups of coffee he drank in an average day. Seven or eight. He'd exchanged one addiction for another. Thinking about the pack of Marlboros in his Tahoe, he folded a piece of Doublemint into his mouth.

He bumped into Wanda in the break room.

"You eat?" she asked.

"Picked up a burger. Looking for something to wash it down."

"Made fresh." She poured him a cup. "Looks like you found those things on your desk. Saw the map on your wall."

"Yeah, thanks. Sorry to make you work late." As he turned to leave, Wanda fell into step beside him.

"What's new on that killing up there at our ceremonial grounds? Dan hasn't mentioned it."

With good reason, Chitto thought. Both murders were not on any officially assigned duty list. Blackfox was operating on a need-to-know basis.

"Don't know anything. How'd you know about it?"

"*What?*" she snorted. "Show me someone who doesn't." She looked toward the map on his wall. "I figure *DW* stands for that murdered guy, Delbert Wilcox. Who's *CC*?"

Chitto rubbed his face. First his mother was pushing him for information on the murder investigation. Now, Wanda.

"Nothing important. And the map's just a new process I'm trying out to keep track of things."

"*Nothing important*—So why'd you need to get it up so blamed fast?"

He ran a hand over his face. "Look, you know how my week goes. When you figure I would've got it done?"

"I got better things to do than your busy work," she mumbled, walking away.

Chitto stared at the map on the wall, wondering if it had been a good idea to put it up. If it was time to remove it from public scrutiny. The phone pulled his attention away.

"Talked to the people out there at that trailer park," Eli Sunday said. "All the men work, most of the women, too. The Carters kept to themselves. Didn't attend church or neighbor much."

Chitto heard a sound on the line, paper rustling, and waited.

"Mrs. Carter has lots of family. Even her grandpa's still alive. Near as I can tell, everyone has an alibi for the time in question." A brief silence followed. "Old timers in the Nation. Honorable people."

Chitto's thinking went to Sonny Boy. How the old mystic had fallen off the wagon, taken a path that was not honorable. His reason? Because of angry rocks. Daughters that wept. Chitto shook his head. For whatever reason, even honorable people could be driven to ignoble choices.

"What about Carter's pickup?"

"Found it yesterday at one of the inlets on Lake Eufaula. Locked. Ground too disturbed to identify footprints. No blood. Hauled it for a closer look. Anything new on your end?"

"Nothing yet. Keep you posted."

"Okay."

Chitto listened to the click on the line. The Creek inspector was not one to waste words.

Chitto carried a stack of pink slips to Wanda's desk. He sorted them quickly, held on to one and handed the rest to her.

"More busy work?" she snapped.

"No," he sighed. Quickly, he briefed her on what needed to be done. Hesitating, he pulled the slip from his pocket. "Might as well follow up on this one, too." The last slip was from Rona Guthrie, someone else who liked to give him the third degree.

"Rona?" Wanda gave him a sharp look. "Think she'd rather talk to you."

"Don't know anything more on that case than last time we talked. She wants more, tell her to call the state attorney's office. Oh, and I'll be out of the office rest of the day. You can reach me on my cell if anyone needs a follow-up call."

Turning away before she could question him further, Chitto walked to Blackfox's office to brief him on what he learned from Tubbe and Sunday.

Blackfox tapped his ballpoint on a yellow pad, absorbing the latest news. "So, both their vehicles were found locked up at the last place the victims were known to be?"

Chitto nodded.

"That means whoever's behind this is planning ahead. Watching the intended victim to learn his habits, how to snatch him without being seen."

Chitto nodded again, thinking about an old Toyota and a pickup truck with a blinky eye.

"Any connections between the two victims? Common friends? Work acquaintances?"

Chitto shook his head. "That's the holdup. We're working on it—and trying to keep our involvement under wraps." He quickly explained that he was taking his work on the Wilcox and Carter cases out of the office.

"You worried that big map you stuck on your wall is getting too much attention?" Blackfox asked.

"Something like that."

Blackfox tapped his pen some more. "You up on other things? Not letting other things slide?"

"No, sir. Wanda's following up on a few things, nothing critical. Mostly digging through old files to find dates and locations."

Blackfox grunted. "Well, if anyone knows where to find it, she does. Not too much she misses . . ."

Hearing Blackfox's voice fade, Chitto waited.

"Been giving some thought to the day Wanda retires," Blackfox said, looking at Chitto. "You think we need to bring in a new person to train?"

Chitto paused, rubbing his mouth. "Well, she is getting up there in years. And that chain smoking's gotta catch up with her sooner or later."

"Yeah, entitled to what time she's got left." Blackfox took a deep breath, exhaled slowly. "But her husband's killer's still out there . . ." He glanced at Chitto. "Feel like I owe her, know what I mean?"

Chitto did.

"Better take care of that map," Blackfox said, returning to his paperwork.

"I'm on it."

★ ★ ★ ★ ★

Chitto found a cardboard box in the break room and packed up his files. When done, he glanced at the blank wall. The empty space would call attention to itself.

He rummaged through a bottom drawer in his file cabinet. In lieu of the map showing tribal jurisdictions in Oklahoma, he put up an oversize version of the Choctaw checkerboard, showing which lands belonged to the Nation and which were owned by other individuals and entities. He labeled a Post-it flag with the initials *SBM,* for Sonny Boy Munro, and placed it near the town of Bokchito. He labeled another one *TW* for Teresa Walker and placed it where the trailer house was located on Highway 70. If anyone asked, he could tell them they were recent incidents he'd been dealing with, neither of which should raise any eyebrows.

Within fifteen minutes, the Wilcox and Carter murder cases, complete with map, Post-it flags and case files, were walking out the door with him. Safe from prying eyes.

CHAPTER SEVENTEEN

Chitto had shoved the breakfast table against the wall as a makeshift desk and hung the *Tribal Jurisdictions in Oklahoma* map above it. The color-coded Post-it flags were back in place, those showing the major fall celebrations scheduled in all the nations and those for the Wilcox and Carter murders. His notebook with his case notes lay on one side on the table, plus photos of the scenes, and his cell-phone charger was plugged into a wall outlet. An improvised office, complete with coffee pot. And out of the public eye.

Glancing at the clock, Chitto realized he had other obligations. After a quick shower, he pulled on clean jeans and pocket T and, over that, a lightweight sports coat that hid his Glock 22. He slipped his feet into loafers, then felt the stubble on his face. Being he was enough Indian, he didn't shave often. Hearing the doorbell ring, he put concerns about a five o'clock shadow out of his mind. The lid to the toilet was another matter, one Mary would not want him to let slide.

En route to the front door, he glanced at the wall clock above the sofa. Five-fifteen. Leslie had split the appointed time evenly. Opening the door, he found her standing on the front stoop, a two-gallon thermos in her hand.

"You ready?" she asked.

"All set." He picked up two bottles of water sitting on the hall table. "I thought of water for the road."

"Mind if I use the john first?" she asked. "Southern hospital-

169

ity requires I get served iced tea everywhere I stop. My eyeballs are floating, and it's at least an hour drive to Sulphur."

Suppressing a grin, Chitto pointed with his chin toward the bathroom. Complete with closed toilet lid.

"Very nice," she said, taking in the living room. "Someone has good taste." She looked at a wall of paintings and prints. "*Very* good taste."

"My wife."

She examined the artwork, nodding approvingly. "Jerome Tiger, Fred Beaver, T. C. Cannon." She glanced at him. "Native Americans; all the works are by Native Americans."

"Right."

She turned her attention to the floor-to-ceiling bookshelves on either side of the fireplace. "This space is different. Not so . . . neat."

"The books are mine. *Mostly* mine."

She raised her eyebrows as she read some of the titles on dustcover spines. "Eclectic. Everything from crime novels to . . . *metaphysics*?" She looked at him.

He shrugged.

"I hear she died suddenly."

Chitto's mouth went dry. "Uh, yeah." He cleared his throat. "Cancer."

Damn. It was still hard to say.

She turned toward the hallway. "I'll just be a minute." She paused mid-step, holding up the water jug. "Oh, and I need to fill this. That Suburban runs hot sometimes. I try to keep this full, in case I'm caught out in the wilds."

"I'll take care of it." He took the water jug from her hand. "Meet you back here."

Busy running tap water into the water jug, Chitto did not hear Leslie walk into the kitchen.

"What's this?"

Seeing her looking at the map on the wall, Chitto shut off the water. "Nothing. Let's head out."

She stood rooted in place. "This is about those murders, isn't it?" She touched the Post-it flags marked *DW* and *CC*. "Those two guys who were found with their heads cut off?"

"How'd you know about them?" His concerns about the anthropologist's sudden appearance resurfaced.

She hesitated. "Think it was your mother that mentioned it . . ."

His mother? Why had she given him the third degree Sunday if she knew about the second victim?

"I remember now," Leslie said. "It was Rhody that I heard talking about it."

This surprised him even more. His grandmother was one of the most reserved people he knew. For her to speak about such things, especially with a stranger in the house, was peculiar behavior.

"Oh, I can't remember." Leslie waved a hand through the air. "I talk to lots of people and things like that spread like a match on a pile of tumbleweeds."

A good answer, but not one that satisfied him. "Just what is *your* interest in these killings?"

She shrugged. "Curiosity, I guess. I was at both celebrations. Matter of fact, I've been to several of these others." She indicated other flags on the map marking celebrations held in other nations.

Chitto relaxed. The woman had a right to be at the festivals. Her anthropological studies required it. And interviewing people about old stories and folktales put her in the perfect place to hear the latest gossip.

She pointed to the flags marking the murdered men's residences. "So, what are these two? Did I miss some festivals?

171

Celebrations?"

Time to shut this down.

"Look, this is police business. Confidential."

"*Oh*—didn't mean to butt in." She flushed slightly. "I'm so used to asking questions . . . well, I'm sorry. Don't worry, I don't talk out of school."

"That goes for my family, too. I'd just as soon my mother and grandmother didn't know about any of this."

"Okay, then," she said, her mouth a straight line.

Chitto followed her outside, thinking about his father's practice not to bring work home. He still believed getting the map out of the office was a good idea, but now he faced keeping the information confidential. There was only one way to make that happen. He couldn't allow *anyone* near the house.

Well, hell, he reflected. Maybe Hattie was right about me needing a watchdog.

CHAPTER EIGHTEEN

It was near dark when Chitto turned onto 177 toward Sulphur. The days were short and would get shorter yet as the planet inched toward the winter solstice. Hardwood and pine forests, mineral and freshwater springs were prevalent in this part of the state. Home to the Chickasaw National Recreation Area, dense thickets robbed the days of even more sunlight.

Traffic was light now that the tourist season was over. The recreation site drew thousands of visitors during the summer. Hunters and fishers. Hikers and Sunday drivers. Maneuvering the narrow two-lane, he was glad the road was quiet. He turned his lights to the bright setting so he could spot the eyes of deer, raccoon and opossum coming out to feed. Periodically, he glanced in his rearview mirror and was relieved not to see a wobbling headlight.

"I do that, too, you know," Leslie said.

He glanced toward the passenger seat where Leslie sat staring through the windshield. Up to now, she had sat silent on the drive from Durant. He figured she had taken his censure about the map in his kitchen personally. Did he come on too heavy-handed? The woman had gone out of her way to set up this meeting with Ward Schmidt.

"What's that?" he asked.

"Keep maps, mark where I've done interviews. Attended celebrations. Healings. That kind of thing."

"Oh." He was unable to come up with anything more to add.

"I got the idea from Ward. He was one of my teachers in college."

"That right?" He wondered if the man's maps would show the sites where cleansing ceremonies had been held. "Think he'll bring his maps with him tonight?"

"*Definitely* not. Academics can be touchy about things like that . . . too." She glanced his way.

The dig made Chitto grin.

She returned the smile. "If we're loose lipped, we won't get invited to rituals and ceremonies. Especially those that are somewhat secretive. Word travels pretty fast on the tribal telegraph."

Obviously, there was more than one tribal telegraph. So far, his remained mute as a stone.

"What determines when a ritual is secretive?"

"Good question." She shook her head, looking thoughtful. "Determined by whoever's in charge, I suppose. Weren't very many at the two cleansings I attended. If I had to describe them, they were more like gatherings of close friends and family."

That would explain why Chitto had not heard about them. Thinking about the family angle, his feeling about a connection between the cleansings and the beheadings grew stronger. He was disappointed he wouldn't get a glimpse of Schmidt's maps.

"What's Schmidt going to talk about tonight?" he asked.

"I told him you were interested in the history of the ceremonies. Where they originated and how they were used in the old nations before the Removal. I'm not sure how willing he'll be to talk about those he's attended locally, unless . . ."

Chitto waited for Leslie to finish thinking about what was on her mind. He had already pissed her off. If he pushed too hard, she could clamp down.

She turned to face him. "*Unless* you were willing to divulge more about your reason for knowing." She continued to stare at him. "This is about those murders, isn't it?"

In the dim light, her eyes were transparent discs, and easy to read. She thought he had tricked her. Maybe he had.

"Let's just say that I'm turning over every stone."

"*God*—freaks me out to think I might've bumped into the killers." She shivered involuntarily, then looked his way. "Okay, here's my advice. Ward loves his field of research, so show genuine interest—at least, *attempt* genuine interest. Otherwise, he'll think the law is looking to shut him down."

He heard the reproach in her words. It was turning into an evening for rebukes.

"There, that's it." She pointed to a building set back from the highway. "The café where Ward said he'd meet us."

Chitto recognized the shape of the building as an old Stuckey's roadside convenience store that specialized in homemade pecan candies. Once numbering in the hundreds, most of the candy shops had been closed down or sold and given a new identity. The building was painted a shade of camouflage green and dubbed *Al's Big-'n-Greasy Burgers*.

Since tourist season was over, the parking lot was almost empty. Ranch hands, he figured, looking at the dirt-crusted pickups and American-made SUVs. He saw guns through the rear window of most of them, hung within easy reach. Noting many were shotguns, he assumed the owners were bird hunters, then changed his mind. Dove was the only thing in season, but this wasn't the right kind of country for dove.

Except . . .

Most hunters after big game scoped out hunting sites in advance. Looking for deer trails. Watering holes. They brought shotguns to take care of less-than-friendly creatures they spooked up, which could range from snakes to wild pigs. He wondered how many of those in the café had field-dressing kits

175

with them, butchering tools like those used on Wilcox and Carter.

"That's Ward's truck." She pointed to one of the vehicles. "The one with the camper shell. Probably waiting for us at the bar."

He pulled into a parking place alongside a faded red Chevy pickup. Its owner was waiting inside. Long-neck bottle in hand, a couple of empties on the bar. The tall, lanky man with graying hair and light gray eyes inspected Chitto with open curiosity.

"Sam, this is Ward Schmidt, who will tell you more than you ever wanted to know about cleansing ceremonies." Leslie touched Schmidt's arm when she finished the introduction, smiling up at him.

Chitto followed Schmidt toward a large, semi-circular booth at the back of the main room, taking in the other occupants along the way. Cowboys fresh from the ranch. Dirt on their jeans, manure on their boots. A half-dozen white men dressed in camouflage pants and dark-colored tee shirts, looking over maps. A couple of white-haired couples at other tables, eating without conversation as couples who had been married a long time tended to do.

He slid into one side of a booth Schmidt selected. Leslie slid in across from him, followed close behind by Schmidt. The server brought ice water, then pulled a pencil and pad from her pocket. Schmidt ordered the dinner special and a dark beer. Leslie copied his order. The server turned to Chitto.

He looked at Schmidt. "How's the burger?"

"Big-'n-greasy," he said, grinning.

Smiling, Chitto ordered a BLT with potato chips on the side, sweetened iced tea.

"So, Lieutenant," Schmidt said. "What's your interest in cleansing ceremonies? Why them in particular, I mean?"

Chitto rubbed his mouth, considering which of two paths to

take—beat around the bush or shoot straight from the hip. Figuring Schmidt was privy to the same telegraph as Leslie, he would know of the murders, too. The trick was not to spook the man into silence.

He looked Schmidt in the eye. "Got a couple of cases that deal with a ritual of some kind. You heard about the recent killings on Choctaw and Chickasaw lands?"

Schmidt nodded. "And you think they're linked to the cleansing ceremonies around the state?"

Around the state? Chitto wondered how many such ceremonies had been held, and why he had no knowledge of them.

"Don't really know. Might know more once I hear what they're all about."

"In all honesty," Schmidt said, "I don't see a connection."

"May not be, but maybe you can educate me on why they're held. I heard about my People's traditions from my mother and grandmother. They learned it from people who came over from Mississippi to teach the People here what they'd forgotten—mostly old stories and myths." He paused to accept an iced tea from the server.

"Sadly, the Removal erased a lot of history," Leslie said.

Chitto nodded. "My family lost people on that march, mostly due to sickness or starvation. Once here, survival took precedence over everything else. I don't remember taking part in any kind of ceremony or ritual when I was growing up."

"Not even a stomp dance," Leslie said, a grin playing at the corners of her mouth.

"Never made sense to me," Chitto said. He turned his attention back to Schmidt. "Maybe if I knew the reason for these ceremonies, I could see if there might be some kind of link."

Schmidt was silent a minute. "I'm familiar with the journey your people were forced to take. You do have a right to know how it was back in your old country." He glanced at Leslie. "As she's probably told you, we're interested in the changes in customs and rituals since the Removal. But everything that's being done now originated hundreds of years ago . . ."

Chitto noticed an abstract look come into Schmidt's eyes. The college professor was about to begin his lecture. He settled back in the booth to hear the history of his People.

"You see, cleansing ceremonies originated as celebrations to welcome the return of a war party." Schmidt nursed his dark lager as he talked, turning the sweating bottle between his hands. "Once men proved their worth as warriors, they returned to their encampment and went through a cleansing ceremony to purge their bodies of dangerous supernatural forces." He glanced at Chitto. "Lots of Native Americans associate death with evil spirits. Maybe you've heard of the Navajo practice of never entering a hogan again after someone died in it. They believe the deceased's spirit remained behind as an evil force. Supernatural, you might say."

Chitto nodded. "Not unlike the old Choctaw belief that people possessed an inner shadow that they called *Shiliup*, which means ghost, and an outer spirit that they called *Shilombish*. After death, the *Shiliup* left on its journey, and the *Shilombish* stayed around the person's house until the funeral ceremonies were completed."

Schmidt smiled approvingly, as he would a student who answered a question correctly. "Yes, that's right, unless the deceased person was troubled in life . . . or murdered. In that case, the outer shadow remained until the problem was solved."

"That's the way I heard it, too." Chitto wondered if the two beheaded men's shadows were still around. Being white men, he decided against it. Marrying Indian women didn't mean they'd adopted the culture.

"So you can understand the need for these warriors to purify themselves after returning from the war path," Schmidt went on. "Cleansing included consuming a purgative, something they called a 'black drink,' which induced vomiting to rid their bodies of evil forces. Then they washed, cleansed and prepared themselves for reincorporation into the village society. This time away from others enabled the warriors, literally and metaphorically, to wash away the blood and power of their slain enemies—and curtail their own spiritual power."

Chitto found his interest growing. "So, these men that killed someone—the enemy—had to go through this ceremony to be accepted again by their own people." He hesitated. "Then what? Life went on as usual?"

"Not right away, at least not for some of the tribes, like the Choctaw. The rest of the ceremony involved the men retiring to a hut some distance from the village. Most times they stayed there four days." He paused. "Four is a number sacred to many Native Americans."

Chitto nodded, thinking of the name he had given the killings. He calculated the number of days the killers would need if they kidnapped the victim after the festival, then held him captive for several days. If they waited to kill him until the fourth day, then put another four days or more into a cleansing celebration, a week could go by. Maybe ten days. Anyone gone for that long would be noticed.

When the food arrived, Schmidt handed his empty bottle to the server and ordered another. He glanced at Leslie. She held up a bottle barely touched.

Chitto picked up his sandwich and talked between bites. "Why would they need to curtail their own spirits?"

"Good question." Again, Schmidt gave an approving nod. "You see, blood by itself didn't appear to have a polluting effect among most of these tribes. But blood connected with creative power, such as the reproductive ability of women and the combat skills of men, formed a potent symbol of spiritual power at work. This power had to be restrained and controlled to prevent possible violence or other mishaps."

"So they wouldn't become bloodthirsty," Leslie said. "Maybe harm their own people."

They ate a while in silence, Chitto seeking a link between the information Schmidt provided and the fourth-day murders— and thinking about the two vehicles that were tailing him.

"See anything to connect to your killings?" Schmidt said, as if reading his mind.

"Not a thing." Chitto sighed. "So that was it? After the purging and cleansing, the solitary confinement, the men returned to their regular lives?" He glanced at the clock on the wall, analyzing the evening. Two and a half hours spent driving to a backcountry café, eating greasy food, and listening to interesting but less-than-helpful information.

"More or less," Schmidt said. "Once they put themselves right."

"What?" Leslie turned to Schmidt. "Aren't you overlooking something? Or, rather, someone? What about the women's role? You didn't describe the dancing either. Or talk about how the ritual might've changed."

Chitto noticed Leslie glance his way. She was asking the questions he didn't know to ask.

"Yeah, I'd like to hear about all that," he said. "And if they ever captured an enemy, brought him back and tortured him."

Accepting a new bottle from the server, Schmidt turned it between in his hands and began the next part of his lecture.

"Warriors did bring back enemies to display, and probably killed them at some point. Most times, captives were tortured brutally, then cut into pieces—except for the hairy parts. These parts were treated as scalps, strung on long poles and carried around by women during the dance. Part of cleansing festivities included warriors displaying trophies of war, especially enemy scalps. And, sometimes, other body parts such as ears or entire heads."

He paused, looking at Chitto. "I believe the two men killed recently were beheaded and their heads left with the bodies. That doesn't fit with the way these rituals worked."

"No, it doesn't," Chitto agreed. "But it's not hard to believe some kind of ritual was being enacted."

"Keep in mind," Schmidt said, "that all I'm relaying to you is the way it was done *prior* to European contact. Cleansing ceremonies these days are less animated. Less frenzied." He grinned at Leslie. "And back then, there *was* a good deal of participation by the women. As a matter of fact, they directed the activities."

Women ran the show . . .

"Like dancing," Leslie said, looking at Schmidt again.

"Yes, displaying the scalps while they danced. Which is why these celebrations were sometimes called scalp dances."

Chitto's mouth suddenly felt dry. "What'd they do with the scalps?"

"Practices differed." Schmidt waved a hand through the air. "After the women danced around displaying them, they might burn them . . . throw them on the top of the hot house to disintegrate." He glanced at Chitto again. "Hot house was another name for the winter house, which had no chimney. The smoke had to find its own way out. These dwellings heated up considerably, as you can imagine."

Chitto noticed Schmidt's face take on a slight glow and attributed it to alcohol. Another way to cook someone's scalp.

"What about changes made to the ritual today?" Leslie prompted.

"Thank you, my dear, for keeping me on track." Schmidt nodded benignly at Leslie and turned to Chitto again.

181

"Today, of course, the rituals are abbreviated from the olden days. Purging and washing take place, but, as you can imagine, today's men—and women, for that matter—are too busy to devote a week to such things." He shrugged. "I see no connection between the murders and the cleansing rituals being held." He paused. Smiled. Said, "Do you, Lieutenant Chitto?"

"Can't say I do."

Chitto wondered if he should ask the question he most wanted answered. Did any of the men attending the cleansing display a small hair lock? But to ask the question would raise more questions—especially from someone like Schmidt—and the scalp lock taken from the murdered men was the one piece of evidence he couldn't divulge.

"And that about covers it."

As Schmidt's yellow-tinged eyes locked on him, Chitto wondered if the man was telling all he knew. If he was deliberately leaving out things. Then he began to wonder if the man was as under the influence as he appeared. If the flush on his cheeks wasn't so much from alcohol as a sign he was enjoying the chase. Wild dogs ripped the genitals off their prey, knowing the pain would slow them down. Chitto never enjoyed head games. He preferred the direct approach.

"Can you identify the men who had to be cleansed?" Chitto asked. "What they did to warrant the ritual?"

"Ah—now we get to the real reason for this meeting." Schmidt made a wry smile. "Sorry, I'm not privy to that level of information. I just record the events, much as Leslie records songs that cannot be interpreted by anyone . . . but God."

From feral dog to priest in the confessional.

"Now, if you had a warrant, I'd have to turn my records over to you. Of course, it's my understanding that it's the FBI that has official jurisdiction in such cases." Schmidt's words trailed off, morphing into quiet laughter. "Anyone want another round before we call it a night?" He looked around for the server.

"Not for me," Leslie said. "I've got an early day tomorrow." She glanced at Chitto. "How about you?"

Chitto was ready to leave, too. "One more question," he said as he slid from the booth. "Leslie mentioned that you keep maps showing where you do your work. I'd be interested in where these cleansings were held. And if you're not comfortable pinpointing the sites, which nation they were held in might be helpful." If he could narrow down where the killers lived, maybe his contacts in the other nations could find out their identity.

Leslie looked at Schmidt. "I don't see anything wrong with that, do you? I mean, these different tribal holdings are really large. The sites would be hard to pinpoint."

Schmidt's smile bordered on a sneer. "You forget what wonderful tracking skills the Choctaw have, which make them excel at hunting." He looked at Chitto. "I'm afraid divulging that information would jeopardize my being invited to other such celebrations. And trust me, word *would* get around." Stretching the long muscles in his back, he said, "Now I have a long drive ahead of me."

The professor had ended his lecture.

As they left the building, Chitto turned to Schmidt. "Thanks for taking the time to talk to me," Chitto said, looking around the emptied parking lot. "I found the information . . . genuinely interesting."

"*Really.* Well now, I enjoyed talking with you, too. It's been a long time since I've had the chance to talk shop." Schmidt turned to Leslie. "And you, my dear. If you need a place to roll out your bedroll tonight, my camper shell accommodates two—as you know."

A flush appeared on Leslie's face. "And my Suburban accommodates one, as *you* know. Drive safe, Ward."

Chitto followed Leslie to his truck, thinking about the coolness she showed Schmidt at parting. Then he began to wonder if she was actually considering sleeping in her Suburban. If so, he should probably offer to put her up in the spare bedroom for the night. It would be too late for her to drive back to his mother's place.

Chitto felt as though a knife were turning in his belly. What would Mary want him to do? Would she want him to bring a woman into their home? Even if she was just a houseguest?

He waited for the darkness that accompanied thoughts about Mary, for her *Shilombish* to appear.

Nothing.

CHAPTER NINETEEN

A full Corn Moon dominated the sky on the drive back to Durant, what some called a Harvest Moon. A time when night and day were equally long. It was the kind of moon that defied description. Right then, it caused him to think about his own insignificance. To think about his grandmother and her talk of stardust. Her rationalization that her story quilt and the Choctaw people would survive the Earth's destruction and become one with the stars, similar in all ways to the previous. History and customs intact, unchanged for eternity. *Ad infinitum.* Without reason, his mind went to Jonathan Swift's poem that mocked self-similarity.

> *"So nat'ralists observe, a flea*
> *Hath smaller fleas that on him prey,*
> *And these have smaller fleas that bite 'em,*
> *And so proceed ad infinitum."*

Chitto considered the concept of microcosm and macrocosm. Smaller versions of something larger. Complex systems seen as single units. That line of thinking progressed to the two murdered men, the similarities in the men while living and their identically constructed deaths. The feeling continued to nag at him that they were not the last, maybe not even the first, that they were part of something bigger. If he kept digging, would he find the original flea, the one at the bottom of the whole thing? Or enough of the pieces to figure out the whole?

"Ward and I were a thing once," Leslie said, breaking the silence. "You know, the proverbial older professor and younger student."

"Oh." Chitto put her comment into the context of the evening. He wondered if she thought his silence was because of Schmidt's parting comment about sharing a sleeping bag. He could think of no further response and, in the ensuing silence, decided she did not expect one.

"Just because Ward and I had a thing once doesn't mean I make a habit of it." She looked at him. "So don't get the wrong idea about me. You know, men and women can be friends. Nothing more, *just* friends."

Chitto nodded, uncomfortable with the disclosure of more personal information. Either his or hers. In spite of that, he attempted to understand the meaning beneath the words. Was she telling him she had no designs on Schmidt? Or was she trying to clarify the relationship, if you could call it that, which was developing between the two of them?

"Ward is a brilliant man," she said, staring through the windshield. "On his way to great things before his marriage disintegrated . . ."

Listening to her words drop off, Chitto waited.

"I'm the cause—at least, I *thought* I was the cause of it." She glanced his direction. "I was one of those brainy girls, you know the type. Bookworm. Not that attractive. Taller than most of the boys in my class. Easily flattered with a man's attention." She sighed. "And slow to mature. It was years later that I realized his marriage had already gone sour before I entered the picture." Another glance his way. "He's hoping this new work will get him recognized again. It's publish or perish in our business. I'm hoping to get published, too."

Chitto found his voice, feeling the need to add something to the conversation. "Yeah, that's the way it worked in geology if you went the academic route. I was more interested in fieldwork. Geologic surveys, that kind of thing."

Her eyes were luminous discs again. "So, how did you end up a lawman—" She threw up her hands. "Nope, not my business."

She evidently recalled his putdown about the map on his kitchen wall. He felt foolish now for having made an issue of it. Clearly, Leslie—many people—had as much knowledge of the murders as he did.

"Hopefully you understand why we're so secretive about things, unwilling to share records." She sighed again. "Ward was trying to be helpful."

"Yeah? Well, I got the feeling he didn't care for me too much."

Her smile was visible in the moonlight. "I think he was a little jealous and showing off a bit. You know, playing the role of brilliant professor, acting like an alpha male establishing his territory—trying to *reestablish* his territory."

Abruptly, Chitto noticed a darkness settle over the night. He wondered if Mary was listening to this nonsense talk about a man being jealous of him and another woman. Looking toward the moon, he was relieved to see a passing cloud shrouded it. A minute later, the darkness faded and the night again assumed its shimmering quality.

"Was it helpful?" she asked. "The information that Ward gave you?"

"It was."

"But you didn't get all your questions answered."

"No." He glanced her direction. "But I got a lot more than I would've if you hadn't been there. Still would like to see his maps."

"I know."

He hesitated. "You said you keep maps, too. I'm assuming you marked the cleansing celebrations you attended."

"You asking to look at my maps?" She gave her head a shake. "Same story as Ward gave you. If we share our work, then we don't get invited to the dance, figuratively speaking. And besides, that wouldn't be ethical."

Chitto blew out his breath. "Yeah, I guess not."

"You *do* understand, don't you? I mean, your mother and grandmother have been so kind to me, I really would like to help. But, I can't do that to Ward."

So that was the reason she set up the meeting. Because of his family, their hospitality towards her.

"It's okay," he said. "I would feel the same way."

"What do you mean *would* feel the same way? You're as protective of your map and records as Ward. No, *worse*. You carry a gun."

Chitto laughed at that. The woman had a way of putting him in his place, but not unkindly. He liked that.

A few miles further on, Chitto thought of other questions he would like answered, ones not taboo.

"I took some basic anthropology courses in school, so I can understand the concept of beheading your enemy. But I don't remember reading about the significance of nudity in rituals."

"Oh, right," she murmured. "The men were not only beheaded, but left nude. Yes, that is interesting."

He could not see Leslie's eyes right then, but envisioned them blinking a lot.

"The first thing that comes to mind is Greco-Roman athletic games. Athletes performed in the nude during competitions in the Coliseum, and since the dead men were found on pow-wow grounds, that could be compared to such events." She paused. "Athletes sometimes battled to the death. You think that could be it?"

He considered the idea for a couple of miles, then shook his head. "I don't think these men were considered combatants."

"Then what?"

Chitto wanted to share everything as he used to do with Mary. To bat ideas around to see which were worth keeping, which not worth holding on to. But though he liked Leslie and felt comfortable talking with her, it wasn't the same.

"Not enough yet to actually determine that," he said. "Call it a gut feeling."

"Okay," she considered. "If not physical, maybe there's a psychological reason for the way they were left."

He frowned. "Psychological?"

"Right. Beheading could mean a simple death wasn't enough. The killers may have wanted to render the victim powerless. You know, separate mind from body, not have the victim able to respond. Talk back, so to speak."

He grunted. "Duct tape would've worked just as effectively."

"But duct tape wouldn't be as demeaning as stripping a person naked and doing things to his body over which he has no control." She glanced his way again. "I understand the men were tied down. Staked out, so to speak."

Chitto sighed, thinking about the efficacy of the tribal telegraph that Leslie was tuned to.

"Or, maybe, it was tit for tat," she suggested. "You know, getting even."

He found that idea worth pursuing. "You mean, like a surrogate? A substitute?"

Were the men left naked and made helpless because they did something similar to someone else? His thoughts went to the girl Nanny Love, impregnated before she got out of middle school. And the Harjo girls, rewarded for their silence with expensive toys and games.

"I was thinking more like object lessons," she said.

"You mean, made an example for others." He found that idea

interesting, too.

"Sort of. You know, similar to the Grimm fairytales."

"Fairytales?" He shook his head. "That doesn't track for me."

"Most people think of fairytales as sweet little bedtime stories, but they were meant to teach a lesson." She glanced at him. "Or scare people into behaving a certain way. Think about the old witch in the woods who baked children into cookies when they strayed too far from home. And the evil queen who fed Snow White a poisoned apple when she became a threat."

"Or the Little People in Choctaw legend," he said, "who lured boys into a cave in the woods where three witches lived."

"Exactly—oh, that's a perfect example. The witches offered the boys different gifts and if they chose the wrong ones, like the knife and bad herbs, they were destined to live an evil life. But if they chose the right one—the healing herbs—the boys became healers of their people." She smiled at him. "Bet you heard that one from your mother, didn't you?"

"Grandmother. Over and over."

Chitto drove quietly, thinking of the lesson the two murders might be intended to teach.

"I'm probably over-thinking things; maybe it's not that complicated." She glanced his way. "At first blush, it sounds like intertribal problems. You know . . ."

"Counting coup," he said. "One tribe seeking revenge against another. In this case, literally."

"I wouldn't have put it quite that bluntly. But then, that could be what the killers wanted people to think. You know, to throw the authorities off track. A man from one nation killed on sacred grounds of another—" She looked at him. "*Aha.* Now I understand why you're doing this *unofficial* investigation. You think that's the first thing the FBI would think, too."

Chitto tried unsuccessfully to restrain a grin. Leslie was batting ideas around on her own, without him divulging anything of importance, and coming up with a lot of right answers.

They drove in silence for another several miles, the highway ahead void of other travelers. Chitto eyed the shoulders of the road for reflections that indicated eyes of deer, coyote, bear. Checking his rearview mirror, he saw headlights, but none close. He ran Leslie's concepts through his mental filter, discarding most of them. But not all.

"What if . . ." She paused, glancing at him. "These killings smack of revenge. Revenge is motivated by a sense of powerlessness. Seeking a solution to a problem, a way to achieve a goal when there's no other solution."

Just what I've been thinking.

"But revenge for what?" She leaned back in the seat, sighing deeply. "This thing is enough to drive a person to drink. I'd say you've got a lot to puzzle through."

Though he said nothing, Chitto agreed with her. The map on his kitchen wall was proof of that.

A bright light in his rearview mirror pulled his attention away from the conversation. He stiffened, watching a sedan with a brown front fender pull around him. The sedan no sooner pulled in front of him than another set of lights appeared in his mirror. A larger vehicle, with a headlight that bobbed like a ping-pong ball.

"Well, hell," he said, half aloud.

"What?" Leslie turned to look at the truck as it pulled alongside them.

"They're boxing us in," Chitto said. "Hang on."

He stepped on the brake, letting both vehicles speed ahead of him. The vehicles immediately slowed, keeping him trapped.

"What are they doing? Who are they?"

"Duck hunters," Chitto mouthed. "Get their plate numbers."

She hesitated. "I don't see any plates."

Chitto figured both drivers had stripped the vehicles of such specific identification, and then laid in wait for him. His thoughts went to Wilcox and Carter.

"Look for a side road where I can pull off. I need about twenty square feet to set this baby down and as much lead time as you can give me. After I come to a stop, I want you out of this truck, as far from it as you can get."

"But—"

"No buts."

She leaned forward, peering into the castoff light from the front vehicle. A minute later, she yelled, "Brake—*now.*"

As Chitto jammed his foot on the brake, the cars ahead corresponded, keeping him boxed in. He cranked the wheel sharply and slid onto a side road. Pulling his service revolver, he fired through his open door. He stopped firing when the gun was empty, watching taillights disappear from sight.

Quickly, he opened the glove compartment where he stashed spare ammo. Eying the pack of cigarettes inside, identical to the one in his Tahoe, he removed the clip and slammed the door shut. Leslie appeared as he reloaded, carrying a branch the size and shape of a baseball bat. He took in the dirt on the knees of her slacks, grass stains on her shirt, eyes round as pie plates.

"Sorry about that. You okay?"

"Yeah," she mumbled, rubbing a hand across her chest. "I'm, uh, I'm okay."

"Good, that's good." Adrenaline pumping through Chitto's temples pounded in his ears. He could feel the sweat between his shoulder blades, smell his armpits.

"You get those sonsabitches?" she said, staring down the highway.

Chitto grinned. "Doubt it. Saw sparks come off metal, but

can't say I did any serious damage. Neither dropped their speed any."

She laughed nervously. "Well, I don't know what you did to them, but you about gave me a coronary."

He smiled again. No two ways about it, Dr. Leslie Anderson was no longer a suspect.

"Man, I could use a drink," she said, still rubbing her chest. "A double shot of scotch. How 'bout you? Oh—Indians don't drink."

"Not all of us," he said. "Nicotine's my poison of choice." Right then, he could've finished off the pack in his glove box.

She faced him, frowning. "Aren't you going to call someone? The FBI should be alerted. I mean, you're an officer of the law—it's their job to protect you."

Chitto thought about the number programmed into his cell. Blackfox had cautioned him the day might come when he would need to call Rodriquez.

But this wasn't that day.

"They're the last people I'd call, especially since—" He felt his way carefully. "Especially since I don't want them to know I'm working their case. No one's to know what happened here tonight. Understand?" Leaning across the seat, he opened the door for her.

"Well, then," she said, holding onto her club as she climbed into the truck. "If I were you, I'd get a bigger gun."

It was nearly midnight when Chitto pulled down the narrow little street where his house was located. The rest of the trip had been uneventful. The pickup with the loose headlight and the Toyota sedan did not make another appearance. He doubted he'd hit either one. He had fired too quickly to be accurate, and they had sped up when the first shots were fired.

He owed Leslie more of an explanation, but he couldn't give

her one. "Sorry you had to get involved," was all he could come up with.

"Yeah, no problem. Only thing is, those people could be the killers. You think about that?"

"Scare tactics," he said, shrugging. "They wanted me dead, they've had other opportunities."

"Oh?" she said. Then, *"Oh."*

Spotting Leslie's gray Suburban in front of his house, Chitto faced another problem.

"Look, I appreciate you setting up this meeting with Schmidt." He listened to the pickup's engine stutter to a stop. "If you need a place to stay tonight, we've got a spare bedroom."

She laughed quietly. "Thanks, but there's a KOA just down the highway. I've put up there before. Showers. Hot water. Even a continental breakfast in the mornings." She made a snorting sound. *"Woo hoo*—instant coffee and donuts."

"I'm not worried about the map in the kitchen any more, if that's what you're thinking. Hell, you know as much about those killings as I do."

She shook her head. "Thanks, but . . ."

Chitto lifted his hands, let them drop. "Look, that's about as close to an apology as you're gonna get."

She rubbed an earlobe. "Sam, it's not because of the map in the kitchen—or the incident on the road. It's because the lady of the house's *Shilombish* hasn't left yet. Her husband won't let it go."

"What?"

"Didn't you hear what you just said? '*We've* got a spare bedroom.' " She looked toward the house. "You're keeping your wife locked up in that ivory tower, just like in a fairytale. I feel sorry for her." She lifted her palms to sign her frustration. "I mean, look at the artwork she chose to fill her life with. So beautiful and . . . and uninhibited." She shook her head as she climbed out of the truck.

Chitto followed her, feeling stunned. "What are you saying?"

"I shouldn't have said anything at all. I do that, look at things with an anthropological magnifying glass." She attempted a smile. "Surely you can understand. You do the same as a law-man."

"Anthropological magnifying glass, my ass. You're saying you believe in ghosts!"

"Oh, that." She glanced away, then back at him. "My work's taught me about things you don't find in books. You're a scientist, you tell me. Can energy or matter be destroyed? Changed, maybe. If transformed, then why not trapped?"

Chitto stood like a stone watching the Suburban's taillights fade, then felt a darkness descend over him. He looked toward the moon to see if clouds were covering it again, but the night sky was cloudless.

He wondered if Leslie was right, if he was keeping Mary trapped against her will. He thought back to the first time he saw Mary. A small, dark, alluring bird. A *wild* bird.

The mid-September moon was about to set, making for a dark night that permitted a star-studded view. Stars winked like beacons. Some bright, some faint. Chitto knew the scientific reason for the difference in size and brilliance, but he imagined them now as souls. Some whole, some incomplete. A small star in the circlet near Jupiter, part of the constellation Pisces, caught his attention.

Wild creatures aren't meant to be caged, said the voice within.

Letting out his breath, Chitto whispered, "You're free." He watched the circlet of light closely, attempting to measure any change in its intensity. The sound of a screen door opening pulled him back to Earth.

"Boycott—git back here. That you, Sam?"

Backlit with the house lights, Chitto could see Hattie craning her neck into the dim light, cotton housecoat clutched at her throat, and a dark shadow moving toward him. Running low to the ground.

"Yeah, Hattie. Sorry to wake you."

"Didn't wake me. Woke Boycott. It's okay; we both needed to relieve ourselves."

Chitto rubbed the back of his neck. "You seen any strange vehicles in the neighborhood lately? Maybe a beat-up pickup with a bad headlight. Old Toyota with a fender painted a different color?"

Hattie laughed. "Hell, Sam. That describes half the vehicles on the block." She paused to look down the street. "Dog woke me up earlier though, seemed upset 'bout something. Growling like a bear." She looked at him. "You think somebody was prowlin' round?"

"Probably nothing," Chitto said, knowing where his tagalongs had been that evening.

About then, the wet-nosed hound named Boycott rammed him in the crotch, causing him to stagger. "I been eviscerated enough for one night," he said, pushing the dog away. "Finish your business and get on home."

"You really need to take that dog off my hands, Sam."

"No, you keep him," he said. "Least for now."

Chitto watched Boycott's shadow shorten until he merged with it at the front porch, then disappear altogether as the light went out. When all was quiet, he found the circlet of stars again and tried once more to calibrate its gradations. To measure some kind of change, however slight. A sign that his letting-go had taken, releasing Mary from her bondage.

It was a loss. Light was fleeting under any circumstance, ephemeral when traversing the galaxy. His sense of true gone, Chitto turned from the night sky and walked into the house.

Standing in its darkness, he realized it was empty. He was now its sole occupant.

Or was he?

Chitto had left the AC running when they left, but now, he caught the feel of warm air drifting in from the kitchen. Removing his gun from its holster, he walked to the back of the house and flipped on the light. The back door was open.

Boycott's barking probably spooked the guy, he thought. Didn't have time to close the door tight.

Checking the kitchen, he found everything was as he left it. Almost. Another sticky note had been added to the map, stuck near the town of Durant. The initials *S* and *C* printed on it.

Holstering his gun, he examined the lock on the back door. It hadn't been jimmied.

"Well, hell . . ." he sighed.

His night visitor had a key.

CHAPTER TWENTY

Chitto wedged kitchen chairs under the front and back doorknobs on Sunday night, and slept with his service revolver on the nightstand. In dreams, he saw himself on a crowded ceremonial ground following an elusive figure that faded like smoke, only to reappear down another path.

He woke early and waited for the east to burn away the shadows. His first awake feeling was one of frustration. An inability to sort through a jumble of information. But something more concrete pushed those thoughts aside.

Keys.

He placed a call to his mother, but she did not know who Mary might have given keys to.

"You lose yours?" she asked. "Can have one made off mine, you want."

He declined because he planned to have the locks changed out. Leaving early, he dropped by Hattie's house to drop off his key so she could let the locksmith inside.

"Don't need yours," she said. "Mary gave me one long time ago."

"See if you still have it, Hattie."

She returned a few minutes later, carrying a key tied to a shoelace.

Chitto grabbed a breakfast sandwich at a drive through and arrived early at the office, hoping the coffee was on. Deprived of companions, the building was quiet, dark in places where light switches hadn't been thrown. Shorter days were eating away daylight hours. The Indian year was almost over. He was running out of time to solve the fourth-day murders.

Hurrying toward his desk, he stopped a few feet away, watching Wanda examine the replacement map he'd put on his wall. Her physical appearance surprised him as much as her presence in his work area. She looked as dried up as a gourd.

"Need something, Wanda?"

She spun around, facing him. "No. It's just . . . this is a different map than the one you had me enlarge. Why'd you do that?"

Chitto was not in the mood for one of her grillings. "This one works better." He set the sack containing his breakfast on his desk. "Coffee on?"

"Do that first thing; you know that." She paused. "Want me to get you a cup?"

"Appreciate it." She didn't move. "Something else?" he asked.

"Well, I was just looking at these stickers on the map. Deal with cases you're working on, don't they? I figure this one marked *TW* is for Teresa Walker, that girl that got raped." She pointed to the one marked *SBM*. "Who's this one for?"

Chitto felt his neck turning warm. Old friend of the family or not, Wanda was overstepping her bounds.

"Nothing to concern yourself with. You gonna get that coffee?"

Wanda's mouth pinched into a tight circle. "Well, it's 'bout time you decided to stick to business. If you'd done it earlier, you'd know that girl doesn't live there anymore."

"What—?"

"That's what Rona called 'bout last Friday, the phone call you palmed off on me—not to mention all those others. She did a follow-up visit and learned the girl moved out." She reached for the flag stuck on the map on the wall. "So, you can take this one down."

"*No*, leave it. I'm not ready to take it down."

Wanda shot him a look. "This have anything to do with Rodriquez coming by Friday afternoon to see Dan?"

"Rodriquez?"

Chitto's first sensation was one of relief. He was glad he'd changed out the maps. One look and Rodriquez would've figured out he was investigating the murder at the old Choctaw ceremonial grounds. The following sensation was of growing frustration with Wanda's prying, her assuming she could take over things he was working on.

"Doesn't have anything to do with the FBI—or you," he said, rubbing the back of his neck. "Look—here on out, please just leave things in my office alone."

Color drained from Wanda's face. "Get your own damn coffee," she snapped, stomping from his office.

Chitto watched her disappear, his mouth open. She had always been feisty—didn't believe in pussyfooting around—but this reaction was extreme even for her.

Had he come on too strong, too direct, he wondered? She'd always been in on internal workings in the department, too— was expected to keep tabs on the officers. And now, he was keeping her out of the loop, keeping something from her—and she knew it. He debated whether to follow her, to give her more of an explanation.

Not gonna happen, he thought, sighing. In this case, that wasn't an option.

But that explanation didn't satisfy Chitto. Recalling Blackfox's talk about finding a replacement for Wanda, he wondered if it *was* time for her to retire. Especially given the physical changes he'd noticed lately.

Was she having health problems? he wondered, considering

the thinness, loss of muscle mass. The vinegary temperament.

It's age, he decided. He had observed the same kinds of changes in his grandmother. His mother. They'd been testy lately, too. And neither of them were spring chickens anymore.

Regardless of the reason, there was nothing he could do about it. He couldn't let Wanda—any of them—in on his activities. She would just have to get over it.

Picking up his coffee mug, Chitto headed for the break room. On the way, he glanced toward Wanda's desk, noted the shoulders stiff as rods and sighed again.

I'll find a way to make it up to her . . .

On his way back to his desk, Chitto knocked on Blackfox's door. The director looked up from his paperwork.

"Hear Raymond paid us another call," Chitto said. "He following up on the Wilcox case?"

"Delbert Wilcox *and* Charlie Carter. Curious about what we've learned." Blackfox looked over his glasses at Chitto. "Which is diddly squat unless you're here to tell me otherwise."

"Diddly squat about covers it. One of the other offices clue him in?"

"No. After Rodriquez left, I called to check. He showed up on their doorsteps unannounced, same as ours."

Chitto took a swallow of coffee. "You thinking what I'm thinking?"

Blackfox raised an eyebrow. "I'm thinking Rodriquez has friends on the inside."

Chitto nodded.

"You ready to give it up yet?" Blackfox asked. "Something tells me you're close to falling off a cliff."

"No, sir, not yet. Like to stick it out through the end of September, when the four-day celebrations end. My gut tells me I need to do that, give it a little more time."

"Well, a man needs to listen to his gut." Blackfox began shuffling through papers on his desk. "Don't let things slide here," he said as Chitto departed.

"I'm on top of things."

Oh, you bet, the voice in his head whispered.

Back to his desk, Chitto went through his phone messages, which were few in number thanks to Wanda's diligence. He made a couple of quick calls, scheduled a meeting with the District 9 officer, then turned on his computer. The first message to pop up was from Tom Murray of the Potawatami Nation.

Call me Monday afternoon. In court all morning.

Chitto spent the morning following up on cases, but his mind strayed to Teresa Walker. He couldn't stop wondering why the girl moved out of her aunt's house. At a quarter to twelve, he closed up his desk. Lunch would be spent paying a visit to Betty Tomlinson.

He drove east on highway 70 toward Hugo, opting not to call in advance. The aunt would probably come up with a reason she couldn't see him. No one liked to talk to the police, not even a tribal officer. If she wasn't at home, he knew where she worked. The local casino—a Choctaw casino. He would have no problem tracking her down.

As he drove, Chitto punched in Tom Murray's number. Finding the Potawatami inspector at his desk, he put his cell phone on speaker.

"Hey, Wheezer, got your message." Chitto used the nickname Murray's jagged-sounding voice bequeathed him. Murray had suffered a damaged larynx several years before in a confrontation with a drunk, causing him to gasp his words. Too stubborn to accept disability, he insisted on working until they nailed his coffin shut.

"That you, Sam? Yeah, thought you'd like to know 'bout somethin' happened after Red Earth. Four days after to be exact."

"Red Earth?" Chitto sat up straighter, thinking about the list of celebrations he put together. "Oklahoma City Convention Center—July?"

"Jogger found this dude on the dance ground. Head cut off."

"How come I didn't hear about that?"

"Jogger called locals; they called Feds. Newspapers played it up as gang related."

"Big, hairy, white guy married to Indian woman, children from a first marriage? Little girls?"

"No," Murray wheezed. "Big, hairy, *black* dude. Ex-military. After discharge married this Potawatami girl. Not even out of school yet."

Doesn't fit the pattern *exactly*, Chitto thought, but close enough. Especially if he was killed on another nation's ground.

"Wait a minute—Red Earth's in the middle of Oklahoma City."

"That's right. Convention Arena. Not far from us, though."

Still might fit the pattern, Chitto thought, then caught a glitch in his thinking. The man was another race, but maybe color of skin wasn't a factor. Then he wondered if Wilcox and Carter were ex-military, if that was the connection between the murdered men. Tubbe and Sunday would have that information or could get it quick enough.

"Sad case," Murray said.

"How's that?"

"Girl got pregnant right off the bat. The dude shot up heroin, beat the crap out of her. Locked her in a bathroom. She lost the baby, 'bout died from infection. Never have any more kids." A long, wheezing pause followed. "Don't seem right, does it? Got to pay all her life 'cause her old man shot up."

203

"Not right by a long shot."

Chitto wondered how long the girl was locked in the bathroom before she was found. If she felt pain when her body aborted the baby. How she might have felt having to look at the undeveloped infant. How she must have felt when she learned it was her last.

"She doing all right now?" he asked. "Maybe getting counseling?"

"What I understand, she went to a healer man. One of ours. You know, *unofficial* counseling."

"This healer's a Potawatami citizen then."

"No, but an Indian. Not sure what nation. Up north, I think. Goes round doin' these healing ceremonies for girls and women. Gets them talking 'bout what happened so they can get it off their chest."

Leslie popped into Chitto's head. She talked about attending healing ceremonies around the state. He wondered if the healer Murray mentioned was involved in the rituals.

"Say, Wheezer, you heard of an anthropologist working up your way name of Leslie Anderson? Doing interviews with old people, capturing their stories."

"Yeah. Working with the Cherokees."

"She's down here now."

"Talked to some of our old folks, too. Nice gal. Highly thought of."

"That's the one." Chitto was glad to get a good report on Leslie. "What about a guy named Wade Schmidt? Older man doing anthropological studies."

A wheezing pause. "Don't ring a bell."

"Okay." Chitto hesitated. "One more question. Anything *unusual* about the body?"

Murray laughed so hard, he took a coughing spasm. When

recovered, he said, "Like a naked dude with no head's not unusual?"

"You got a point . . . but, I was thinking of something else." He listened to static for almost a minute.

"Had a chance to gas with the medical examiner that did the autopsy," Murray said, hesitating. "Was *one* little thing."

Chitto swallowed. "How little?"

"Oh, 'bout the size of my thumbnail. How'd you know 'bout that?"

Chitto explained the link to the other two murders. "What'd the FBI do with that case? You know if any follow-up was done?"

Murray answered with another wheezing laugh.

Cold case file . . .

"Thanks, Wheezer. Needless to say, the missing scalp isn't for public consumption. Appreciate it you'd send me the name of that girl and the victim, the date he was found."

"Can do."

"And the name of that healer man, too."

"I'll check around." A pause. "Say, Sam, you get the feeling someone might be doing us a favor?"

Chitto hesitated. "You mean, like an act of kindness? What makes you think that?"

"Not sure. Maybe 'cause I got two little girls at home. Something happened to me, I'd like to think someone would step up to the plate."

"Hang tight, brother," Chitto murmured.

After disconnecting, he thought about the way this murder broke the pattern. A first marriage for the young widow. No young daughters involved. Just a dead baby and no more in her future. It was enough to make you say to hell with the human race.

He sighed, feeling as if he were still chasing dream shadows. Then his thoughts went again to the healer the girl went to. He

205

wondered if he was at the healing ceremonies that Leslie attended.

Only one way to find out.

A blue Chevy sedan was parked in front of the singlewide trailer on U.S. 70. Chitto parked behind it and walked to the front stoop. Betty Tomlinson answered his knock, a small woman with jaundiced skin and dark circles under the eyes. She wore the garb of a cleaning woman and a look that said she was tired to the bone.

Chitto shook his head slightly, wondering what her story was and knowing it by heart. Didn't finish school. Married young. Husband left her. Married again. A damaged record returning to the same old scratch.

He looked around the room as he sat down. The furniture had been righted; there was no peanut-butter-and-jelly sandwich lying uneaten on the kitchen counter. And the dog was missing.

"Where's Domino?" He looked toward the back door.

"She took him with her."

"Good dog." Chitto waited to see if she would say where Teresa had taken the dog. A minute passed before he decided he was going to have to do the talking.

"I'm following up to see how your niece is doing. We do that, make follow-up calls."

Not entirely true. He'd turned the case over to the U.S. attorney's office and, so, done his duty. His official duty. He cleared his throat, a cue it was her turn to talk.

"Told the county lady last week Terry was gone."

Terry. Teresa-with-no-H had a nickname.

"That would be Mrs. Guthrie. She wanted to get Teresa into some counseling. You know, someone to help her through this bad time."

"She is gonna be okay."

"Teresa's a tough girl, all right. Where'd she go? Back home?"

She frowned. "*This* is home. She is just staying with a friend right now. You know, for a little while."

"Letty Munro," he said, more a statement than a question. She did not deny or confirm his conclusion, but the look she gave him said he had guessed right. "Be good if Teresa got some help. Professional help."

"She is gonna do that, real soon."

"Well, that's good." Chitto wondered if the girl contacted Rona after all. But that line of reasoning didn't stack. Rona would have called the office, let him know the girl had contacted her. She was good at keeping tabs on her cases.

"I got to go to work." She looked toward the door.

Chitto stood. "When you see Teresa, tell her I came by to check on her. You do that . . . tell her I came by?"

She nodded.

At the front door, Chitto turned to face her. "Your husband—*ex*-husband. He leaving you alone?"

"Yeah, he is leaving me alone."

"Good. He shows up again, give me a call. Not too late to file that restraining order."

No response.

He handed her a business card. "Give me a call, you decide you want to do that."

She closed the door, but not before he read the blank look in her eyes.

As Chitto returned to the office, he wondered if Betty Tomlinson would consider a native healer capable of providing professional help. Then his thinking went to something else the aunt said: *This* is home.

Even more confusing was her reaction to the restraining order. It was as though she knew nothing about it.

CHAPTER TWENTY-ONE

Chitto scrambled eggs absentmindedly, thinking about the updates he had made to the map on the kitchen wall. Two more Post-it flags, blue in color, now marked information about Victim Number Three.

No, number one. Unless others showed up.

One of the new Post-its was in the vicinity of the Oklahoma City Convention Center, marking where the body of Dewan Baldwin was found. The other, in Potawatomie County where Baldwin lived with his girl-wife, Katie Ward Baldwin. Age seventeen. A girl not yet grown, destined to a life without children.

Tom Murray had phoned him the information late the previous day. Murray also had found out the name of the healer man conducting ceremonies around the state. Justin Arnett.

Arnett lived in the northeastern corner of the state, in the Quapaw Nation. Several years before, he had started counseling abused women, using a combination of traditional ways and modern therapy techniques. According to what Murray found out, Arnett recently had begun counseling women outside his region.

Murray also described the ceremony. At sunset, as a fire burned over a pile of large rocks, a prayer man welcomed dead ancestors, then women victims gathered inside. Arnett smoked the sacred herb in his pipe, following which the women prayed and talked. Afterward, the women washed themselves clean.

Spiritually cured.

"Hear tell he's helped a lot of 'em," Murray said.

Chitto wished it were that simple. Many abused women went to professional counseling for years and never healed.

He turned his attention to dates as he scraped eggs onto a plate. Baldwin, the murdered ex-airman, was found on the third of August. Four days after the Red Earth Festival. The next body, Delbert Wilcox found the first week in September. A month later. Charlie Carter in mid-September. A week after Wilcox. No consistency in timing.

So, unless there's victims we don't know about, he thought, this thing's just ramping up. If that's the case, now's the time to shut it down.

Chitto wished the military-duty connection had panned out, but it didn't. Calls to Tubbe and Sunday confirmed that neither of the other murdered men served in any branch of the military.

He ate slowly, his mind on the particulars of the cases. Because the men were not known in the area their bodies were found, the murders appeared to be random. Opportunistic. But if that were true, what was the occasion that caused them? The motivation? And why those particular men?

Sighing, Chitto ruled out opportunistic. All three murders were carefully planned, the men chosen deliberately. The connection between them was what he was after. That would lead to the one calling the shots in this macabre game of craps. The tripwire.

Finishing breakfast, Chitto stacked the dishes in the sink. He needed to make a phone call before he headed for the office, where he was scheduled to meet with two field officers, back to back. He punched in the number by heart.

"Morning, Mama. Dr. Anderson there?" Chitto used Leslie's professional title deliberately, hoping to dampen his mother's matchmaking tendencies. "Need to talk to her."

209

"She's not here. What you need to talk to her about?"

He shook his head, not wanting to start his day with a confrontation with his mother. Here lately, every woman he talked to was a challenge.

"Following up on something."

"What?"

Chitto sighed, wishing he had gotten Leslie's number when he'd had the opportunity. "Remember Dad's policy of not talking work?" He listened to the pause on the line, then wrote down the ten-digit number his mother read off. "Thanks. Tell Grandma I said 'Hey.' "

"Wait a minute. I'm down there for a meeting today. Want to meet me for lunch?"

"I'm really booked. Been covering for another lieutenant and have two field officers coming in today. Maybe another time?" He listened to the silence on the phone, reading what it was saying: *What son doesn't have time to see his own mother?*

"Okay. I'll give Wanda a call," she said. A click on the line.

Chitto hung up the phone, feeling somewhat nonplussed. No one reacted predictably these days.

At seven thirty, Chitto pulled into the parking lot. He'd tried calling Leslie on the way, but the line was busy. Departing his car, he was surprised to see her pull into the parking space next to him.

She walked toward him, smiling. "Mattie said you needed to talk to me?"

The busy phone line cleared up. Since he wouldn't talk to her, Mattie called the anthropologist.

"What'd she want?" he asked.

"Damned if I know," she said, brow wrinkling. "I've been staying down here this week. She asked what I've been up to, when I was coming back up that way, if I'd run into you. That kind of thing."

"What'd you tell her?"

She affected a Texas drawl. "Well, pardner, what could I tell her? I figure you didn't want her to know about the shootout at the OK Corral."

He grinned. She turned serious.

"You were working unofficially that night we talked with Wade, so I told Mattie we went to dinner. Which wasn't a lie—" She let out a moan. "Oh, no. I hope she doesn't read anything into that."

"She won't," he said, then realized his and Leslie's stories did not jibe. He had implied his business with Leslie was official. Leslie had indicated it was personal. His mother would read *a lot* into the dinner meeting.

"So, what'd you want to talk to me about?" she asked. "I was on my way out to Highway 70 and thought it would be faster to drop by. Being cell-phone reception isn't great here."

"Yeah, I tried reaching you."

A police car pulling into the parking lot got his attention. Seven was here for the first scheduled appointment.

"Say, I'm on short time right now. Can we meet up later? What I want to discuss is complicated. How about lunch?" Remembering he had declined his mother's lunch engagement, he amended his offer. "No, make that supper."

She nodded. "Yeah, lunch wouldn't have worked for me anyway. Where you want to meet? And what time?"

"You choose." He had been out of the game too long.

"There's a place on the highway by the KOA. Mexican food."

Mexican food. Chili peppers at six, bicarb of soda at ten.

"Yeah, I know it. Six o'clock?"

She waved as she pulled away.

Chitto considered Leslie's remarks as he walked to the steps, wondering what she would be doing on Highway 70. He recalled

211

the list his mother had given her on that first Saturday he met her. Bokchito was on Highway 70. She was going to see Sonny Boy Munro.

He smiled, hoping Leslie liked pigs and knew how to make a decent peanut-butter-and-jelly sandwich.

Seven sat across from Chitto, fingers tapping a staccato rhythm on the arm of the chair.

"Almost done," Chitto said, looking over the results of the polygraph test. "Looks like your boy was telling the truth . . . for the most part."

Seven leaned forward. "What's that mean?"

"Didn't spend the night with his girlfriend the night of the robbery, like he said he did."

"Hot dog!" The young officer's grin faded quickly. "But this isn't admissible in court, is it?"

"No, but that doesn't mean you can't use it to good advantage. If not with the suspect, then with his girl. Wasn't she his alibi?"

The grin reappeared. "Yeah, and she was real nervous the *first* time I talked with her. This time, she'll crumble like a cracker."

Chitto printed off a copy of the report and handed it to Seven.

"You got an envelope I can put this in?" Seven said. "Don't want to give my perp any advance warning."

"All out. Check with Wanda."

"Passed her going down the stairs when I came up."

"Wait here. I know where she keeps them."

Chitto pulled on the desk drawer where Wanda stored manila envelopes. Locked. He found the same true of the supply cabinet. He noticed Junior Wharton searching for something, with the same result.

Blackfox rounded the corner, eyeing the situation. "What's goin' on?"

Wharton quickly explained the dilemma. "Nothing critical. I'll come back later." He returned to his desk.

"Wanda must've had a senior moment," Blackfox said, looking at Chitto.

"Don't think so, Dan. She's mad because I wouldn't fill her in on these cases I'm working on. But you told me to keep things on the QT and so I told her to . . ."

". . . back off? Probably the first time anyone told her that." Blackfox sighed. "I'll have a talk with her. Whole department shouldn't pay because she's got her tail in a crack."

Chitto read the look on Blackfox's face as he turned away. He was thinking again that it was time for Wanda to retire.

And maybe it was.

Back at his desk, Chitto rummaged through his trashcan. "Just threw this envelope away," he told Seven. "Used, but it'll do the job."

Seven stuffed the report inside the recycled envelope and walked toward the hallway.

"Wait up, Seven," Chitto said.

The young officer turned, face serious. "Something wrong, Sam?"

"No, something right. Nice police work on that killing up there at the old capitol. Noticing the victim's clothes had just been washed and hung out to dry was good. Real good."

Seven's face flushed, obviously pleased. "Anything new? My district's buzzing about those killings. All kinds of speculation."

Those killings. Word was already on the street about the second victim.

"Lot of the jerks up my way are getting real nervous. Looking over their shoulders. Wondering why those guys were picked." Seven laughed. "Wondering who's next."

Chitto would bet big money they were nervous. That was the way object lessons worked.

Seven's demeanor turned serious. "Why *were* they killed, Sam?"

"Have to ask the FBI. Officially in their hands."

"Yeah, that's gonna happen." He paused. "Oh, and that fabric softener my wife uses is called Final Touch. You wanted me to let you know." Giving a wave, he left to retrieve his suspect.

Chitto chuckled. Whoever was running the fourth-day murder spree had a sense of humor. Then he sobered. Final Touch was not a choice at the washateria. He assumed most local laundries purchased from the same vendor; there were only so many that did that kind of thing. That meant someone was washing the victim's clothes at home. Someone with a strong stomach.

Or a cold heart.

CHAPTER TWENTY-TWO

Twelve-ten and Chitto's next interrogation was at one o'clock, the second one that day. He wasn't looking forward to this one. Leon Messina was barely twenty, but not an amateur like the previous one he'd helped question.

Messina and his family lived in northern LeFlore County, one of Chitto's favorite places for rock hunting. Rugged country, full of wrinkles. Two fault lines ran through it: the Choctaw and the Winding Stair. Chert, black shale, fossilized sponges spoke to an ancient life. The former home of pre-Columbian people. The mound builders.

The Messinas had a long history there, too. Fingers in everything from drugs and prostitution to land swindles. A half-blood, the boy's mother had been a member of the Choctaw Nation, which entitled the boy to membership, too, and was the reason the tribal police could bring him in for questioning. The boy's mother died prematurely in an accident, leaving his upbringing to his father's family. Vincent, the boy's grandfather, claimed rights over the entire region, ruling like a provincial crime boss. Chitto's father had run himself ragged trying to put Vincent Messina behind bars but, thanks to the convoluted legal system, could never get anything to stick. One thing Chitto knew for certain: the kid would be a pro when it came to lying.

The clock now read twelve-fifteen. Lunch would be in a paper bag again.

Hustling downstairs, Chitto was surprised to encounter his

215

mother standing on the curb outside the Choctaw complex.

"Where you going?" she asked.

"To get some food." He pointed in the direction of Main Street. "You waiting on Wanda? She left a while back."

"Something came up so Rona's picking me up. This was the easiest place for us to meet. Come with us. Be better than greasy-gut food."

"Wish I could." He nodded at a car driving up the street. "But, if I'm not mistaken, my next appointment just drove up."

Because the ride down was a long one and he was not officially under arrest, Messina had requested he be allowed to ride up front. Chitto looked into Messina's face as the District 4 tribal police car pulled into a parking spot. The dark-haired, dark-eyed kid in the passenger seat had the pallor of a dead carp, an indication to Chitto that his activities didn't occur in the bright of day. Seeing a coldness in Messina's eyes, he wondered if evil was an inheritable trait.

"You feel that?" Mattie wrapped her arms around her body. "That cold wind?"

"It's ninety degrees in the shade, Mama," he said. Glancing toward a sky that excessive heat had turned crystal clear, he rubbed a hand across goose bumps on his arms.

Her eyes opened wide. "It was your father's *Shilombish*."

His silence triggered a frown.

"Don't give me that sour face, Sam. I know you don't believe in such things, but your father's spirit's still here and won't leave 'til his killer's found." She looked around cautiously. "He's here; I can feel it. He's trying to tell us something."

Chitto shook his head. "Hey, look, I've got to go. Need to interrogate the man in that car in a few minutes." He pointed his chin toward Main Street. "A burger's all I have time for."

"Okay, you go now. At least you'll eat good tonight. I dropped off a pot roast at your place and a pie your granny made."

"My place—How'd you get in? I had the locks changed."

"Hattie let me in. She had a new key made for herself, one for me and your granny. I put everything in the fridge." Spying Rona Guthrie's car, she waved it toward the curb. "You coming home this weekend?" she asked as Rona pulled to a stop.

"Not sure." Curious why she didn't comment on the changes he'd made, he said, "You find everything all right? In the kitchen, I mean?"

"If you're talking 'bout that sink full of dirty dishes, I washed 'em. Be a disappointment to your granny, you don't come home. Leslie will be back, only here another week. Returning to Washington pretty quick."

Chitto stared in surprise. "She already finished that list you gave her?"

"No. She teaches up there at that school," Mattie said. "She's gonna finish up the interviews next year." She walked to where Rona was double-parked, then looked at him. "Leslie could prob'ly use some home cooking, too. Ask her over for supper; there's plenty for two." As she slid into the passenger seat, she looked at him again. "Bring home my pie plate and roasting pan Sunday." She waved as Rona pulled away.

As he drove to Carl Junior's, Chitto thought about Leslie's upcoming departure. It hadn't occurred to him that she would return to D.C. so soon. Then he latched onto the other thing his mother said. She left food at his house. Both he and Leslie could eat home cooking that evening. Since Leslie had already seen the map, there was no harm done if she saw it again. And the house was a better place to discuss business than a busy café.

The line was long at the drive-through, which gave Chitto time to make a call. As he waited for his order, he punched in Leslie's cell-phone number. Getting her voicemail, he told her about the change in plans. His place, six o'clock.

★ ★ ★ ★ ★

Chitto returned to his office with a sack lunch on the seat beside him. Sunshine reflecting off changing leaves made the day glaringly bright. He paused after parking, observing construction activities. The site looked like an anthill that had been kicked up, with workers scurrying everywhere. The sounds of their hammers beat a staccato rhythm that was jarring.

He glanced at the sky as he exited his SUV, thinking about his mother's explanation for the cold wind she'd felt earlier—and her interpretation that it was his father trying to tell them something. After his father's death, he occasionally sensed his dad's presence, but he knew those times were triggered by memories. A sense of loss.

The problem was, he'd felt that cold wind, too. What did it mean? Some sort of premonition? A warning?

"Bullshit," he muttered, blaming his mother's superstitions for his lapse in rational thinking. But as he proceeded up the steps, Chitto's apprehension grew. If his father's spirit *had* made an appearance, why now?

As he approached his desk, Chitto eyed a manila envelope lying on his chair. Picking it up, he noticed how light it was. Feeling for contents, he fingered a small object at the bottom. A closer look confirmed his suspicions. Charlie Carter's scalp lock.

"Well, hell," he mumbled, thinking about the cold wind he'd felt earlier. Irrational as it was, he couldn't help but wonder if there was a connection. That thought was followed with another.

Then why didn't I sense Dad's presence when Wilcox's scalp lock was left for me to find?

He was still studying the object at the bottom of the envelope when Four appeared at his desk.

"All set downstairs, Sam." The young field officer looked at the sack from Carl Junior's on Chitto's desk. "Want me to stall

218

a few minutes?"

"Nope," Chitto said, locking the manila envelope in the bottom drawer. "Just lost my appetite."

As Chitto followed Four to the interrogation room, he put his attention on the task awaiting him. A boy-looking man with the eyes of a dead fish who had been raised up with evil.

"You think we got enough file for a search warrant, Sam?" Four asked. "I'd bet my bottom dollar his granddad's got a dog-fighting pit out there at his place."

Four had picked Leon Messina up in connection with a dog-fighting ring in the county. The kid had blown through a stop sign, causing a hay truck to clip his rig in the rear. The impact put him in the ditch and spread the contents of his trunk along the right of way. Chains, wooden sticks, buckets, antibacterial soap—items used in dog-fighting operations. A look inside Messina's car revealed a bloodied pit bull wearing a studded collar. The discovery was quickly tied to another incident that a sheriff's deputy had just called in. An older pit bull had been found less than a mile away, jaws taped shut with duct tape and one leg lacerated to the bone. A bait dog. Past its usefulness, the older dog had been used to train younger ones. Beyond help, the injured dog had been tied to a post and left to bleed to death. The two incidents occurring so close together tipped the scale of coincidence. The two investigating officers figured Messina had dumped the dog and was speeding to put some distance between him and it. Four hauled him in for further questioning. When he couldn't get the kid to admit to anything, he called Chitto to assist.

" 'Fraid the lie detector test didn't show much," Chitto said. "He still sticking to his story that the pit bull was covered in blood because he'd been hunting and the dog killed a rabbit?"

Four nodded. "Like a pit bull is a hunting dog," he snorted.

"Not for rabbits, anyway," Chitto commented.

"So, what do we do?" Four asked, pausing outside a door behind which Leon Messina waited. "I'd really like to nail this kid."

Chitto took a minute before answering, wishing he knew more about his father's investigation of the Messina family. Their habits. Routines. Addictions. Weaknesses. Regrettably, his father had strictly enforced his rule not to discuss business at home. Bottom line? They were walking into a blind canyon.

"Push him hard. See if he'll let something slip," Chitto said. "He's out of his home territory, doesn't have his family to fend for him. Young as he is, maybe he hasn't set hard yet. Got to have a weak spot somewhere."

"Be glad to," Four snorted. "I'd love to crack him wide open."

Chitto let Four take the lead in the questioning, offering comments occasionally to assist. The kid had been well trained. Hard as a tack. Unshakable. Seemingly amused at their efforts. As time went on, however, Chitto noticed he began to glance at his watch now and then.

"You got an appointment to keep?" he asked finally.

The kid grinned his response.

An hour later, Chitto could sense Four had reached the end of his rope. He had, too. The kid was a stone block. He signaled Four that he wanted a turn at him.

"Know what people that'd do this to a dog deserve?" Chitto said, laying the pictures of a dog with its muzzle torn off, one leg hanging on with sinews, in front of Messina.

"What?" Messina said, barely glancing at the photos.

"A bullet in the head."

A hint of a smile showed on the kid's face.

"You find that funny?" Four snapped.

Messina laughed outright. "Comin' from him, I do," he smirked.

Four didn't get it. Chitto did. The kid had let something slip all right, but it didn't deal with *dogs* trained to kill. Chitto's father and Bert Gilly had been killed by *men* trained to kill. Hit men that put one bullet behind the ear. But that was confidential information, not shared beyond a few, and never to the press or public. How was the Messina kid privy to it?

Chitto stared at Messina a full minute before sensing Four staring at him, looking confused. "Time to wrap this up," he said, gathering his investigative materials. "Drop by my office before you head back, Four."

En route to his office, Chitto thought again of a cold wind on a blistering hot day. *Was* his father's spirit trying to communicate something to him? If so, what? Did he want Chitto to accomplish what he never could? To put a stop to the Messina crime family? Or was it something more basic? More urgent?

Chitto came to a dead stop at the top of the stairs, hit with a chilling thought. Was his father telling him someone was in danger? His dad had harassed old Victor Messina for years, trying to put him out of business. Did he and Bert Gilly die because of it?

Chitto's heartbeat pounded in his ears. Had old Victor Messina been his father's executioner?

Proceeding toward his office, Chitto reviewed what else the kid might've let slip. The watch, he thought. Why was the kid so interested in what time it was? Unless . . .

"Aw, hell . . ."

Reaching his desk, Chitto placed a call to the dispatcher, arranging for the field officers in District 7 and 9 to intercept Four and provide armed escort back to his home district. Hanging up, he wondered if he had overreacted. But another part of him knew it paid to be cautious on this job. His father and Bert Gilly were reminders of that.

Four appeared at his desk a few minutes later. "You said to stop by before I left, Sam. I'm ready to roll. I got a long drive ahead of me and a snake for company."

"You'll have other company. Seven and Nine will be escorting you. Your car equipped with a cage?"

"Yeah . . ." Four frowned. "Why?"

"Because that's how I want you to transport this kid. And keep a shotgun on the seat next to you. Two in the chamber."

"You trying to tell me something, Sam?"

Chitto paused. "I think maybe somebody is."

And I'll sure as hell be spending more time in LeFlore County in days to come . . .

CHAPTER TWENTY-THREE

Chitto checked on the pot roast warming in the oven for the third time in fifteen minutes. He had not heard from Leslie and worried that she hadn't gotten his message. The doorbell brought a sigh of relief.

He smiled as he opened the door. Leslie stood on the front porch, clothes wrinkled and damp hair curling in ringlets around her face.

"Sorry I'm late. Mr. Munro let me use the shower out back of his place. I changed clothes, but these are the only shoes I brought." Flushing slightly, she looked at her feet. "I'm afraid they smell of barnyard. You mind if I shuck them here? They need a good airing out."

"Not a problem. You work up an appetite?"

"Ohmigod, *yes.*" She walked inside in stocking feet. "Only I hope we're not having pork. I formed a deep bond with a lot of little pigs today."

Chitto laughed at that. "Sonny Boy has a shower out there at that hunting shack?"

"He lets hunters in there, too? But yes, an outdoor shower that's lined with peeled poles." She grinned. "Private, but air-conditioned."

She stopped at the kitchen doorway. "Did you take down the map, or should I sit with my back to the wall?"

"Seems the information on it isn't as privileged as I thought," he said. "Tribal telegraph."

"More efficient than cell phones." She looked at the table. "So, what's so important it got me invited to this great-looking dinner? Somehow, I didn't picture you a cook."

"Mama brought it down." He pointed her toward a chair at the table. "Grandma sent the pie."

"Hope you appreciate how lucky you are."

Chitto contemplated her comment as he set the roaster pan on the table. He had not considered she would have no family back in D.C. But then, other parts of the country were different from this place. Extended families had not broken down in the Nation, in part because of the benefits offered to those meeting the qualifications of the Dawes rolls, the late nineteenth-century government judgment that determined the fate of allotment Indians. Over time, the Nation tried to improve the fare of its citizens. Medical care at clinics. Assistance with food and shelter. Higher education for those that wanted it. The practice, while not entirely replacing what was taken away with the Removal, made for a system that took care of its own.

Sometimes too well, Chitto thought. What started out as a way to empower the People had morphed into red welfare for some. Dole junkies, growing fat, lazy. Addicts to handouts and drugs. Women soaking up alcohol like sponges and squeezing it into unborn babies . . .

"Those, uh, these new stickers mean what I think they do?" Leslie asked, face ashy.

"Happened in July," Chitto said, dishing up plates.

She chewed on her bottom lip. "The Red Earth Festival in Oklahoma City . . ."

Chitto noticed her green eyes blinking with a steady rhythm. She was absorbing information, attempting to translate it into something she could understand.

"I don't know what to make of it," she said, looking at him. "What does it all mean?"

224

He nodded to the plate he had set in front of her. "Food first. Talk later."

"I'm for that," she sighed.

Chitto noticed Leslie's eyes return to the map periodically during supper. He knew she was trying to overlay his map with the maps she kept. Looking for patterns, just as he was. As he dished them both a second helping of beef and pan vegetables, she broached the subject.

"I am sufficiently restored to think straight, so give. Why am I here?"

He rubbed his mouth, thinking how to begin. "It's these healing ceremonies. I'm beginning to think they play a role in this . . ." He pointed with his chin toward the map. "Need a quick lesson in what they're about."

She continued to eat. Chewing slowly. Eyes displaying a mind at work.

"Well, let's begin with a few basics," she said a couple of minutes later. "There are differing opinions, of course, but I think they can be traced back to the old Green Corn Ceremony."

"The festivals going on right now are based on that," he said. "A celebration of the beginning of our new year."

"Yes renewal of the annual cycle. It's associated with the return of the next summer and the ripening of the new corn." She paused. "Only the ceremonies today are truncated. In olden days, they lasted much longer and were more elaborate. Brush arbors were constructed around a square where men sat facing one of the four directions. A ring-mound of earth encircled this square and in the center of all this was the ceremonial fire, which was referred to by a lot of different names. But my favorite is Grandfather Fire. This fire was the central focus of the songs and prayers of the people and was considered to be a living, sacred being that transmitted the prayers to the one above." She pointed skyward. "The Creator. The entire ceremony's focus was on relighting this ceremonial fire."

"And today, about all that's left is the singing." Chitto thought of Sonny Boy. "Which is the same as prayers."

"There was a lot more to it than just the Grandfather Fire, of course. In early times, a ribbon or ladies dance was held on the first day. On the second day, the men got up early and removed the previous year's fire, cleaned up the ceremonial grounds, that kind of thing. Then they danced throughout the day. In the meantime, the women cleaned out the cooking fires, which were relit with hot coals from the newly established ceremonial fire."

Chitto refilled iced-tea glasses and indicated she should continue.

"Well, these ceremonies went on for days, with fasting and singing, ceremonial cleansing of their bodies. At midnight on the last day, a stomp dance was held, with more fasting and dancing through the night. This ceremonial feast, commonly referred to as the Green Corn Ceremony, was very central to the Muskogean people, as well as other tribal nations. It represented not only the renewal of the annual cycle, but of the community's social and spiritual life as a whole. It was a healing ceremony for everyone."

"And all that was lost with the Removal," he said. "Well, maybe not all of it. Thanks to people like you, a lot of it's being restored."

She flushed slightly. "I just don't see any connection to *that.*" She lifted her chin, indicating the map of murders. "I mean, this ceremony was to the Muskogee peoples what the Year of Jubilee was to the Israelites. A time of release. Freedom. When offenses were forgiven." She hesitated. "Well, let me amend that last statement. *Almost* all offenses were forgiven. But surely, none of the old stories, the old rituals I've talked about, could have caused anything so . . . so terrible." Again, she looked at the map.

"I don't see any connection either." He cleared the table and brought out the pie, along with fresh plates. "You slice. I'll make coffee."

As they finished the meal, Chitto brought up her pending departure.

"Yes, after the Muskogee-Creek festival," she confirmed. "I'm not looking forward to that long drive back to D.C. Or the winter months. Or freshman students—especially not freshman students." She grimaced. "But we all have to take our turn."

A feeling of displeasure came over Chitto. She would be gone eight to nine months. He would miss the happy-go-lucky anthropologist, and a lot could happen in that time. Damaged relationships could mend.

"Schmidt going back at the same time?"

She nodded. "We tag team on long drives in case of car trouble." She glanced at her watch. "I have to get going. Early day tomorrow and Mr. Munro kept me pretty busy. Used muscles I forgot I had."

Chitto stood at the front door, watching Leslie tie shoelaces "You get a chance to interview Sonny Boy?"

She looked up at him. "That's not why I was there. He's hosting a healing ceremony at his lodge this Thursday night, and I wanted to see if I could attend. Mr. Munro's the prayer man."

Prayer man? Why did that surprise him? Only an honorable man was allowed to be the prayer man. Chitto recalled what he knew of the prayer man's role. Lighting the fire and dousing the rocks, to create steam. After the ceremony ended, waiting for the fire to die. The last one to leave.

"You, uh, you know the name of the healer man leading the rituals?"

She looked at him, eyes guarded. "Same one that's led all the others. Justin Arnett. He was there this afternoon with some other people, talking about who will be attending."

Chitto's eyes narrowed. "You know who that was? The people he met with, I mean?"

She shook her head. "A girl and a woman. The older woman sounded like she was coming down with a cold. Had a real bad cough. I'm not permitted to get involved in that piece of it, so I wasn't introduced to them. Why?"

He rubbed his face. "Suppose they'd let another person attend?"

She frowned. "Same answer as before, Sam—don't dare take the chance."

"It's okay," he said to calm her anxiety. He had enough anxiety for both of them. He needed to connect the dots and do it fast.

Leslie extended her hand. "Thanks for the meal. Suppose I'll see you this weekend?"

He nodded. "Yeah. Mom ordered me to return her dishes."

She grinned. "And I have to find chocolates with soft centers for Rhody. No nuts."

He smiled at that. Watching Leslie walk down his sidewalk, red hair an aura in the reflected light, he remembered one question that had gone unanswered.

"Leslie," he called out. "You said almost all offenses were forgiven at the old Green Corn Ceremonies."

She turned to look at him. "That's right. Two offenses were considered unforgiveable. Rape and murder were executable sins." Waving through her car window, she drove away.

Chitto swallowed as he watched her disappear. Without knowing it, Dr. Leslie Anderson had just connected the dots.

CHAPTER TWENTY-FOUR

Chitto cleaned the kitchen after Leslie left. Afterward, he sat at the table, studying the map on the wall. Making suppositions, drawing conclusions in an attempt to apply an empirical process to an irrational chain of events. Result? A premise he couldn't prove in a court of law.

He picked up the phone and punched in a number.

"You got any idea what time it is?" Blackfox said, sounding groggy.

Chitto glanced at the clock on the wall. One fifteen.

"This couldn't wait, Dan. Figured it out—I know who's behind these murders. We need to talk—now. Better we do it here, my place."

"Why can't it wait 'til morning?"

"Man's life could be on the line." He paused. "And, Dan, you're not gonna like what you hear."

"Put the coffee on," Blackfox said.

Dressed in a gray sweatshirt and faded jeans, Blackfox sat down at the kitchen table. He looked at the map on the wall, then at Chitto. "Beginning to think I made a mistake lettin' you run with this thing."

Chitto laughed softly. "Hold that thought." He poured two cups of coffee, set them on the table and took a seat across from Blackfox. "Need to fill you in on a few things before I begin."

He told Blackfox about the two men following him, the scalp locks left for him to find, being mugged in the parking lot, the sticky note left on the map on the wall. He pointed out the initials *S* and *C* on it.

Blackfox leaned forward, eyes glinting. "And you're just telling me this *now*?"

"Warnings," Chitto said. "Had to be warnings, else they would've taken me out long time back. Now why would someone go to all that trouble?"

"You got my attention." Blackfox leaned back in his chair, cradling his coffee cup.

Chitto rubbed his face. "Remember our talk about someone on the inside clueing Rodriquez in?"

"This the part I'm not gonna like?"

"Yes, sir." He pointed his chin at the map. "Think I better start at the beginning. It's complicated."

Blackfox held his cup out for a refill.

"First off," Chitto said, refilling both cups, "we're dealing with a fluid organization. People from thirty-eight tribal nations. Each one knew part of the problem and, because someone acted as overseer, became part of the solution. Regular people from every walk of life. People easy to overlook, not perceived as a threat. And because of the distance from each other, hard to identify as links in a chain."

"I need to make notes?" Blackfox pulled a notebook from his hip pocket. "Start writing down names?"

"Not yet. Just hear me out." Chitto leaned back in his chair, staring at the map. "Organizational structure's . . . complex. A network, including people with access to legal records that identified abused girls and women, victims of rape."

"Access to records." Blackfox frowned. "Like who?"

"People fed up with the justice system."

"Crap . . ." Blackfox laughed without humor. "Who's that leave out?"

"Exactly," Chitto said. "Picture it like a spider's web."

Blackfox looked at the map again. "Damn big web."

"It is. Others involved felt they needed to look after these abused women—their daughters and sisters—to ensure they wouldn't be harmed any more. Even if it meant allegiance outside the law. Ever hear of something called the Four Mothers' Society?"

Without waiting for a response, he filled Blackfox in on Leslie Anderson's work around the state. The work of the heritage societies that spun off from the old, original organization.

"Damn," Blackfox said. "My wife's a member of the local society." He eyed the map, shaking his head. "Those groups are everywhere."

Chitto nodded. "My mother and grandmother belong to one, too. They tried to warn me away, but I didn't understand why 'til tonight. Don't think they knew everything, just picked up enough to know I was sticking my nose where it didn't belong. This thing's widespread. People from all the nations."

Blackfox looked at him. "Go on. Who else we talkin' about?"

Chitto told Blackfox about the healer, Justin Arnett, and Sonny Boy Munro. "They and probably others like them—felt the victims needed *more* than legal justice. They needed a fresh start, to begin the new year cleansed of nightmare memories."

"And those ceremonies took place right in our backyard?" Blackfox shook his head, looking incredulous. "Even for those killings committed in other nations?"

"Figure it was for convenience and to create confusion. Killings were done by those who wanted justice so bad, they were willing to act as substitutes for wronged women. Cherokees. Apaches. Creek—didn't matter." Pointing to the map again, Chitto filled him in on the cleansing ceremonies held around

231

the checkerboard. "The abused girls were strangers they didn't know but under the skin, they were sisters to *their* sisters who suffered similar injustice."

"Stand-in murderers," Blackfox commented, looking dazed. "Proxies."

"*Executioners* in their eyes, enforcing laws that said rape and murder are unforgiveable." He shared what he learned from Leslie about the old beliefs. "Girls like Nanny Love and the Harjo girls received the justice they deserved for the sins stepfathers committed against them. Katie Ward Baldwin received justice for the murder of her unborn baby."

Blackfox held out an empty cup.

Chitto filled their cups and continued talking. "And then there's the one at the top. Someone who understood how the checkerboard works. Who believed following the process wouldn't rectify things. Someone who knew how to bury evidence under a mountain of paperwork. Someone who could block me because she knew every move I made. Why? Because I told her every move I made." He gave Blackfox a long look. "And you ordered it."

"*Shit.*" Blackfox leaned back in his chair.

"Has to be her. Checkerboard justice, administered through one linchpin in a strategic position."

"What clued you in?" Blackfox asked, rubbing his face.

"Medical examiner's report on Teresa Walker, that rape case I investigated. I overlooked something important on it."

In his mind, Chitto saw the report: *NAME: Teresa Inez Walker. AGE: 15. PLACE OF RESIDENCE: 15903 OK HWY 70. NAME OF PARENTS: Deceased.*

"It was the link in the chain I skipped over," Chitto said. "The Walker girl didn't call her own mother from the clinic because she was dead. She called a friend, Letty Munro. Letty told her grandfather, Sonny Boy, who called someone in the heritage society. And that someone called—"

"Wanda," Blackfox said, "who mothers everyone 'cause she and Bert never had kids of their own."

"Yep, a mother to the Nations."

Or a deadly vine giving its poison to the little people . . .

"What in hell would drive her to . . ." Blackfox shook his head. "Wish it didn't, but it makes sense. Would account for her behavior recently, too." He waved a hand toward the map. "You said another man's neck was on the line."

"Could be. Need to put my mind on how to handle that." Chitto glanced at the clock on the wall. Four twenty-five. "What do you want me to do?"

"Need some time to consider the implications of this situation." Giving the map a last look, Blackfox pushed out of his chair. "One thing I know for sure. I'm gonna keep a close eye on you. Can't believe you kept me out of the loop."

"Dan, if you'll let me explain—"

"No ifs, ands or buts," Blackfox said walking to the sink. "You *will* keep me informed here on out."

Chitto waited, watching him dump cold coffee down the drain.

"Call Wanda later. Pick up your messages." Blackfox leaned on the counter, talking with his back turned. "Take care of what you have to outside the office. Carry on as usual when you do come in." He faced Chitto, face drawn. "Don't want to alert her we're on to things 'til we figure out how to proceed. Keep in touch with me on my cell—not her. Here on out, she's out of the loop."

Nodding, Chitto walked him to the door.

"Aged a lifetime tonight," Blackfox said, fading into the awakening light.

★ ★ ★ ★ ★

Chitto attempted a couple hours of sleep, took a hot shower, made a fresh pot of coffee. He kept the call to Wanda brief, had her follow up with what she could to keep her out of the way, then handled the most important issues from the road. It was noon when he made it to the office.

"You eat?" Wanda asked when he walked in.

He held up a McDonald's sack.

She frowned. "What'd you do that for? Pot luck today."

"Forgot." Walking to his desk, he sat with his back to the hallway.

As the office cleared of people and noise, he stared at the map of the Choctaw Nation on his wall. He had a duty to perform. A legal duty. Rubbing tired eyes, he tried to fathom where in the thousands of miles comprising the whole of Indian territory another man waited to die.

One flag on the map drew him like a magnet. The one designating where Sonny Boy lived. The old mystic would be singing another prayer soon. Or had that prayer already been said? That prayer would put in motion cogs in a wheel.

He reviewed upcoming celebrations, the last ones to be held that year. The Wyandotte Nation's festival had been held the previous weekend, September 14 through 19. Four days ago. Had Sonny Boy been there? Had he sent a prayer to the Creator already? If so, who was the man destined to be executed? Or would the next man's fate be postponed until the following week when the Muskogee-Creek Nation's event was scheduled in Okmulgee?

He hoped desperately for the latter option, that the Muskogee-Creek event would be the next one chosen. An extra week gave him time to determine where to look. Figure out how to intercede.

Abruptly, he looked at the map on the wall again. Even if the man were abducted, maybe he could save him. The healer man, Justin Arnett, was scheduled to conduct a healing ceremony that evening. Starting at sundown.

He began closing down his desk. He had not done a good job up to now of being the hunter, but tonight that would change.

"Where you off to?" Wanda said as he walked past her desk.

Same place you were yesterday, he wanted to say. Recalling Leslie's description of the two women who met with Justin Arnett, he knew Wanda was the older one with a bad cough. Which was why she couldn't have lunch with his mother. But he didn't say this. He didn't want to alert the chief cog in the wheel he was about to gum up the works.

"Following up on something that came up this morning," he said.

"Bet you got time for dessert." She held up a plate containing berry pie and a Styrofoam cup of steaming coffee.

"Wrap it up. I'll take the coffee with me."

Wanda set the plate on her desk, picked up a pencil and looked at him. "Supposed to let me know your whereabouts. Dan's orders."

Not this time . . .

"Give you a call from the road," he said, walking toward the stairs. This time, the duck hunters were going to have to look hard to find him.

On the way out the door, he put his mind on how to approach Sonny Boy's place unseen. That required he become a sneaky devil.

CHAPTER TWENTY-FIVE

Before leaving the tribal complex, Chitto checked the checker-board map in his glove box to see who owned property adjacent to Sonny Boy's. Coy Mapes, a farmer he bought hay from, had pastureland that backed up it. Wasting no time, he called to get permission to park his rig there. Turning off his cell phone, he drove a back way to his house.

Parking his Tahoe in the garage, he debated whether to take his Remington 879 or Colt AR 15. Deciding on the shotgun, he put it in the gun rack in his pickup. If cornered, the Remington would cover more area. For backup, he carried his Glock and spare clip.

Driving to the stable, he hitched up his trailer and loaded his horse, Blue. He needed to get out of sight quick. As he drove, he checked his rearview mirror but saw no one following him. Since it was a workday, he banked on his hunters having jobs.

Taking back roads to Mapes's farm, he called Blackfox. "Told Wanda I'd call her with my whereabouts, but I'm leaving my phone off unless I need to use it. You'll probably hear from her."

"Already did," Blackfox said. "Came in bugging me about not being able to reach you, wondering where you were. Told her it was none of her business. Made her so mad, she started coughing up blood. Rushed her to the hospital and that's when she let loose that she's got lung cancer. Terminal. Weeks at the most. I was a bettin' man, I'd say days. Got a call in to Hospice;

she's moving in this weekend."

Chitto pulled up an image of Wanda. Brittle as a dried leaf.

"Answers one question," Blackfox said. "Why she did it—the reason she dreamed up this cockeyed scheme. Ten years is a long time to wait for justice to be done. 'Specially when you're running out of time."

Chitto felt a sharpness in his chest. A knife turning.

"You there, Sam?"

"Yeah . . . yeah. Just floored, I guess."

"Need to think on this one," Blackfox said. "How to handle it, I mean. Maybe it's time to let the FBI have it. Some cases might belong in a file box stuck in a basement. And if Wanda *is* the one dealing the cards . . . well, this thing will fold soon as she's out of the picture."

Wanda would never be out of the picture. The checkerboard was a land of ghosts. Her shadow would hang around until Bert's killer was found.

Chitto felt both sorrow and regret as he shut off his phone. Disease and death were affecting his life again. All he could do was put his mind to the job at hand. Wanda was Dan's responsibility for now. He had his own row to hoe.

Coy Mapes was stacking hay inside his barn when Chitto climbed out of his rig. The old man's skin was as brown and furrowed as the land he'd farmed for fifty years.

"How you doin', Coy?" Picking up a hay hook, Chitto helped stack the last of the bales. The sun was starting to dip low in the west. "Surprised you're storing those bales inside. Dry as it is, they'd weather fine in the field."

"Ordinarily, that's what I do. Ain't no ordinary year." He told Chitto about an NPR program he listened to recently where a local sheriff placed a GPS device in a hay bale to track thieves.

"You're pulling my leg," Chitto said. "Hay rustlers?"

237

"Well, think about it. Price of a bale went for fifteen, twenty dollars before the drought. Now, same bale goes for sixty-five to seventy. Bale of alfalfa used to run forty-five to sixty dollars will cost you a hundred forty to a hundred-and-a-half. Already raised my prices, prob'ly do 'er again." He cracked a grin. "Most years, barely break even. Who would've thought a damned drought had a silver lining?"

"Damn, Coy," Chitto grinned, too. "Maybe I better buy fifty, sixty bales while I can afford it." He dropped the ramp on the back of the trailer, released Blue's halter from the tie down and tossed the lead rope over his back.

"Not a bad idea," Mapes said, watching Chitto throw a saddle on Blue. "You want, I can load up other side of the trailer while you're out riding. Would leave me more room in the barn, too. Be damned if I'm gonna resort to bugging bales of hay."

"Yeah, do that." Chitto inserted the Remington into the saddle holder. "But here's the deal." He explained he would likely be gone until morning and needed his rig out of sight. "I'm not back by morning, appreciate you calling this man. Tell him to come looking for me and Blue." He handed Mapes one of Blackfox's business cards.

Reading the card, Mapes eyed the long gun and turned slitted eyes on Chitto. "You need another hand? Can still knock a tin can off a fence post at fifty yards."

"Not expecting trouble." He hoped that wasn't false hope. "Just taking precautions."

"All right then. Pull 'er in the barn."

Chitto parked his horse trailer inside the big hay barn and took off across country, hugging tree lines that shielded him from passersby. If the duck hunters were looking for his truck, they'd be hard put to find it. And if they did, he'd bet money they weren't prepared to trek through the countryside on foot. Or come face-to-face with a Remington.

★ ★ ★ ★ ★

Chitto found a large clearing with a good stand of tall fescue to tether Blue. To make the horse comfortable while he was gone, he removed the saddle and hauled a bucket of water from a nearby creek.

"Fill your belly," he whispered, feeling the velvet softness of the horse's muzzle. "Don't be calling out to me; you'll give away my hiding place."

Making a snuffing sound, the horse put its nose to the ground.

In dwindling light, Chitto began the final half mile to Sonny Boy's place. If he had guessed right, he would come out in back of the wooded acreage surrounding the lodge. Plenty of cover to hide his presence, and his dark clothes would blend into the brushy shadows.

He traveled light. A pack held water and field glasses, a flashlight for later when he returned to Blue. He wore the service revolver on his belt, the extra clip in his pocket and the Remington slung over his shoulder.

Making his way quietly, he reached a place that gave him a good view of the dome-like hut back of Sonny Boy's place. A covering of willow branches and blankets muted the voices inside. He smelled wood smoke, burning tobacco. The healer had started the ceremony.

He did a quick sweep of the area to make sure he was the only trespasser outside the lodge, then settled in to wait. Soon, he heard the voices of women talking. Then, the chant of prayers. Watching mist rise over the lodge, he knew Sonny Boy was pouring water over hot stones to create steam. The steam would make bodies sweat, empty out pores that had become clogged with waste left from a bitter time.

Time passed. Chitto inched closer to the lodge so that he could monitor progress. He did not want to listen to the words being spoken, for that would be a violation to the women.

Ceremonies were sacred, not meant for public scrutiny. Checking his watch, he was surprised to find how late the hour was. Ten fifteen and the ceremony continued.

Around eleven o'clock, he sensed a change in the mood coming from the lodge. A calmness. A man emerged from the blanketed doorway. He assumed it was Justin Arnett. Women followed, small size designating some were girls. Chitto watched Arnett lead the women to a round contrivance, lined in poles. The outdoor shower Leslie had described.

Chitto studied the dim shapes of the women standing in the shadows, concern growing. Leslie's tall, slender figure and red hair were not among the group.

Arnett spoke with each of the women, then left. Through his field glasses, Chitto watched him proceed down the dirt track toward Sonny Boy's house, listened to the sound of an engine starting, heard a car driving away. The ceremony was over. The healer would make the long drive back to the Quapaw Nation, his part in the process complete. The women would bathe themselves under a moonlit sky.

Hearing voices from the road, he crept closer. Spotting two men, both carrying long guns, he smiled. The duck had outsmarted the hunters. As he watched, the men walked toward an old pickup and a smaller vehicle with an off-color front fender.

He crept closer to get a look at their faces in the headlights. One of the men wore a ball cap, turned backwards. The other, long hair slicked back in a single braid.

What the hell—

Ernest and Bennie, the two buddies who wrecked the Red River Tavern, started their vehicles and disappeared down the dark road.

★ ★ ★ ★ ★

Chitto returned to the lodge, where smoke escaped between willow branches. Pushing aside the blanket covering the opening, he slipped inside.

"Grandfather," he said, speaking quietly so as not to frighten the old prayer man. "Am I allowed to sit with you as the fire dies and the stones grow cold?"

Sonny Boy pointed out a place for Chitto to sit. "I have been waiting for you."

"You knew I was coming?" Chitto removed his pack, laid it and the rifle to one side.

Sonny Boy grunted, showing no concern. "You have questions for me."

"Yeah. You, uh, you remember that day I brought you home, Sonny Boy? The day I asked you about the tracks to this lodge? You said you didn't know if anyone had been here."

The old man looked at Chitto, face thoughtful. "I remember. You asked me if someone had hunted here." He lifted gaunt shoulders, let them drop. "No hunters."

Chitto shook his head. He had dropped the ball. The first rule as a scientist or lawman was to ask the right question.

He watched the old man for a while, seeing his ancient body, naked from the waist up, shine in the darkness. Sonny Boy stared into the fire, looking like a seer. Was he?

"Tell me, Sonny Boy," he said, feeling his skin grow damp. "How did you know I would be here tonight?"

"She tell me, when she bring this to give to you." Sonny Boy pulled a brown paper bag from beneath a blanket at the back of the lodge.

Inside the bag, Chitto found a box of candy, chocolates with soft centers, and an envelope. He read by firelight.

Sam,

 I figured it out, too, and know my involvement contributed to what has happened, which means I have broken my oath as an anthropologist not to interfere with a native culture. I only meant to document changes, not cause them. I look upon them as stories, beautiful, old stories. I failed to take into account the fact I was dealing with a people who needed to make those stories live again.

 Please deliver the chocolates to your grandmother and support the excuse I gave your Mattie. I called and let her know that I have returned home early, saying my teaching obligations demanded it.

 I don't know if I will be returning to finish my work next year. There is much to think about.

Your friend,
Leslie

Chitto folded the note and returned it to the envelope. As he did so, he noticed the letterhead was printed with the address of the university where Leslie taught. He hoped the choice of paper was intentional.

He turned his attention to Sonny Boy. One final question needed an answer.

"Grandfather, I need to know if you sang at the Wyandotte festival last weekend."

Sonny Boy nodded. "It is hard to hear the women's prayers. Listen to all those bad things that happened to them, hear them cry. So, I pray." He stared into the dying fire. "It is in the Creator's hands now."

Chitto sighed. The old man's talk about weeping daughters now made sense.

"After the fire is out, I cannot sleep," Sonny Boy said.

Chitto mulled this over. The women who attended the healing ceremony were released from their pain, but the old man absorbed it. Just as the rocks absorbed the heat from the fire. Glowing red, some so hot, they cracked. Angry stones.

Sonny Boy looked at him. "Whiskey helps me do that. They close down my likker place. You take me to find new one?"

Chitto contemplated the drunks he had chanced upon lately. Rapists. Child abusers. A holy man. How could souls shaped by the same Creator's hand have diverged so radically, yet fallen into the same chasm? He sighed. Sometimes it didn't pay to dissect the paths of others. Especially one who could barely see light atop the rim of his own abyss.

"I can't do that, Grandfather. But I will stay with you until morning."

"Okay," Sonny Boy said a minute later. "Together, we wait for daybreak."

As the old man returned to his meditation, Chitto felt a heaviness in his chest. He would learn no more from Sonny Boy; he was but the prayer man. Others handled the rest of the process. All of which meant, he was too late to save a life. Somewhere, a man was held captive. Sustained on alcohol or drugs. Hands and feet bound. Clothes freshly laundered to remove evidence.

He did not know where the ritualistic execution would take place, only that it would happen on ceremonial grounds. He could not contact all the nations. His only option was to call the FBI. They were the only ones with enough people to cover the territory.

Did he want to do that?

Chitto pulled his cell phone from his pocket, pulled up Ramon Rodriquez's number and stared at it in the digitized light.

Did he have a choice?

Through the laths of the hut, Chitto heard a voice he recognized. Carefully, he pulled aside the blanket and looked toward the improvised shower stall. A slender girl with long dark hair emerged in the moonlight, wrapped in a towel. The bruises that discolored her body the last time he saw her were healed. And from the look on Teresa Walker's face, her body was not the only thing made well.

Chitto recalled a time two years before when he had taken Mary to see a healer. Though that healer had not been able to help Mary, the healer tonight had helped this girl. A strong girl who fought back had regained her dignity.

Seconds later, the impact of the girl's presence hit him. He knew the identity of the next man to be executed—no question in his mind. He let the flap to the lodge close again, his thinking digressing to the first day he'd met Teresa Walker, the helplessness he'd felt as he read Buster Tomlinson his rights. He remembered the legal words that he had spoken to the man who had raped his niece. Officially authorized words.

But he had made a promise.

Chitto stared at the cell phone in his hand, at the number for Ramon Rodriquez.

"Grandfather," he said, pushing the *Off* button. "I need a cleansing ceremony. I have just killed an enemy."

Sonny Boy took a pack of Camels from his pants pocket and held the pack out to him. "First, we pray."

Chitto reached for the pack, then waved it away. "Your prayers are powerful enough for both of us," he said.

As day broke, Chitto peeled the shirt off his back, used it to mop away the sweat, then pitched it aside. As he watched the fire turn to embers, he absorbed the last of its heat, feeling muscles relax, perspiration seep from his skin. Slowly, he became aware that he felt no remorse for what was to happen. No remorse about not preventing it. The Creator chose the prayers he would allow. Who was he to interfere with a prayer being answered? Those matters were outside his jurisdiction.

Sitting next to Sonny Boy, Chitto watched the fire die, listened to round granite stones, millions of years old, groan as they gave up their heat and grew peaceful again. In that stillness, he planned his next steps.

He and Sonny Boy had already discussed a cleansing ceremony. When to meet again to make it happen. Where Chitto would spend a few days in solitary confinement.

He would also talk to Tubbe, Sunday and Murray, and share with them what he'd learned of the executions conducted across their nations. He would tell them of the decision he had made this night, of the path he had decided to walk, make it clear they had to choose their own. But he could predict what that would be, for they were not just lawmen. They were men of justice.

And that left just one loose end to tie up.

CHAPTER TWENTY-SIX

Chitto parked outside a house on a tree-lined residential street. Deep letters cut into the wooden sign out front had been darkened with black stain. He read the word *Hospice*, skipped over the rest and walked up a pitted sidewalk buckling with age. Recognizing two men walking out the front door, he lifted a hand in greeting.

"Hey, Sam," Tommy Rideout said.

"How's she doing?" Chitto asked.

Rideout cleared his throat, then stared at the ground.

Chitto turned to Junior Wharton. "Not too good, huh?"

The K-9 officer shrugged. "We brought flowers and tried to joke with her like we used to, but . . ."

"Okay," Chitto nodded. "See you back at work."

The house had been outfitted with a lobby of sorts. A sofa in one corner faced a fat, cathode-ray TV. Next to it was a magazine rack filled with copies of *Oklahoma Today* and *House Beautiful*. A sign above the sofa said *No Smoking*. Chitto approached a woman with a badge on her shirt that read *Volunteer* and asked where Wanda Gilly's room was.

"Down that hallway to the right." Washed-out hair framed a wrinkled face. "Can't miss it—looks like a florist's shop. People coming in constantly. Lot of police. Wanda calls them her kids."

"Thanks." Chitto turned to walk away.

She pointed through a window. "Little garden spot back there. You want to, you can take her out. We managed to keep

246

the pot plants alive in spite of the drought." She attempted a smile. "Seemed important."

As he walked, Chitto glanced through the window at the garden. Wooden chairs sat under an oak that looked to be a hundred years old. A mange of Bermuda grass spreading across the ground. Plants in flowerbeds had dried to stalks.

He paused at the doorway to Wanda's room. The scent from baskets of flowers was overwhelming; colored foil around pot plants assaulted the eye; an intimidating guest book demanded signature before entry. A funeral.

Flipping through the book's pages, he saw his mother's and grandmother's names on the first page. On subsequent pages were names of everyone in the department and most of those in the tribal complex. He recognized other names from across the checkerboard, even from the Texas side of the state line. Closing the book, he walked to where a rag of a woman sat in a wheelchair.

Seeing him, Wanda wheezed a sigh. "Thank God you didn't bring more stinking flowers." Though weaker, her voice was still grating. "Go get those Marlboros out of your glove box. I'm dyin' for a smoke."

He smiled at that. A nurse's aide in the corner was not so amused.

"Now, Mrs. Gilly," she said. "Doctor made it clear: no more cigarettes."

He walked to Wanda's wheelchair and kicked the brake off. "How 'bout we visit the garden where we can talk in peace."

"I stand on the fifth amendment," she said as he wheeled her out the door. "I don't know nothin'."

He grinned. "We both know that's not true, Wanda." He pushed her chair through a door built to accommodate the handicapped. "But don't worry, I'm not wired."

She managed a chuckle and waited patiently as he positioned

her near thick shrubbery that still held onto a few leaves.

"So, where'd I screw up?" she said as he adjusted the pillow at her back.

He thought a minute. "Think it was the missing soap and fabric softener." Spotting a pot of wilted red geraniums on a picnic table across the yard, he retrieved it and set it on a table next to her. "Didn't make sense that one of the cleaners would risk his job over something so small."

Wanda nodded. "Shouldn't have taken that stuff out of the office. Almost brought it back in Monday morning. Figured that would be a bigger mistake. Didn't want to risk someone spotting me."

Chitto leaned towards her, sniffing her robe. "You really use Final Touch?"

"Why, have for years. Hides the smell of smoke on my clothes . . ." She glanced away, blinking, then looked at him. "*That's* what messed me up?"

"How'd you know that stuff was in my office anyway?"

She smiled, dull eyes taking on a sparkle. "Who do you think that guy was went into the washateria? Practically stripped himself naked, his brother, too, so he'd have something that looked like wash."

Chitto laughed outright, then rubbed his throat. He'd been *that* close to his hunters and didn't even know it. "Don't suppose their names are Ernest and Bennie."

She grinned. "My nephews, pretending to be construction workers. When you got secretive, I had them tail you to see what you were up to. About scared the pea wadding out of them that night you emptied your gun on them. They dropped that last envelope off at your desk, too."

"The last one." He tilted his head, as if thinking something over. "So *you're* the one that dough-popped me in the parking lot?"

248

"Element of surprise," she said. "Dumpsters crammed with scrap two-by-fours. Damn crows helped, too. Made so much noise, you didn't know I was anywhere around."

Wanda was *Hoklonote'she*, the telepathic shape-changer. Except she didn't need to read minds because he'd let her know his every move.

"Pack a hell of a punch for a little woman." He rubbed the back of his head. "I don't get it," he said. "Those boys got arrested for wrecking a tavern because of a girl problem."

She snickered. "Wasn't any *girl* problem. Problem was an old man who developed loose lips when he got drunk. Tried twice to discourage Sonny Boy; it didn't work. Only thing left was to close down his watering trough."

Sonny Boy's wallet full of money became clear.

"Funny thing is, you helped get them outta jail." She laughed softly.

"Yeah," he said. "*Real* funny." He rubbed a hand across his face. "Those boys were busy tailing me. That means it had to be you broke into my house."

"Didn't break in," she said, raising a finger in protest. "Mary gave me a key long time back."

"*Jeezuscrise*," he said, thinking Mary's attitude toward house keys had been overly liberal.

"Wouldn't have let any harm come to you, if that's what you're thinking," she said.

"So, you're saying my neck was never on the line?" He raised an eyebrow. "The long guns those boys were carrying said something different."

"Well . . ." She stared into the distance. "Guess we'll never know now, will we? If Dan had let Rodriquez take on the case in the first place, would've made things simpler."

"Yeah, I figured that out, too."

Chitto picked up an Adirondack chair and moved it closer.

249

Easing into the chair, he felt shoulder muscles loosen. Tight neck muscles relax. What was it about Adirondacks that fitted the body so well, he wondered. The angles, he decided, crossing on ankle over his knee. Some old carpenter a long time ago had figured out how the human body was meant to bend. Reaching into his pocket, he withdrew his pack of Marlboros and a book of paper matches.

"Oh, good Lord—*bless you,* Sam." Wanda's hand shook as Chitto lit her up. When he handed her the rest of the pack, she slid them into the pocket of her robe and repeated, "Bless you."

"There's a cost."

She raised an eyebrow. "Ain't there always." She inhaled, blew a coil of smoke out her mouth. "I'm not giving you names."

"That's not it."

"Then . . . what?"

"This scalp dance ends now. I'm tired of looking over my shoulder, and . . ." He picked up her loose hand. "I expect you to finish the journey. No need for your *Shilombish* to hang around. I plan to stay on the trail of Bert's and Dad's killers, won't stop looking while there's a breath left in me."

She took another drag on the cigarette, looked at him through a whirl of smoke. "You've been making noises about giving up this last year, quitting the force."

"Not anymore." He looked her in the eye. "Let me take care of things."

Suppressing a cough, Wanda flipped cigarette ash into the pot of geraniums. "That a promise?"

"You can take it to the bank." Chitto could read in Wanda's eyes that she knew he spoke true.

"Well, all right then." She took another drag on the cigarette, waving smoke away with a hand frail as a dragonfly's wings. "One more question before I end this dance."

"What's that?"

"You could've stopped that last one." She looked at him with eyes sunken in their sockets. "Why didn't you?"

He laughed softly. "Seemed like a good day to be indigenous."

ABOUT THE AUTHOR

Scalp Dance, A Sam Chitto Mystery evolved naturally for **Lu Clifton** as she was born in and spent her early childhood in southeastern Oklahoma. While not a member of any nation, she has Choctaw and Cherokee ancestors in her maternal and paternal lines and a long-standing interest in Native American myth and folklore.

After completing a B.A. and M.A. in English at Colorado State University, Clifton worked in the business and journalism fields. She currently lives in northern Illinois and dedicates her time to her two favorite things in life—spending quality time with family and friends and writing fiction.